A Hallway
of
Gallows

Trudey Martin

Copyright © 2020 Trudey Martin

ISBN 9798621324049

The brickwork as red raw as they are within
A seeping mould invades the floor's horrid hide
Juices corrupt walls and peel back their foreskin
The ceiling grows weary of never being dried
The hallway of gallows, great shingles on its skin
Doors and windows forever cried

That was them

Excerpt from Freddie Smalls
Alexander Yalnif

LINCOLN

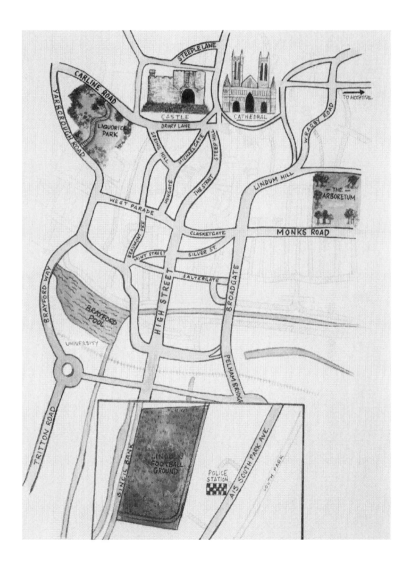

I was scared. Really scared.

My legs were heavy like stones. Shards of barbed wire stabbed into my brain. I was sure that I had been drugged, although I couldn't remember it. In fact, the last thing I remembered was running, running fast and determined to get somewhere as quickly as I could. But I couldn't drag a sensible thought into my brain and I had no idea why I had been running, or where.

I tried to adjust my position, but it was impossible to shift as much as an inch. Tight knots chaffed at my wrists and ankles, securing me to a wooden chair. The muscles in my legs and arms tensed in an attempt to cope with being pulled back unnaturally behind me. Ropes around my ankles tightened and rubbed with every move I made, the trickles of blood tickling as they ran over my foot and between my toes. Restraints of some sort forced my arms back and dug deep into the skin around my wrists and elbows. Piercing pain ran up all four limbs from being wrenched too sharply at such unusual angles and my legs shook uncontrollably with the effort of keeping them in such an abnormal position.

I had no feeling in my left foot. The shoe had fallen off and the top of my foot had gone numb from being wedged against the cold damp concrete floor. Something, a piece of rag or cloth, had been stuffed into my mouth and no matter how hard I tried I couldn't dislodge it with my tongue. Swallowing was impossible with my mouth forced so far open and the rag was soaked, saliva dripping down my chin. I struggled for air; my laboured breaths pulling in what oxygen they could, but it wasn't enough to quell the rising panic, and my lungs burned with the effort. My jaw twitched, stiffening from being wedged uncomfortably wide. I'd no doubt been like this for a while, although I had no idea how long. It could have been anything from a few minutes to a few hours.

My eyes resisted my initial attempts to open them, a tough crust welding them together. As I forced them apart, the dry lids scratched at my eyeballs and daylight assaulted my senses. I looked around and took in the outline of a vast warehouse. Way up high near the roof, a few small windows let in a little soft summer sunshine. The light threw shafts of sunbeams across the floor, which danced on pools of water gathering beneath the dank and dripping roof. The place smelled old and wet. Patches of moss grew out of cracks in the concrete, and near the walls, tall weeds made an attempt to reach the sunlight.

I concentrated on staying alert; on not letting my fear overwhelm me. But with each passing second the shaking in my limbs and the numbness in my foot was intensifying. The blood pulsing through my arteries was deafening. I looked around for something to focus on; trying to figure out what this massive building was used for. It was the size of a hanger but, as far as I could see, there wasn't a door big enough to get a plane through. A pile of broken pallets leaned against the wall to my left, and some damp cardboard floated on air currents created by holes in the wall. Maybe it was used for storage, although as far as I could see there was very little here. Apart from me.

A loud crashing noise behind me interrupted my efforts to calm myself, instantly creating waves of panic that rattled through my body. My breathing quickened; my pulse followed suit. An echo of footsteps grew louder as they came closer towards me.

Then, a gritty male voice shouting, 'Steve! Steve! Where the fuck are you?"

A door flung open at the far end of the room and a man, who I took to be Steve, came scurrying out, puffing on a cigarette and putting on a quilted sleeveless jacket as he hurried through the door.

"We're up in ten minutes," the first man shouted in a gruff, tobacco hardened voice. "Get her in the room, ready."

Shit. Ready for what? My chest tightened once again. I struggled in the chair; wriggling and pulling at the ropes tying me down, scraping my wrists and ankles even more. I didn't know what I was hoping to achieve but I had to try something. If I had been drugged, then the drugs had definitely worn off now and I was fully alert. And I didn't like it at all.

The man called Steve threw his cigarette on the floor and marched over to me. The gruff man appeared at my side, and I turned round to look at him. He leered back down at me and grinned, showing several missing teeth as he did so.

"You're in for a treat," he said and gave a short snort that I took to be laughter.

I struggled more forcefully, but Steve kicked out at the chair, pushing it to the ground. I fell backwards, the cold air rushing past my ears, my bound limbs struggling in vain against their restraints as I landed with a crash on the cold, damp concrete, just managing to hold my head up enough so that it didn't hit the floor. Pain tore through my arms as they were crushed between the floor and the weight of my body on the chair. I cried out but the gag in my mouth turned it into little more than a whimper. Steve kicked the chair again, turning it so that I was on my right side. My arm took the brunt, scraping across the concrete, as the momentum of the kick dragged the chair across the sodden floor and I gasped desperately for air through the rag. My breath and saliva mixed, catching in the back of my throat, chokes and vomit threatening to rise into my gagged mouth. The more I struggled to breathe, the harder it became, my head beginning to float off as my brain lacked the oxygen it needed. Just as I thought I could no longer bear the piercing pain ripping through my trapped biceps, the gruff man reached for the binds and my arms were suddenly free. As I pushed myself up to release the weight, a wave of pins and needles tore down my arms and into my hands. My nostrils flared as I struggled to take in deep breaths through my nose, trying to bring my head back down to earth. Steve bent down and grabbed me, pulling me into a sitting position with my feet pulled awkwardly to one side, still attached to the chair. He fumbled roughly with the ropes at my ankles, sawing further into my flesh as he struggled to release them.

Once my feet were untied, the two men pulled me upright and started dragging me towards the doors at the far end of the warehouse. My remaining shoe fell off after a few paces, leaving me barefoot. My feet, heavy and still numb scrambled for purchase on the floor but I could barely move them, and it was a struggle to stay upright. The two men lugged me along regardless and my feet flailed as they tried to keep up.

Steve held my arms behind my back whilst the gruff man took some keys from a pocket and opened one of the doors. I tried to kick back at him but I couldn't move my foot, let alone coordinate it, and it just scraped along the floor. A bright light assaulted my eyes as Steve pushed me into the room—a complete change from the dank, dark atmosphere of the big room. As my eyes adjusted, fear sank to the pit of my stomach, taking complete control of my body. It was all I could do just to keep control of my bladder.

And then it all came back to me, a rush of images pouring into my brain. Why I'd been running, and exactly where I had been running to. The memory did nothing to allay my fears. And as I looked around, my legs buckled underneath me and the men holding me fought to keep me upright.

I tried my best not to lose my composure completely and prayed to anyone who would listen that Sam Charlton had been right when he'd said he knew where this place was.

Wednesday

2

I only took the job because of Charlton. The woman who had turned up to see me had said that she couldn't afford to pay my normal rate but she was desperate. Apart from thinking that I needed a job that paid more, I also thought that it was beyond my capabilities. But when I'd spoken to Charlton about her, he'd persuaded me to stretch myself.

"You've just tied up that case you were working on. Well, this is similar. It's a missing person too isn't it?" he'd said when I had explained it to him that evening.

"Well, yes," I'd admitted. "But it's a little more complicated than that."

It was a lot more complicated than that, actually.

The woman had been quite distraught at our first meeting in Café Santos. This was one of my favourite cafés in my hometown, Lincoln. It was a friendly independent and I preferred giving them my money than the chain coffee shops that were everywhere. And besides, their coffee was amazing. She was already there when I arrived, anxiously wrapping the end of her cotton scarf through her fingers. I recognised her from her description of herself – short, slim, early forties and with a blonde ponytail. I went over and shook her hand.

"Verity Spencer," I introduced myself.

"Hi," she said in a quiet, small voice. "Linda Watson."

I went and ordered a coffee and then returned to sit down beside her. She turned to me, and before she had even spoken her eyes were welling up with tears.

"Thanks for agreeing to meet me," she whispered.

I nodded and smiled in what I hoped was a reassuring way. I had dealt with a few distressed people since tumbling into this line of work just under a year ago. It still felt like a whirlwind, how I'd got to where I had since my husband, John, had died. About three months after his car crash, I'd got involved in a set of circumstances that Charlton always referred to as 'the incident'. I'd managed to uncover a scandal involving some prominent Lincoln individuals and I'd developed a taste for investigating since then. But I hadn't ever dealt with anything quite like this before.

I glanced at the woman beside me and sensed that this was going to be a difficult meeting. I touched her arm lightly.

"Just start at the beginning," I said.

She wrung her scarf once more between her fingers and swallowed.

"Well, it's for my daughter I'm here." She paused. "She's convinced something bad has happened. I mean, really bad. It's starting to affect her schooling and her social life. She did try talking to the lad from the home, but then she suddenly stopped doing anything. She just stays in. I'm concerned for her more than anything."

I waited a moment; after a few seconds her hands laid still on her lap and she swallowed, looking down at her fingers. "What is it that your daughter thinks has happened?"

"She doesn't really know. But she thinks there are some people who know something." She gave an ironic little laugh. "I'm sorry, that doesn't make any sense." And then she flicked her eyes up at me momentarily and sighed a really heavy sigh before carrying on, "Gloria is a girl I've been fostering, she's been with us for just over two years now. I've been a foster carer for the county for about twelve years, since Sarah, that's my daughter, was about three. We've had dozens of children over the years; babies, toddlers, teenagers. I'm used to dealing with children. Some only stayed a few days and some stayed for a few years. I treated them all equally; not the same, children are so different, but I tried to set them on the right path, give them love and consistency. Most of them had led very difficult lives."

She took a sip of her coffee and looked back up at me.

I nodded, encouraging her to continue. "Tell me a little bit about her. What is she like?"

"Gloria was different to any of the others. She'd come to this country from Africa, Congo actually, as an eight year old. She'd seen her father, her uncles and her older brother die when rebels took their village, and her mother was raped. Her mother died some time after from an untreated infection they think she contracted when she was raped. The family had to flee their home and—" She thought for a moment. "I think they lived in a refugee camp for a while."

She paused and stared out of the window. I followed her gaze; passers-by were rushing from one shop to another, seemingly without a care in the world.

"Gloria told me that she was proud and grateful that her remaining family had persuaded an uncle to bring her to Britain. They settled in this area—he was an accountant, so he soon got work. Gloria attended a local primary school, which she said she'd enjoyed. But her uncle struggled with the transition, he couldn't cope with all the death and violence he'd seen. He got more and more depressed and one day Gloria came home from school, I think she was about ten, and he'd disappeared. They found him at the coast in his car, a hose pipe feeding exhaust fumes in through the window."

I struggled to keep my features free of emotion, difficult though it was. It was a tragic story. I said nothing and just allowed her to continue.

"Gloria went to a foster family the other end of the county and had to change school. She said she hated it and the family weren't very friendly. She started kicking off and she was moved. She had a couple of quick changes after that, and in the end she went to a children's home in the city. After a year or so a new social worker came on the scene, Gloria liked her and they worked on some of her issues.

Anyway, the social worker thought she'd do better in a proper, loving family and Gloria agreed. And that was when she came to live with us."

"How old was she then?"

"She'd just turned thirteen. She was such a bright thing. She tried kicking off with us, but we just told her it wouldn't get her anywhere; she was here now and she'd stay here whether she behaved or not. She settled down and she and Sarah just, well, bonded." The tears appeared in her eyes again. "They just get on so well. They're like real sisters. They fall out and argue, but they have so much fun together. Well, they did. Gloria had her dark moments and as she developed into a teenager she began to have some very moody periods, but the two of them were so close. I mean, until recently and it all started to go downhill."

"What happened?"

"Gloria suddenly started wanting to be on her own."

"I guess that's not unusual for a, what, fifteen year old?"

"It wasn't just that. It seemed to start out of nowhere. She started getting really moody, slamming her door and staying in her room for ages and, we later found out, climbing out of the bedroom window in the night. She started going back to the children's home and hanging out with the young people there. Not that that's necessarily a bad thing but there were some troubled young men there at the time." She stopped, looking lost in thought. "Even Sarah couldn't get through to her." She paused again and gazed into nothingness.

"What do you think was going on?" I prompted.

"I really don't know," her voice shook and she hung her head, whispering into her chest. "Sarah thought she had a boyfriend at the home. She started to stay out overnight. I always called the police and they often brought her back from houses where she really shouldn't have been. I don't know if she was with a boyfriend or not."

"Did she tell you anything about what she was doing?"

"She wouldn't talk to anyone." She glanced up, her brow deeply furrowed. She looked as if just talking about it was causing her some pain. "Everyone tried," she continued, "the police, the social worker. She'd always got on well with the social worker, but she stopped responding to her too. She just locked herself away. She was staying away longer and longer and going further. They found her in Leeds once, and somewhere in Kent. She'd be away for days at a time, then leave again almost as soon as she got back. The social worker had said they were going to talk about her at some meeting, some…um…I don't know, important high up people who deal with this kind of thing. But I don't know what they thought they could do, or how they might help." She shrugged her shoulders. "Whatever they said, it didn't change, she just kept disappearing."

Linda paused. She glanced around the room, her eyes darting from one thing to another. Her gaze rested on the ceiling, and she pulled her lips in tightly before covering her mouth with her hand as if she were trying to stop the words from coming out. She looked back down at her hands and swallowed, then wiped her eyes with her scarf. "Then one day she just never came back." And with that she burst into uncontrollable sobs.

I wasn't great with big shows of emotion but I leaned over and gave her a hug.

I was thinking that this might be a job too far for me. I'd taken on some difficult cases over the last few months, but nothing like this. After 'the incident' the media had been quite interested in what had happened. Although my name was kept out of most of the reporting, the local press had mentioned my involvement. As a result, I'd been approached by a woman who'd been convinced I could help solve a marital mystery. It had been easy money. I'd tailed her husband for a week or so and had discovered that he'd had a second 'wife' and family in a town fifty miles away. I'd presented the woman with the evidence and banked the money she had gratefully handed over. After that, she'd told people, and they'd told other people, and jobs had just started to come along with remarkable regularity. And never once had I found myself regretting leaving the boring job I'd had lecturing at the local college. The money I earned wasn't great for someone just the wrong side of forty, but with the pension from John's job it was easy to make ends meet. And I really enjoyed the work.

Linda sat back in her chair. She told me the police had done what they could. They'd looked in all the known places, everywhere they'd found Gloria in the past. Spoken to all her friends. But very quickly the trail had run dry and they'd had no further leads. The police had hundreds of crimes to look into and she wanted someone who could dedicate themselves to finding the one person who mattered so much to her daughter.

"When was the last time you saw her?"

She checked her phone, looking for something, a reminder or a prompt of some sort. I could see her counting the days. "Four weeks ago, yesterday," she pronounced. "The police all but gave up a week or so ago, and Sarah has been begging me to do something. To be honest, I'm worried that she might get involved herself if I don't get a professional in."

It took me aback to be called a professional. It still didn't really feel like a proper job.

"The social worker?" I asked

"Yes she's been good. She's been in touch a few times but, you know, people can't dedicate their lives to it when they have twenty other children who need their attention, right here."

"Do you have a name?"

"Oh, yes, she's called Joy Mahoney, she's based in an office in the south of the city, not that she's there much, but she does get back to you if you leave a message, which is more than some of my other children's social workers have done."

"Do you have a photo of Gloria? Any possessions?" I asked.

Linda shared a picture from her phone; it instantly landed in my photo album. The technology of modern mobile phones never ceased to amaze me. I examined the picture. Gloria was a tall, slim, vibrant African young lady, with a smile that seemed infectious. She wouldn't have looked out of place on a catwalk.

"Well, there's probably some things in her room," she added. "If you've got time later, maybe you could call round. Sarah will be home from school about four. I'm sure she'd be happy to talk to you, too."

I still wasn't sure if I felt capable of taking it on, but I agreed to call round later. She wrote down the address and rushed off out into the street, leaving me looking at my phone and studying the smiling face of a beautiful, disappeared, teenager.

3

I walked back up the hill to my house in the area of Lincoln known as the Bailgate, as I'd need the car later. I reached the cathedral and, although it wasn't far to Steeple Lane from there, I decided to pause before heading home. The sun was high in the sky, the cobbles and the pavements radiating heat. Passers-by were peeling off layers and I bought myself an ice cream, hoping it would cool me down a little. I walked over to the cathedral and sat on the wall outside, eating my ice cream and gathering my thoughts about what Linda had told me. Images of Gloria filled my mind and I fished out my phone, looking again at the picture that had been taken, Linda had said, 'just before she stopped smiling'. As I finished up my ice cream, I sat there watching the people milling around for a while and then I walked home.

It had taken me a while to build up the confidence to want to get behind a wheel again after

John's fatal accident. Until quite recently, I had just hired a car if I'd needed one, but it had become obvious a while back that I really needed my own car if I was going to be able to do my new 'job' properly. So, a few weeks ago I'd recruited my good friend Robert, and his reluctant partner Keith, to help me find something suitable. Keith's contributions had mostly consisted of commenting on economy and value for money. Mine were more about whether I liked the colour or not. So, I'd relied on Robert knowing what he was doing and steering me through the salespeople's talk of horsepower, litres, and torque, and I'd ended up with a rather lovely, powder blue Fiat 500, which I'd christened Frank. I knew cars were supposed to be female but this one just didn't feel like a girl. Robert had protested quite vehemently, "A powder blue car is not male". But I hadn't taken any notice. He was Frank, and in my mind, he always would be.

I pottered about at home for a while, then jumped into the car and headed off to the south of the city to talk to Sarah about her missing friend. The family lived in an area just off Doddington Road. It was a funny little place, sandwiched between a social housing estate and an industrial area. The house was semi-detached and had a little bay window at the front, a neat gravel drive with a small well-kept garden, and a garage. I pulled onto the drive, parked up and rang the doorbell.

A young girl answered the door, and I assumed that this was Sarah. She was mid-teens, petite and had her mother's blonde hair, pulled into a similar ponytail.

"Sarah?" I asked.

"You must be the lady Mum told me about. You're going to help us find Gloria?"

"I'm not sure yet if I'll be able to help," I said, thinking it best to be honest.

Her mouth drooped, and her eyes welled up, so I quickly followed up with, "But I've come to find out a little bit more about her, to talk to you, to see if I think it's something I can get involved in."

Sarah smoothed down her hair and ran her hand across her face. Her grey skin and the dark circles under her eyes gave her a look of haunted exhaustion. She took a step back and gestured that I should come in, keeping her eyes fixed on the floor as if it might give her some answers. I wondered where to start.

"Thanks," I said. "Is it possible to have a look at her bedroom?"

She led me up the stairs. There were three bedrooms, two at the front and one at the back. The one at the back was clearly Sarah's. A jumble of clothes and make-up formed a torrent that spilled across the carpet, clearly visible through the half open door. Toiletries were strewn across the bed, the bedside cabinet, and quite a proportion of the floor. Not an uncommon teenager's bedroom. We doubled back along the landing towards the front of the house and she pushed open a door into Gloria's bedroom. I was taken aback—it didn't look like the bedroom of a fifteen year old. The bed was neatly made, the floor was clear and there was precious little to personalise it.

"Have you tidied it since she left?"

"No." Sarah shrugged. "She always kept it like this. She never really made a mess." She paused. "We put her clothes away, washed stuff and put it in the drawers, but it's more or less how she left it."

"Do you mind?" I gestured vaguely around the room.

She shook her head, so I started looking around. There wasn't much, considering the room belonged to a teenage girl. On a pinboard near the bed there were a few photos of her and Sarah, a poster of a band I had never heard of and a leaflet about an online counselling scheme called Kooth. *Online counselling?* Whatever next. On the bedside table a little plastic ornament of a Disney figure stood, keeping watch over the bed. It was the princess from The Little Mermaid. I picked it up.

"She brought that over from Africa," Sarah said. "I think it's about the only thing she has from when she lived there."

I put it back down, carefully, just as I'd found it and carried on around the room. On the windowsill there was a healthy-looking cactus and a copy of 'The Catcher in the Rye'. My favourite book. I flicked through the pages; it was well read with pencil markings. Keeping page was a short school report, signed by the school headmistress.

"We're doing that for GCSE English," Sarah offered, without me asking for an explanation.

I worried that having to study a book might put youngsters off it, but I said nothing and carried on. I moved over to the chest of drawers and opened them one at a time. All the usual—underwear, socks, vests, pants. There was a drawer full of T shirts and another with long sleeved tops. I moved over to the wardrobe and browsed through the contents – school uniform, a couple of summer dresses, some tops. And then a dress caught my eye. I picked it out. It looked new, and expensive. I checked the label.

"Did she normally buy Paul Smith clothes?"

Sarah came over and examined the dress. "I've not seen that one before," she said. "Although she did suddenly start getting new clothes and other things. Look at this." Sarah went over to the chest of drawers and pulled out some underwear.

Some of it still had the labels on. I hadn't noticed before when I'd just pulled the drawers open – I didn't like to rummage too much. It was all expensive stuff, and way too grown up for a teenager.

"Where did she get it from? Did she have a job?"

"No. I don't know. She would never say, but she got a brand new iPhone too." She looked down; it was obviously hard for her. "I asked her the first few times she appeared with something new, but she just shouted at me and got angry. I wanted to keep our friendship, so I stopped asking, hoping we'd go back to normal." She tailed off, the fact that the normality never returned didn't need saying, I could see it in her face. She slumped down on the end of the bed. I sat down opposite her.

"When she ran away, or when she stayed out all night, do you know where she went? Or why?"

Sarah shook her head and stared at the bed cover. Tears welled up in her eyes, and I thought she was going to cry, but she looked up and said, "I think she had a boyfriend. I think he would text her and she'd go and meet him. She didn't say but she had her new phone with her all the time. She was obsessed with looking at it and not missing anything. Sometimes, we would sit here and chat, and I'd think we were going to get back to how it was, then the phone would ping and she'd cut me off, throw me out the room and close the door." She smoothed out imaginary creases in the duvet. "I think it was someone at the home. I went up there and spoke to one of the guys, but he wouldn't say anything. I'm not sure if he was her boyfriend, but maybe he was protecting her, I don't know." She shrugged her shoulders and gave a great sigh of resignation. "But then one of the older lads, who'd left the home I think, came and found me after school one day and threatened to beat me up." She glanced up at me, and then looked immediately at the door as if it might have grown ears all of a sudden. "Don't tell Mum that, please."

'I won't." I took her hands and looked her in the eyes. "But it is important. Do you know any of these people's names?"

"The boy from the home is called Liam, but I don't know his friend's name."

"How old are they?"

"I think Liam is about seventeen, maybe eighteen. I don't know the other one. Twentyish maybe."

"Is there anything else you can tell me? Anything? Where she went, how she got there?"

Sarah looked back down and shook her head. "I'm sorry," she whispered.

I finished off my sweep of the room. I looked in the drawer in the bedside table. There was a keyring style token and a passport. I picked them up. The passport showed a slightly younger, but equally stunning Gloria and I flicked through it but there was nothing in it other than the picture and a folded piece of paper. I held up the token and showed it to Sarah.

"It's for the gym." She took it from me. "You programme it and then put it in the different machines and it knows what you need to do. Then it collects all the data and tells you how close you are to your target." She passed it back.

"Did she belong to a gym?"

"Yeah, the Tritton Road one. She went quite a lot. All children who are looked after by the council can get free gym passes. We do too if we want. Families who foster, you know, so we don't feel left out and so it seems like we have some kind of reward for giving up our home and our parents to other kids." She sighed again. "I'm sorry. I know all these kids have gone through a hard time, but it's not easy sharing Mum with them all. Free gym access is nothing really. Sometimes I just want my Mum all to myself."

I nodded and smiled. It had to be hard to share your home like that. "Do you mind if I take a few things? Just to remind me, and so I have something to go on?"

She didn't say anything, just gestured around the room with both hands as if to say, take what you want if it will help.

I picked up the passport and the gym token. I took a couple of the photos off the wall, photos of Gloria and Sarah. I went over to the windowsill and picked up the book, then back to the chest of drawers and found one of the pieces of underwear that still had a tag attached. I added that to my stash. I looked around the room, there was nothing much else there. I hadn't seen anything that was giving me any clues at all about where Gloria had gone, or who she had gone with, but I didn't want Sarah to feel that all hope was lost, not just yet. My eyes landed again on the Little Mermaid princess, and I leaned down and scooped it up, placing it on top of the expensive underwear. Sarah found me a paper bag that had had some fruit in from the supermarket, and I decanted Gloria's possessions into that, said a hopeful farewell, then left.

4

"Verity," Sam Charlton said after I'd explained it all to him on the phone that evening, and expressed my doubts about my abilities. "You'll be fine. It's definitely time for you to take a step up. It'll be challenging."

"I'm not sure I'm ready for challenging," I said, tucking my feet underneath me as I sat on the sofa. "I'm rather fond of boring."

"Hmmm, yeah," he reflected. "I wondered what it was you liked about me."

"That's a bit presumptuous," I countered. "It might just be that I find you useful."

"Ha! I doubt that," and he laughed. "The thing is, you can't just tail philandering husbands and wives forever."

"I don't just chase husbands and wives, Sam, as you know very well. What about the recurrent shoplifter I helped identify? Or the son I reunited with his mother recently?"

I thought about how, over the last few months I had got quite used to meeting people and listening to their stories, often sad and involving family rifts or arguments. The job I'd just completed had been searching for a son. His mother hadn't seen him since Christmas Day two years before when he had stormed out halfway through dinner after a row got overheated. He had never returned. It had taken me seven weeks and three days of research and dogged determination but I had eventually tracked him down to a village in southern Spain where he was working as a barman. He'd not wanted to return that Christmas Day due to pride and, somehow, the longer it went on, the harder it had been to go back. He'd broken down in tears of relief when I'd explained that his Mum had hired me to find him, and I'd returned him to the thankful arms of his family.

It was at that moment that Charlton interrupted my thoughts by pointing out that the two cases were both missing people. And therefore similar. I sighed. What had I got to lose? Apart from my reputation, that is.

"Okay, okay," I said, throwing my hand in the air, even though I was on the phone.

"So," Sam continued. "What have you got so far?"

"A distressed foster sister, a few random possessions that probably mean very little, plus a passport, and a couple of photo booth pictures," I replied.

I valued Charlton's insight and his gentle guidance. I'd met him during 'the incident' and we'd kept in touch periodically since. He'd been working as a detective inspector in the Human Trafficking Unit when we met and had since transferred to a CID in Central London. Once in a while I'd call him for advice and every now and again we'd meet up for dinner if I was in London. He was always supportive and encouraging, giving me tips when I was at a dead end.

"Okay," he said. "Who are you going to talk to first?"

I mulled that question over after we'd hung up. I wasn't entirely sure, so I started to make a list of people, or places, I knew had some connection to Gloria.

Liam ?? – residential home
Liam's older friend?!
Joy Mahoney – social worker
Mrs Fielding – headteacher, Welton Road Academy
Tritton Road gym - ??

Linda had told me that it was council policy that every time Gloria went missing she had to call the police. The police would look for her and, when they found her, would bring her back. Linda knew most of the local police who had, at some time or another, brought Gloria home. She'd said that some were better than others. Some had treated Gloria as if she was deliberately causing them hard work, but others better understood the troubled emotions of a child in care. There was one older policewoman who Gloria had developed more of a rapport with, and who used to come into the house with her, have a cup of tea and make sure that Gloria was okay. Her name was PC Deborah Keal so I added her to my list of people connected to Gloria.

It really didn't feel like much, and I hadn't got a clue what I was going to ask anyone, or where I should start. I sat on the floor in my living room and leaned against the sofa. I spread Gloria's possessions on the carpet around me and gazed at them, hoping for some kind of inspiration. I picked the passport up. It had been issued by the embassy of the Democratic Republic of Congo, and flicking through I found a letter from the Home Office which stated that Gloria had leave to remain in the UK until she was eighteen years old.

I looked at the pictures of Gloria and Sarah. They had been taken in a photo booth, a run of four pictures. Gloria was tall and Sarah petite, so Gloria's face was above Sarah's in most of the pictures. They were larking around, sticking out their tongues and making faces, generally having fun. I could sense their closeness through the camera. What had driven Gloria away? And why hadn't she been able to talk to Sarah about it?

The gym token told me nothing, other than that Gloria had free membership of a gym. I tossed it back down on the carpet and picked up the knickers I'd taken from Gloria's drawer. The label, still attached, said that they were from Agent Provocateur, and a quick search of their website informed me that they cost £295. *How much?* I looked at the image on my laptop and compared it to the tiny knickers I held in my hands, and there was no doubt that this was the same skimpy red thong with crystals that was for sale online. I'd bought the occasional piece of racy underwear before but could honestly say that I had never paid anything close to almost three hundred pounds for a pair of pants. What was a young teenage girl doing with such expensive designer underwear in her possession? And a Paul Smith dress? Where on earth had she got the money from? Both Linda and Sarah were adamant that she'd never had a job. Maybe one of the reasons she had kept disappearing was because she was shoplifting? Shoplifting and selling the clothes on, perhaps.

I opened the front page of the book and read the first sentence. It had had me hooked from the start as a young adult and I had read it in one or two sittings. I wondered if Gloria was enjoying reading it. She was about halfway through, her page marked with the short school report. I didn't have children, so I'd never had to read school reports, but I imagined they were probably a drag for teachers to write for the majority of pupils. You know, 'could try harder', that sort of thing, as a code for 'your son never does any work and I wish he wasn't in my class'. Or maybe teachers really enjoyed their jobs and I was being harsh. I had become very jaded in my old lecturing job at Lincoln College. The courses had been too prescriptive and students could pass simply by churning out the right few phrases without really understanding what they were learning. Thankfully, I hadn't had to write reports.

This was clearly some sort of mid-term report, and just had a line or two saying that Gloria was doing very well, her grades were good, her effort was outstanding and that she was heading towards obtaining a 6, whatever that meant these days. The report had been written at the end of the autumn term, just before Christmas. That was barely half a year ago. It just didn't make sense. I carefully replaced the report in the page it had been marking. If we found Gloria, she'd want to finish the book and I didn't want to lose her place.

The little Disney princess smiled up at me from the floor. I couldn't remember her name and had to Google to find it—*Ariel, of course*—the Little Mermaid. I pictured a small, scared, orphaned Gloria leaving her home and travelling across the continents to an unknown land, leaving chaos behind her and clutching the tiny model in her hand. It seemed poignant that she still had it and that it had been standing there, keeping watch over her while she slept. I reached over and picked up the smiling princess, with her pale skin, enormous blue eyes and her luminous red hair, and I wrapped my hand around her. I uncurled my fingers and looked down, asking Ariel if she had any idea where Gloria was, but she just smiled up at me enigmatically. She had no more clue than I did.

Thursday

5

The following morning I headed out for a coffee as soon as I was up and showered. We were having a lovely hot sunny spell and even though it was early it was warm enough to leave the house without a coat or even a jacket. The sun was already dragging itself up and over the city, bathing Lincoln in a bright, clear light; the blue sky prophetic of a scorching day to come. There were plenty of coffee shops at my end of town, but they weren't open this early and I needed to buy other things too. So I headed past the cathedral, down Steep Hill and into the city centre.

I sat down with my coffee and fished out the list I'd written the day before. It was a bit early to call anyone; no one would be at work yet. I grabbed my phone and tried to work out some email addresses so that I could, at least, start to contact people. The social worker was easy, I knew the format of council emails having emailed them on numerous occasions to try to get someone to sort out cars and other vehicles owned by people who thought it was perfectly acceptable to park in such a way as to make access to Steeple Lane almost impossible. I never got very far, but at least I knew the format of their emails. I didn't hold out much hope; I knew social workers were busy people, but Linda had said she'd been good at getting back to her so, who knew. It was a start.

I dithered over what to write and deleted about a dozen efforts ranging from two pages covering everything I knew to one line. I settled, in the end, for short and sweet.

> *From:*<Verity@SpencerHelp.com>
> *To:*<j.mahoney@lincscc.gov.uk>
> *Dear Joy,*
>
> *I'm sorry to bother you, but Gloria Kasongo's foster carer has asked me to help try to find her. I know the police seem to have come to a dead end, and she is really concerned about Gloria's welfare. I wondered if I could have a quick chat with you?*
>
> *Please call or text on the number below with a time to meet/ring.*
>
> *Kind regards,*
> *Verity Spencer*

Next I used my phone to search for the Welton Road Academy. They had quite a polished website, with several pictures of smiling teachers and radiant youngsters. The pupils all seemed to be engaging really well in lessons and the teachers appeared to be thoroughly enjoying the experience of teaching them. It looked like a place you'd go to relish your learning, soaking up everything you were taught, and emerging as a well-rounded, well-educated young adult ready to conquer your dreams. I wondered if that actually applied to many of the real students, and whether education had really changed that much since I'd been at secondary school. Some of the teachers at my school had seemed to positively enjoy inflicting humiliation and suffering on the more sensitive children, probably scarring them for life. I selected the menu and found a page detailing all the staff members then sent off an email to the headteacher, cutting and pasting what I'd written to the social worker.

Then I sent an email to Detective Sergeant Mike Nash from Lincolnshire Police. He'd helped me out once or twice in the past, so it was worth a try. Nash had interviewed me at the start of 'the incident'; after I'd discovered an elderly man dying from a gun shot wound. Occasionally he'd passed on information that would have sat in a file somewhere and never seen the light of day again. Nothing confidential, and it wasn't an entirely altruistic act. Police were busy people, with several cases on the go at one time, meaning that some would constantly get shuffled to the bottom of the pile. By helping me, he was also actually helping the force as it meant fewer, lower-level unsolved cases on their books. I knew they had looked into Gloria's disappearance, but I could understand that, amongst all the other crimes they had to investigate, someone who had gone missing and turned up several times before was unlikely to top their daily to-do list. Especially as the trail appeared to have run completely dry. I fired off an email to Nash with a few details, hoping that he might be able to add something to the limited information I currently held.

It was still early by the time I'd finished my coffee so I decided I would walk over to the Tritton Road gym. I knew where it was—it was part of one of those out-of-town shopping areas, about twenty-five minutes away.

I set off down the High Street, under the stonebow – a Tudor arch that spanned the pedestrian area – and headed towards the Glory Hole. Aside from its merriment-inducing name, this was a convenient little cut through that led down the side of the river towards the university. It ran alongside another Tudor building, the High Bridge café, spoiled by being next to the red brick monstrosity that was Marks and Spencer. I walked along the side of the river and past the university, keeping close to the water as it dipped towards the south of the city and then headed towards Tritton Road and walked along until I reached the area where the gym was. The gym was in the far corner of a largely deserted car park, which sat away from the main road. The screech of metal on metal set my teeth on edge as a young man across the car park lifted the shutters on a large retail outlet. As I walked towards the gym, a couple of uniformed staff were letting themselves into various shops, preparing for imminent opening. A café was open, but apart from that and the gym, everything else was still closed.

I opened the door of the gym and a blast of icy air hit me, sending goosebumps up my arms as I escaped from the heat outside. I shivered and rubbed my arms as my body tried to adjust to the sudden change in temperature. The building was quite modern, large and open plan with the main gym immediately behind the reception area. Half of the running machines were occupied; people pounding the treadmills before work. I looked at the sweaty runners and decided that they would probably be grateful for the air conditioning. One wiry woman on a rowing machine rowed as if her life depended on it, and a few men lifting weights looked as if they were expending as much energy watching themselves in the mirror as they were lifting the weights.

I walked over to the reception desk. A young lady wearing a light tracksuit greeted me with a broad smile. She was holding a pencil in her right hand and twirling it inadvertently between her fingers. A name badge on her chest informed me that she was called Christina Jones.

"Good morning," I said. "I'm looking to talk to one of the trainers who works here."

"Okay," she mused, and furrowed her brow. "Was there anyone in particular, or can I help?" She took the pencil and placed it behind her ear.

"Well, I'm not sure," I admitted. "I'm looking for someone who might have worked with a particular customer. She's a member here, and disappeared about four weeks ago. I'm helping her family try to find out where she is." Okay, that was a little white lie but I wasn't going to go into all the details of Gloria's care history.

"Oh." She looked up, raising her eyebrows as high as they would go. "Do you think we'll be able to help?" She retrieved the pencil from her ear and began twirling it once again.

"I don't know," I replied. "I'm not sure at the moment who'll be able to help, so I'm just trying to find out a little bit about her to see if I can figure out where she might have gone."

"I see." There was a note of considerable doubt in her voice and she stared quite intently as she lifted the pencil to her mouth and started chewing on the end of it. I was so distracted by her pencil antics that I missed what she said next.

"I'm sorry?" I asked.

"Do you know who her personal trainer was?"

"Does everyone who comes here use a personal trainer?" I asked, doubtfully. I had been a member of a gym in the past but had never used the services of a trainer. Mind you, I had mostly used it for sitting in the steam room so you probably didn't really need a trainer for that.

"Everyone is assigned to a trainer, if they want one. Not everyone uses us. Some use us all the time." She smiled and began twirling the pencil again.

I fished out my phone and showed her the picture of Gloria. "This is her. Do you recognise her?"

Christina's face broke into a grin and she said, "Oh yes, Gloria!" Then she furrowed her brow and said, "Is she alright?"

"That's what I'm trying to establish," I said, trying to sound patient but falling short of the mark. "Do you know who her trainer was?"

"Jack," she said. "Jack Clayton. She saw him quite a lot. But he's not here at the moment, sorry. He'll be here later if you want to call back. Midday, or early afternoon is a good time. The gym is less busy then." She swung her arm to indicate where she meant, as if I might not have noticed it there behind her.

"Thanks," I said. 'I'll call back later." And I left her chewing the end of the pencil with a frown of concern wrinkling her forehead.

I had got so accustomed to the chilled air of the gym that the wave of warmth that hit me as I left took me by surprise. I blinked against the bright morning sun, shielding my eyes with my hand until they adjusted. I was just crossing the car park to get back to the road when my wrist vibrated. I had bought an Apple watch a while ago and wore it all the time, mostly to keep a track of my daily steps. I glanced at my wrist and saw it was a text from Keith.

Don't forget you're on desserts tomorrow. See you at 7 x

It was a good job he'd texted—the fact that it was Friday the next day had passed me by. For the last six to twelve months we had developed a loose arrangement whereby we had a Friday Food Night every couple of weeks, and we took it in turns to host, and to do different courses. Sometimes there would just be me, Keith and Robert and sometimes there might be an additional mouth or two. Tomorrow it was the three of us and it was their turn to host. I had already decided I would make a tiramisu and I had the ingredients ready, I just needed to find the time to prepare it.

6

I had walked another fifty yards or so back towards the city centre when my watch vibrated once again, this time a phone call. I hastily grabbed my phone.

"Mike, hi," I said, surprised that Nash was getting back to me so quickly.

"Verity, how are you?"

"I'm good, thanks," I replied. "And you?"

"All good. Listen, I'm just in Grantham for a meeting, then I'm heading back to Lincoln. I should have half an hour to spare you. It'll probably be about 11.30ish. Is that ok?"

"Absolutely," I said. "Where are you based these days? Hasn't the police station just closed?"

He laughed. "It has, Verity, it has indeed. I'm in the new place, down on South Park. Do you know it?"

"Yes, the old fire station? I'll come down there for 11.30. Thanks, Mike."

I looked at my watch, it was just after 10am. I weighed up my options. It was probably about a 40-minute walk home. There was no point heading that way, only to have to head back to the south of the city again almost as soon as I'd got home. I thought about getting a taxi home and starting on the tiramisu but after a couple of moments of prevarication I doubled back to the café near the gym and grabbed another coffee. I found a seat and scanned my emails hopefully, but there were no replies yet. The music in the café was deafening. I couldn't think why they needed to play it so loud, as if the caffeine wasn't enough to get people going in the morning.

Whilst I waited I sent my friend Collette a message.

Hi darling. All ok? X

Collette had been a great source of comfort to me after John had died, scooping me up when I needed it and really looking after me. We still saw each other frequently, at least once a week. But she was preoccupied by her children. If I was being honest, although I was godmother to her two daughters, seeing Collette in a constant state of agitation with one thing and another, made me think I'd maybe had a merciful escape not having the worry of offspring.

Within seconds a reply came back.

Ok, ta. Sophie off ill. Don't forget Charlotte's birthday on Thursday. 5pm x

Blimey, good job I'd messaged, I'd have completely forgotten otherwise. I put a note in my calendar for Wednesday to remind me to buy a present and sent a quick thumbs up back. I picked up my phone and looked up the new police station on google maps, which informed me it was a 25 minute walk away, so I lingered over my coffee and then set off just before 11 o'clock.

The new police station was a 'hub', which housed the fire station and ambulance service as well. I walked into the reception area, which still smelt new, and joined a couple of people in a queue to sign in. It was impossible not to hear that the first man had come to prove he'd changed his tyres after being stopped by a patrol earlier in the week, and the second young man, barely a man, was here to report as part of his bail conditions. After I'd been handed a visitor's pass I paced about, looking around as I waited for Nash. As far as it could be for a police station, the reception was reasonably welcoming.

I stood and perused a picture on the wall, obviously drawn by local children. It had all the local icons – the red arrows in the sky above the cathedral, the university, the Lincoln Imp – and some friendly police officers greeting the locals.

"Verity!" Nash's voice broke into my thoughts. "Come through." He indicated for me to go ahead of him through the door. We walked down a short corridor and he peered into a room to the right but it was occupied.

"Follow me." He gestured through another door.

We walked past the locked steel door of the custody suite and into 'interview room one'.

"Sorry it's a bit formal," he apologised and indicated that I should sit down.

Everything in the room was screwed down—the chairs, the table, the recording machine. I imagined in case detainees became over-agitated. I sat down on one of the fixed chairs, positioned just too far back from the table to be comfortable.

Nash had a folder in his hands, which he placed on the table and he sat down opposite me.

"Thanks so much for seeing me," I said.

"Not a problem," he replied. "Now, you're trying to help find Gloria Kasongo?"

"Yes. Her foster carer came to see me, to see if there was anything I could do to help. She did mention there was a PC who got on okay with Gloria, PC Keal?"

"Ah yes, Deborah. Do you want me to ask her to give you a call?"

"Please, that would be really helpful. Nash, I know someone was investigating and drew a blank. Is there anything you can tell me that will help?"

"Well, in the interests of finding Gloria, I can tell you a little bit about the investigation. I mean, I'm limited in what I can say, obviously. But, actually, Verity, we don't know much anyway and our officers have enough cases where they do have solid leads. We have our ongoing social media campaign, people do sometimes respond to them, although there's nothing yet. You know, if we get any new information we'll obviously look into it but as things stand at the moment, we really have exhausted our options."

He opened the file, careful not to let me see the contents. "Ah yes, her phone. We did find her phone."

The new iPhone that Sarah had mentioned. She was apparently glued to it. This didn't sound good. "Where did you find it?" I took my notebook out of my handbag.

"It was in a house in Lincoln. A well-known address." He looked up and anticipated my next question. "I can't, obviously, tell you the address, but I can tell you that it isn't relevant anymore anyway, so even if I could it wouldn't be of any use to you. The couple who lived there have been evicted."

"What was her phone doing there?"

"It was an address we were all too familiar with, I'm afraid. A couple who had a constant stream of young people visiting. They used to give them alcohol, cannabis, probably other drugs as well. Neighbours complained about the amount of unsavoury visitors coming and going. The noise. Shouting, screaming. Taxis calling at the house at all times of the day and night. Drug dealing, antisocial behaviour. They received a couple of harbouring notices."

"Sorry, a couple of what?"

"Ah, yes, child abduction warning notices. It prevents them from having a particular child at their house."

"So what were these people doing?"

"A bit of drug dealing, that's for sure. With all the activity, and knowing the young people involved, we think they were involved in some form of child sexual exploitation. You've heard of that?"

"Like in Rotherham?" I frowned. I had read articles in the press, but hadn't really gone into all the details. I remembered Asian men and young white girls and very little else.

"Well, not quite. There are many forms of CSE and we think this couple were being used as a kind of hub. They kept the kids, fed them drugs and alcohol and then taxis came and collected them and took them, well who knows where." He shrugged, palms up, as if it could have been anywhere in the world.

"Where did they go? And what happened to them?"

"We're not sure, Verity, not sure at all. Problem is the young people won't often tell us. They get into this because they're vulnerable, lonely, often in care. Sometimes they believe one of the involved people is their boyfriend. They're wined and dined, treated like an adult, they think they're in love."

"But how can someone make someone else believe they're their boyfriend when they're not?"

"Just by giving them a bit of affection, Verity. Some of these young people are quite isolated. You know, few friends at school. Bit of bullying. Parents who don't really care. You come along and tell them they're beautiful and special. Bob's your uncle, so to speak. They're so pleased to be able to tell everyone they have a boyfriend. And to believe that they really are special to someone. Then their 'boyfriend'"—he made the inverted commas sign— "decides that if they really loved him they'd have sex with his friends. And his friends' friends." He paused, looking as if he was thinking about the sadness of this.

"And they don't refuse?"

Nash sighed and rubbed his cheek with his hand. "They don't have the ability to refuse. By that time they're in too deep, thinking this is how love works. By the time they build up the courage to question what's going on, they're probably being forced to have sex with men, pose for pictures, videos, prostitute themselves. That's often when the violence starts. And the threats."

"Jesus."

"Or sometimes they get them dependent on drugs and they have to have sex with others to 'pay' for the drugs. They're often intimidated, threatened, too scared to say anything, told they'll be deported for criminal activity. These young people don't know the law."

"So they could get help?"

"If they knew where to go, but generally they don't. They believe what they're told, especially if they're alone here and English isn't their first language." He picked up the file and tapped it against the table, then rested it back down. "Sometimes they're given phones, jewellery, other gifts. For a lot of them, they come from violent, dysfunctional families and they think it's all normal, even when it's clearly an abusive relationship." He sighed a heavy sigh as if he'd seen these patterns too many times.

"Gloria had a new iPhone apparently," I said, thinking aloud about what he'd said. "And some expensive clothes. Would they be connected?"

"They could be, Verity, they could well be. The phone we recovered was an iPhone. It didn't give us many clues, though. There were a few calls to one particular taxi firm. There were some photos of Gloria in various stages of undress − not selfies, posing, and taken from across a room although we couldn't place where. The photos had all been sent to one number, probably for distribution on the Internet, but we never traced the number. It'll have been trashed soon after."

"Which was the taxi firm she used?"

"That would be A Star Taxis. Down the High Street, just past the court. Do you know it?"

"I have a vague idea." I wasn't really that familiar with the area. "Nash? Gloria's foster carer said she'd been found in Leeds and other places. What do you think she was doing there?"

"She did start being found further afield, Leeds, yes, several times. Trouble is, she was always found in a public place like a park. And she would never say where she'd been or who she'd been with, even though she was sometimes quite upset. We, that is the strategic child exploitation group, had a meeting with professionals from Leeds but with so little information we didn't have much to go on."

"Why didn't she say anything?" I couldn't understand why someone could be hurt by others and not be shouting for help.

"Thing is, Verity, the thing is that these young people are extremely vulnerable. Often they give off vibes of being streetwise and clever for their age – that's why some of my colleagues are not as patient with them as they should be—but truth be told, they are very damaged, traumatised. They've often suffered a lot in their lives. They're desperate for attention and that makes them very easy to prey on."

I thought about what Linda had said about Gloria's life as Nash continued to talk.

"Gloria may well have thought that her foster carer would throw her out if she found out what she was up to, or that she'd be deported back to Congo." He shook his head. "These people find the weakness, they prey on the vulnerability, threaten them with the things they know the young person is scared of, make them think no one will believe them. They have all the power, Verity, all of the power."

"Where do you think she is?"

"Honestly, Verity, I have no idea. My guess is that she's in a house somewhere, completely off the radar, being made to turn tricks to make money for some slimy bastard. I think she'll just turn up one day, somewhere we're not expecting. She'll have reached the limit of her usefulness, or she might run away, who knows?" He stared off into the distance, then he shook his head as if to free himself from the thought. "There are some evil people out there, and whilst she's making them money, I think she'll stay hidden."

Nash looked at his watch and jumped up. "Sorry," he said. "I need to get going but let me know how you get on."

We retraced our steps back to the reception area.

"Have you heard from Sam Charlton recently?" he asked as he held the door open for me.

"We were chatting the other evening," I said. "He persuaded me to take this case on." I shrugged my shoulders and smiled.

"Ah, well give him my regards won't you if you speak to him again soon."

I will, Nash, I certainly will, I thought, but I just nodded and headed back out into the sunshine.

7

I looked at my watch and wondered if Jack Clayton might be at the gym yet. I decided to give it a go and headed back the way I had come.

I found Jack behind the reception desk, his name badge negating the need for further enquiry. I looked him up and down and decided that if you were to draw a personal trainer, there was a good chance you would draw Jack Clayton. He was around his late twenties, maybe early thirties, with short, dark, close-cropped hair and arms that were bigger than my thighs. He looked up as I approached and asked if he could help. He had a bunch of keys hanging from his shorts with more keys than your average jailer. They jingled melodically as he spoke.

"Hi, yes, I'm hoping so. I'm trying to locate Gloria Kasongo and I hear you were her personal trainer."

He arched his right eyebrow and gave a short nod of his head.

I carried on, "I gather she's a regular here and I'm just trying to find out a little about her."

"What can I say?" He shrugged. "She comes here, I set her programme, she trains, she goes home. Nothing more I can tell you." And he folded his enormous arms across his ample chest as if to close down the conversation.

"Did she ever tell you anything about her life? Where she went? Who she knew?"

Silence. He just tilted his head back.

"Anything at all? It's just that she's been missing for over four weeks and people are concerned about her." I thought I saw a slight twitch in his left eye, but I couldn't be sure. It could have just been the light.

"No," he said. "There's nothing I can tell you about her."

I wasn't getting anywhere. "Well, if you do think of anything, please give me a call." I wrote down my number, thinking, not for the first time, that I should get some business cards printed. One of my friends worked at a local printing firm and I resolved to ask him the next time I saw him.

Jack Clayton remained impassive. He stood there with his arms still folded across his chest whilst I wrote down my number. He left the piece of paper where it was, on the reception desk, and said nothing as I headed back towards the door.

"Thanks," I shouted back, in the cheeriest voice I could muster, but I got no response. Jack was already reaching into his pocket. He brought out his mobile and lifted it to his ear, ignoring me and concentrating on the call he was about to make.

I was getting hungry, so I set off back up the hill towards home for some lunch. I called in at one of the little supermarkets for a ready-made salad, and when I got home I sat in the garden with a glass of lemonade and ate it straight out of the container. After I'd eaten I went back into the house and opened up my laptop. I'd received an email from the social worker suggesting that we could meet up tomorrow morning around 10am, if that suited. So I emailed back and said that would be fantastic. She was based in an office at the south end of the city so I could walk if the weather held up. I opened up the weather app on my phone and looked at the forecast. Tomorrow was predicted to be fine and bright, with high temperatures again. After that, there were increasing chances of thunderstorms.

8

I only had a little garden, but I enjoyed looking after it. Most of my flowers were in pots and when it was hot they need a lot of attention. I went outside and deadheaded and watered for a while, standing back every now and again to admire the show of petunias, geraniums and fuchsias, now getting well established and beginning to tumble down the side of the pots. I had just finished and gone back into the house, when I heard the familiar sound of an email arriving in my inbox.

It was from the school. Gloria's form teacher, who was also Head of English, had emailed and asked if I could go in and see him tomorrow morning before school started, around 8.30am. The headteacher had obviously forwarded my email to him as it was there in the trail. Welton Academy was to the north east of the city, and I thought about the timing. I worked backwards from needing to be with the social worker in the south of the city for 10am and, even if I took the car, I'd be cutting it fine. I responded saying that I couldn't make that time but I could go after school either today or tomorrow. I waited for a response, and it wasn't long before an email pinged back saying that today would be better, how about 4pm?

I glanced at my watch—that didn't give me too long, so I ran upstairs and showered, dried my hair, got changed and set off for Welton Academy.

Mr Ian Moorehouse sat in an office that had his name, followed by 'Head of English' inscribed on the door. The receptionist abandoned me outside the classroom, with a vague waft of her hand. I poked my head around the door and Mr Moorehouse scuttled over and ushered me into the office, where, before introductions could take place, we were momentarily interrupted by a timid young lady who had missed her bus home. Mr Moorehouse directed her to run after the receptionist and ask her for help, and then returned his attention to me. He looked far too young to have had time to go through university and then teach for enough years to attain 'head of' status, although I guessed he was probably mid-thirties. He ran a hand through a headful of big hair, revealing the end of a tattoo peeking out of his rolled-up shirt sleeve.

He indicated a seat on one side of the desk, which I sat down on, and he took the seat at the other side. He linked his hands together in front of him, tapping his index fingertips together, and leaned back in his chair. He gave the impression of a man with little time to spare to deal with people coming in to see him, least of all people who didn't even have children in his class. So I cut any prevarications and got straight to the point.

"I'm helping Linda Watson," I began. "I'm trying to find out what has happened to Gloria Kasongo."

"Such a shame about her," he said, giving a short laugh. I couldn't make up my mind if it was nervous or cynical. "Such a bright young girl." And he tapped his still-linked fingertips against his chin.

"Do you have any idea where she might be?" I asked.

"Me?" His eyebrows shot up and he opened both hands, palms towards me, and lifted his shoulders. His voice rose high. He sounded incredulous. "Why would I know where she was?" And a little defensive.

"You are her form teacher. I thought you might have some insight into what was going on for her."

"Ha." Another of the short laughs. This time, definitely cynical. "I'm sure she just went off the rails," he proclaimed as if it happened all the time.

"Off the rails?" I parroted, trying to keep the surprise out of my voice.

"She started making quite dubious choices," he stated, and this time he placed the fingertips of both hands lightly on the desk and started drumming them in turn. "She was choosing to hang around with the wrong sort, you know?"

"The wrong sort?" I was just repeating what he was saying back to him.

He raised his eyebrows and tilted his head, as if I should know full well the type he was referring to.

I changed tack. "You said that she was a bright girl."

'Hmm." He looked off to one side, leaned back in his chair, relinked his hands, and returned both index fingers to his chin. "She was talented, clever. She was going to get top marks." He gave another snort, then paused and looked directly at me. "But in the end she chose having fun over getting good results, didn't she?" It sounded almost like a challenge, throwing down the gauntlet—*ha! top that!*

I spent a moment mentally comparing him to the teachers in the pictures on the school's website. It wasn't a favourable comparison.

"A policeman I spoke to said that when children do that it's often because they're vulnerable. Traumatised," I ventured.

"I don't think she was vulnerable." He put his hands down flat on the desk as an emphasis. "She was a leader if anything. She and that young lad from the home." He drew a circle in the air with his finger as if indicating where the home was. "They were a pair. Thick as thieves. Once she got in with him she stopped caring about school. She'd turn up, then just as soon as she got here, she'd leave. She was more interested in surfing social media on her phone." He looked off to the side again and gave another cynical laugh. "Sometimes in class she'd just ignore me, start looking through her phone and then just stand up and leave." He said it as if he was more concerned about the slight to his teaching than for any worry about Gloria and what might have been going on for her.

"She walked out of class?"

"Many times." He slapped his hands down on the desk as if to signal he was getting ready to close the conversation. I got the impression he'd only agreed to meet me to please the head teacher. He didn't seem to have much inclination to find out what had happened to Gloria. But I wasn't done yet.

"Do you think she was getting messages from someone? Do you think someone was telling her to leave?"

"Well she didn't have to, did she?" He stood up. He was clearly bored of the conversation.

I didn't seem to be getting very far, so I stood up too and made to leave the office. I turned round at the door. "Did you ever see where she went?"

"No," he pondered. He put his hands in his pockets. "Although I did see her getting into a car one day. She just walked straight out of the classroom, not a word, just got her things and left. We were in 23B and the windows look over the road. She waltzed out quite the thing, and got into a sports car. I remember because just as she was getting in she turned round and looked up at the window and waved." He shook his head. "Brazen," he said. "Utterly brazen."

I walked home, thinking about what he'd said. His description of Gloria was a world away from the vulnerable teenager Nash had described. I needed to do some research. But not now. Right now I had a tiramisu to make.

Friday

-9-

The following morning I didn't wake up until nearly 9am—almost a first since John had died. I still didn't sleep too well and I rarely slept past 7 o'clock, but perhaps it was all the walking I'd done the day before. In many areas of my life I was getting back on an even keel. I wasn't relying so heavily on my friends to keep me entertained when I was alone and, since being forced to leave my home during 'the incident' I had definitely reassessed some of the important things in my life. Good, deep sleep, however, still alluded me on most nights, and I often had fitful dreams about John. Most of the time they were nice dreams, and although they disturbed my sleep, I enjoyed them. It was almost as if I got another chance to see him, another chance to cuddle into his arms, to feel his breath on my face, to smell him. I never woke up feeling sad after one of those dreams, always happy that I'd experienced seeing him one more time.

It took me a second to comprehend the time, and when I did, I jumped out of bed, headed into the shower and then got my things together ready to drive down to the social work office. It was far too late to walk.

The office was situated not far from a school and the last few, tardy, parents were just leaving as I arrived so there was plenty of parking space on the road. I parked up and headed into the office. A friendly receptionist greeted me, and I told her I was here to see Joy Mahoney. She asked me to wait whilst she let Joy know that I was there, waiting for her.

The waiting area was a mixture of a doctor's waiting room and nursery. A box piled with toys sat in the corner, looking as if it hadn't been disinfected in months. You could almost see the bacteria crawling over the toys. Posters filled the walls, detailing who you could call if you were being domestically abused. Or maybe you were privately fostering a child, or a teenager needing to talk to someone. You certainly wouldn't go short of a helpline number, that's for sure.

My contemplations were interrupted by the door lock clicking and then opening. A round, smiley face appeared, looked at me and said quizzically, "Verity?"

I stood up. "Yes, that's me."

"Joy," the large, cheery woman announced, and she offered her hand. "Joy Mahoney." She pronounced it like the Americans do, May-O-Ney.

Joy Mahoney led me through a rabbit's warren of corridors, her large but short frame swaying in front of me as we went. A shock of tight black curls formed a halo around her head, and they bounced magnificently as we walked through the maze of corridors, surely designed to disorientate anyone who wasn't supposed to be there.

Eventually we arrived at our designated room, and Joy opened the door and indicated that I should go in. Joy plonked herself heavily on a chair and indicated that I should do the same. I moved to the opposite corner of the table and sat down so that I was facing her.

"Now then." She smiled. "Gloria. Let's talk about Gloria."

I told Joy a little about what I was hoping to achieve.

"Obviously there are things I need to keep confidential," she explained, but then said she would obviously help as much as she could. She was clearly concerned for Gloria and hadn't heard anything from her in several weeks. We chatted for a while about what a lovely girl Gloria was, how she had been living in the home when Joy had met her and how she had come to persuade Gloria that a family would be a better place for her to be.

"And she settled in so well," Joy sighed. "It was all going fantastically…" She looked off to the side. She gave another sigh.

"Where did it start going wrong?"

She shook her head. Her curls twirled around her face. "I don't know." She closed her eyes for a moment as if she were trying to remember. "I'm not sure. I remember getting a phone call to say that she'd gone missing one day. I was really surprised. I mean, some of my young people do go missing, but with Gloria…well…it came as a bit of a shock."

"Do you know where she went?"

"Not that first time. I think she came back fairly quickly that time, probably just stayed out too late. But then she started going more frequently. It escalated quite quickly. We found her a few times in houses around the city, where she was really in some danger. There were people there who are not good to be mixing with. But generally, she wouldn't say where she'd been, or who she'd been with. Or what had happened to her. To start with she would at least text me to say she was okay if I sent her a message. But then she stopped responding. I was really worried about her. She was staying away longer, and we were finding her in places further and further away." Joy rubbed her temples as if massaging her brain might give her some answers. "She just clammed up. I'm not sure if she was scared, or…or what."

I got the impression that Joy was actually quite worried about Gloria. It didn't feel as if this was just a job to her. These were young people that she cared about and wanted the best for.

"Her teacher said he thought the boy from the children's home had led her astray," I suggested. "And Sarah, the foster carer's daughter did say she'd been seeing more of him. I think she said he was called Liam"

Joy pulled her mouth to one side and shook her head. "I don't think Liam had anything to do with it." She shook her head again, releasing the curls once more. "Liam's been excluded from a few schools, he does struggle with large classes, but he's never really been in any trouble. And as far as I'm aware he's never gone missing. I mean, he's late back at the home sometimes, like most teenagers, but he's never been missing overnight." She paused and looked towards the ceiling. "And we never found the two of them together after one of Gloria's missing episodes."

"Didn't she say anything about where she was going?"

"No, nothing." Joy's mouth curled downwards. "I tried. I tried everything. I'm used to teenagers, but there was something... We used to have a good, open relationship and I just don't know what happened."

I looked at Joy. She had a round, open face. A face that would be easy to pour out all your troubles to. If she had lost Gloria's confidence, then I could imagine few others would be able to get her to open up.

"Do you think she was being exploited?"

Joy nodded. "Undoubtedly. Yes, undoubtedly. I think there was some sexual exploitation going on. We did find some photos suggesting that. And I do think she might have been given drugs or alcohol." She paused, glancing to her left, thinking. "I also think someone was hurting her. One time when she was brought back from...I think it was from Leeds...she looked in pain. I thought she was just upset to start with, but when she walked, it was obviously really hurting her somewhere." Joy looked down and she hung her head and sighed. "I tried to persuade her to talk to HSL, thinking that she might prefer someone she didn't know, but..." She let her shaking head do the talking.

"HSL?" I asked.

"Ah, yes, Hope, Strength, Lives. It's a specialist service we have here in Lincolnshire. It's for young women who are unaccompanied asylum seekers and at risk, or who are vulnerable. It's why we have more young women here. Most young people seeking asylum, as I'm sure you know, are boys."

I didn't know this, but I nodded anyway.

"But we have the HSL service. It's a charity, separate from statutory services, but it gets money from the government too. It's quite successful, actually, but obviously you have to persuade people to talk to them first."

"And Gloria wouldn't?"

She bit the corner of her lip and shook her head. "I couldn't get her to talk to anyone."

"Do you think Liam would talk to me?"

Joy brightened up a little at this suggestion. "I'm sure he would," she said. "And as a matter of fact, I need to go up to Plumtree house, that's the home. If you give me five minutes, I'll nip and ring him up and ask if he's okay to talk to you. He has a home tutor so he's not in school at the moment." She glanced at her watch. "But the tutor is only there for a couple of hours each day—she'll have gone by now." And Joy finished this sentence by raising her eyes to the ceiling, shrugging and shaking her head. A gesture of despair that indicated Liam was not getting the education he should.

Joy rushed off, leaving me alone in the little room, and then burst back through the door about ten minutes later, carrying some car keys in her hand. She had a big work bag on her shoulder, brimming over with an untidy mess of paperwork and notebooks. Joy's ample frame filled the door and she held it open, saying, "Come on, I'll give you a lift up there."

10

Joy left through the staff exit, and I followed her out into the car park. A nearby car winked its lights as she flicked the remote control. I went round to the passenger side and opened the door. I was about to get in, but I was greeted by a seat full of empty sandwich packets, water bottles, takeaway coffee cups and crisp packets. As Joy flopped into the driver's seat, she looked over.

"Oh, excuse the mess," she said brightly.

I didn't get the impression that this was an unusual state for the car to be in. Joy scooped up most of the packets and threw them into the back of the car, where they joined piles of notepads, newspapers, blankets and dog hairs.

"Just throw everything onto the floor," she said.

I did as I'd been told, pushing the rest of the mess into the footwell and arranging my feet on top of it. Joy's car didn't appear to have functioning air conditioning, so it was stiflingly hot. We wound the windows down and drove along with the wind blowing our hair and having to shout to hear each other.

Plumtree House was a large Victorian detached house on a road called Carline Road which ran from just below the castle out towards the north-west of the city. We pulled into a small car park and parked at the front of the house, near what looked as if it was, indeed, a plum tree. Although I couldn't be sure. Along the side of the house, a steep grass verge led to a long rambling garden with fabulous views looking down to the south of the city and beyond. Joy rang the doorbell, and a young lady in jeans and a t-shirt answered, greeting Joy by name and inviting us in.

"Coffee? Tea?" she asked, but we both refused, just asking for water.

Joy introduced me, identified the young woman as Abigail, then asked her if Liam was about. Abigail left us in the hallway and headed up the stairs two at a time. She soon returned, trailed by a teenager I took to be Liam, in a grey hoody and khaki cargo trousers, his hands in his pockets. How he wasn't fainting from heat I didn't know. Just as Liam reached the bottom of the stairs, a door opened to our right and a slim, thirty-something woman with short dark hair and glasses came out.

Joy gestured towards her and said to me, "This is Amelia Macdonald, the manager. Amelia, Verity Spencer." Joy announced that she was going to talk to one of the young people and that she'd come and get me when she was done, and then she took the stairs towards the first floor, placing both feet on each step as she heaved her way up.

Amelia Macdonald smiled and shook my hand. She tipped her head sideways and raised her eyebrows as if to ask what I was doing there.

"Hi," I said awkwardly. "I've come to have a chat with Liam. It's about Gloria Kasongo."

Amelia gestured towards the room on the opposite side of the hall. "Please," she said. "Let's use the lounge. You don't mind me joining you? It's just that Liam is only seventeen and I can probably help too."

I shrugged and looked at Liam to see if he minded, and he shrugged back so we all went and sat in the lounge. The promised water never arrived. The lounge was a large room overlooking the car park at the front. Two comfy sofas and a couple of easy chairs were arranged around a coffee table, and it felt like a normal, homely space. Books and board games were scattered across and beneath the coffee table. A very modern looking television, with a games console underneath, was screwed to the wall. I sat down in one of the chairs, and Amelia and Liam sat on a sofa at a right angle to me. I thanked Liam for seeing me.

"Do you have any idea where Gloria might be?" I came directly to the point.

Liam shook his head and looked at the carpet.

"Do you know where she went when she ran away?"

He shook his head again. This was hard going.

"Were you friends when she lived here?"

At last he looked up. "Yes," he said softly. "We were really good friends."

"What did you do together?"

"Well, it's a couple of years ago, we weren't very old. We just, like, hung around."

"There was the club, wasn't there?" Amelia suggested.

Liam nodded. "Yeah, we used to go to a club, you know, activity club after school and in the holidays."

"Did you miss her when she moved out?"

He slowly nodded his head. Amelia gently put a hand on his knee and said, "You struggled a bit to start with didn't you?"

Liam nodded again. He looked up, and across at me. "She was, like, a really good friend and we kept up on Facebook, but I missed her. It felt like she didn't need me anymore, like she had her new family and didn't really want me." He pulled at his hoodie, pulling it closer round his neck.

"So you lost touch?"

"Yeah."

"But you became friends again? How did that happen?"

He started pulling at the loose fibres on the arm of the sofa. "I got thrown out of school." His head sank into his chest and he tugged once again at his hoodie. "I lost it with one of my teachers."

If they were anything like Mr Moorehouse, that didn't surprise me in the least. I could imagine quite vividly punching him on the nose, but I didn't voice that out loud.

"Anyway," he carried on, "I was ranting on Facebook and she, like, told me to shut the fuck up." He looked at Amelia. "Sorry," he said.

And she patted his knee again.

"She was right, really, I s'pose but we got chatting and I went and met her in town one day."

"How long ago was that?"

He shuffled his feet on the floor. "Maybe a year. I'm not sure."

"When she went missing, did you ever go with her?"

He shook his head.

"Sarah said that when she came to see you, she thought maybe you and Gloria were boyfriend and girlfriend?"

He didn't say anything, but he picked a little more furiously at the sofa arm, and shook his head slowly. I got the impression he might have liked to have been her boyfriend.

"Did she have a boyfriend?"

He looked down and shrugged his shoulders. "Maybe. I think, maybe, yeah."

Just then there was a knock, and Joy's smiley face appeared around the door. "Can I borrow you for a moment, Amelia." She glanced over at me. "Won't be long. Ten minutes, is that ok?" She looked at her watch as if she were about to start a countdown.

"That's fine," I said.

Amelia stood up and started to leave. As she crossed the floor, I asked Liam, "Did you ever meet Gloria with an older boy? Someone who used to live here?"

"Noah," Liam started to say, but Amelia cut him off.

"I'm sorry, but we can't talk about other people," she said, then quickly added, "confidentiality," by way of an explanation. She flashed a friendly smile and then left the room to go and talk to Joy.

Liam ignored her advice. "She was quite friendly with Noah when she lived here. But, um, I don't know if she saw him again after he left. Maybe." He shrugged.

"Could he have been her boyfriend?"

He sank further into the sofa and shrugged again. "Maybe. I dunno." He shook his head as if he really didn't want to think it could be true. "Maybe," he whispered.

"Did Noah threaten Sarah, Gloria's foster-sister?"

"He may've done, he could be like that sometimes." He shifted a little in his seat. "But I'm not sure, we lost touch a while ago."

"Where did he go, when he left here?"

"He moved into a flat, I think. I know he was working, but I'm not sure where."

"I could do with talking to him," I said, more to myself than to him.

"Sorry. I don't know where he is. There are records in the office of where people go when they leave, but it's all kind of locked away."

"Did you know that Gloria was leaving school in the middle of lessons?"

He shook his head again and looked down. His eyes became damp and he started blinking rapidly. He wiped his right eye on the back of his hand, and I wanted to take this boy who, for whatever reason, couldn't live with his family, and hold him and tell him it was okay. I wasn't sure it was okay, though, him alone with just social workers and residential workers to look after him. I mean, I was sure they did a fantastic job, but I could see why Joy had thought that Gloria would be better living in a family.

"I think she did have a boyfriend," Liam eventually said. "I don't know who it was, but I think it was someone older than her." He paused and stretched his hands out on his knees, examining them whilst he searched for the right words. "I think that's why she started running away. To be with him. She stopped coming round here, and we stopped meeting in town. So, I don't really know, but that's how it seemed to me." He let out a great sigh.

I wondered if he'd ever really admitted that to himself before, that she might have had a boyfriend. Someone other than him.

"Okay," I said, and I stood up. "Thanks so much for talking to me, Liam. If you think of anything else, or if you do hear from Noah, can you give me a ring?"

He nodded, so I wrote down my number and handed it to him. He scrumpled the piece of paper up and shoved it into a pocket in his trousers. I wasn't sure it would ever see the light of day again. We walked out into the hallway.

"Did Gloria ever give you a hint? Did she say anything that might give a clue as to what was happening?"

"She started saying something once, about going out at night, but when I asked her more she wouldn't answer. Then she stopped coming round not long after." His shoulders slumped and his body drooped once again.

"Can you remember anything of what she said?"

"Not really. Um, I think she said something about not knowing people. You know, people turn out to be different to what you think, but I can't really remember exactly."

Just then Joy reappeared so I said goodbye to Liam and thanked him once again. Joy and I crossed the car park and climbed back into her hot and untidy car. This time we were heading south and the sun glared in through the window. I fished about in my handbag but I didn't have a pair of sunglasses with me, so I closed my eyes to block it out and hoped it didn't blind Joy too much as she drove back.

Outside her office, I bid Joy goodbye, thanked her for her help and ran across to my car. It was mid afternoon and I needed to get ready to go out.

11

I sat at Keith and Robert's dining table, waiting for the main course to arrive. I had arrived a few minutes after 7pm, having decided at the last minute to take my car as I hadn't wanted to carry the tiramisu down Steep Hill. Keith and Robert lived in a modern apartment near the canal, which was about a half an hour walk. I had decided to drive there and then walk back so that I could have a drink. Or two. It was a lovely summer evening and it would be nice to stroll back up the hill later.

I sat on my own, watching in silence as Robert and Keith worked together on final preparations for the dinner. Robert was pulling food from the oven, and Keith providing plates and utensils seemingly without the need for communication. Before scooping up the food they paused momentarily, turned to each other and embraced. I felt very privileged to have them as my friends.

Robert and I had known each other for years. Soon after I'd married John, and we'd moved to the house on Steeple Lane, I'd got my first job at the local college. Robert had worked in the same department, ordering all the supplies we needed and guarding the stationery store with a zeal that couldn't have been stronger if he'd paid for the stock himself. We'd become firm friends and, even though we only worked together for a year or two, had remained so ever since. He'd met Keith a couple of years later and we had all shared each other's ups and downs. They had been my rocks in my most down moments after John's death.

"How is your mother-in-law?" Robert asked as he brought through a magnificent beef wellington. He could remember her when she was a vibrant and funny lady, telling me how to do my garden and bringing round a constant stream of cuttings and seedlings.

"Not good." I said, taking a sip of my wine. I helped myself to roast potatoes and vegetables as Robert carved up the beef. He was a great cook and it was done to perfection. "She doesn't really do a lot now, just sits and looks out the window, watching the birds. She doesn't know who anyone is. She doesn't remember having a child. She often says that she's waiting for her mother to come and collect her. It's so sad."

"Do you get to see her much?"

"Not really. I went about three weeks ago, I guess." John's mum was living in a nursing home and had been there for some time. She required care twenty four hours a day. "She has no idea who I am. I go because I think I ought to, really. And because there's no one else." Her only child had died, and she had no other family. It was tragic, although she was very well cared for and always seemed content when I went to see her. "The carers are really good with her," I added. "They've put a bird table and feeder just outside her window. It's really nice, but she's just not the same. She can't remember anything. It's like her whole life never happened."

"I hope I never end up that way." Keith shuddered. "I'd sooner go quickly than sink into dementia."

Later, after he'd cleared away our empty plates, Robert asked, "How's the car?"

"Frank? He's fabulous," I said, clapping my hands together. "Great choice, thanks so much for your help."

Robert shook his head. "I really don't see how a powder blue, Fiat 500 could ever be considered a boy. It's not exactly macho."

"Well, he is," I said. "Maybe he's in touch with his feminine side?"

"A gay car!" Robert exclaimed. "Only you could have a homosexual car."

As we waited for our main course to digest a little, Keith asked, "And Sam Charlton? Are we going to get to meet him anytime soon? You keep telling us about him, but we still haven't actually met him. You're becoming mysterious." And he gave me a wicked grin and a wink.

"Enough!" I said. "All in good time. And don't smile at me like that."

And then, a couple of hours and another bottle of wine later, we sat contemplating the half-eaten tiramisu. It was late, the sun had gone down a while ago, and I stood up and thanked them for a fabulous evening.

"I'll decant the tiramisu and then you can take your bowl with you," Robert said and carried it through the open-plan dining room and into the kitchen area.

"I'll put it in my car on the way past, and then I can walk up," I said. "I'll come back down in the morning and pick the car up."

We said our farewells, kissed, hugged and waved. I walked the few hundred yards to my car. I passed an elderly neighbour calling his cat in for the night, and said hello. As I reached my car I put the bowl under one arm and rummaged in my handbag for the car keys. I was absorbed in thought, raking through my bag.

A rush of footsteps startled me. Someone was really close. I hadn't heard them until they were right upon me. I glanced up and started to turn round to see who it was that was in such a hurry, but before I had time to do so the bowl arced out of my arms as a pair of strong hands shoved at my back. My hip fell heavily against the car, and although a stabbing pain ripped through my thigh, I was more concerned that I might have damaged the door of the car.

"Fuck off," a deep, male voice shouted as I fell forwards.

I had no time to put out my arms to break the fall and a burst of pain exploded in my knee. The bowl had shattered into a thousand shards of glass and they dug into my skin. I cried out and tried once again to turn round to see who it was, but an elbow jabbed into my back and the skin on my hands shredded as I was pushed down into the remains of the glass bowl.

"Fuck off," he said again, bending into my ear. "Fuck off home where you belong, bitch!"

Sharp needle points pierced my knees as they scraped on the glass whilst I struggled to stand up, my brain grappling to make sense of the sudden turn of events. My arms trembled and worked against me as I tried to push myself upright and regain my balance.

"Hey!" A shout came from behind me; the elderly neighbour I assumed. "Hey! You! What are you doing?"

A final shove from behind forced me forwards, and I fought to stop myself from falling to the ground once again. The neighbour must have seen what had happened and the old man was lumbering towards me as fast as his ancient legs would allow. My assailant ran off, his back to me and his hoodie pulled tight over his head. There was no way I could see his face. I ran after him, my quivering legs slowing my speed. He was fast and he'd already sped off down the road, yanking over a bin that someone had left out, and scattering empty packets and decaying food across the pavement. I came to a stop. There was no way I would catch him. As I peered down the road and into the distance, he disappeared round the corner and headed along the main road. All I'd seen of him was his black jeans and a dark hoodie. Nothing identifiable at all.

I sat down on the side of the upturned bin, leaning my elbows on my knees and regained my breath whilst the old man drew near. As he approached, I examined my arms and hands. Droplets of blood were dripping from the many, small cuts that peppered my skin.

"Are you okay?" the old man said through laboured breaths, as he bent down to help me stand up.

"Just a bit shaken, I think," I said, running my hands across my body to check that everything was still in the right place.

"You need to be careful," he said, the concern showing in his wrinkled brow. "We've had a spate of burglaries recently, I think it's druggies, needing stuff to sell," the old man continued, as he took my arm and guided me back down the road. Without saying anything, he was steering me back the way I had come. "Bloody idiots," he added.

He left me as we approached Keith and Robert's flat, and veered into his house, wishing me well. I thanked him for his support and rang Keith and Robert's doorbell.

"Forget something, sweetheart?" Robert said as he answered the door. He looked down at my arms and his mouth fell open. Concern wrinkled across his forehead as he took my arms in his hands, ushering me inside.

Once I was sitting at the kitchen table, wipes, plasters and cotton wool appeared almost instantly and Robert set about cleaning my arms. It was clear that there was no real damage. All the cuts were superficial, although they stung like crazy.

"You can't go home, darling," Keith proclaimed. "You're too shaken up. The spare room is all made up. Why don't you stay here?"

I reluctantly agreed. It didn't seem sensible to head home, and if I was being honest with myself, I did still feel quite unnerved. I didn't admit that to anyone else, though.

"We have had a problem recently," Robert agreed, when I told him what the neighbour had said about the spate of burglaries. "There's been a couple of the houses broken into. I think we're okay as we're in a flat. It's harder to get into the properties."

And with that, we all headed towards the bedrooms.

"Thanks for having me," I said as we parted ways at the door. I went into the spare room and sat on the bed wondering if it was a random drug addict, or whether I'd seen someone in the last couple of days who wanted me to back off. And if so, why? Why would someone not want a vulnerable teenager found?

Saturday

12

The bright morning sun streamed in through the window and woke me early on Saturday. I lay in bed for a while, confused as to where I was. Then I remembered that I hadn't actually made it home, and I spent a little while pondering on the events of last night. I mentally went through all the people I'd spoken to over the last couple of days, but no one stood out as a potential for sending someone round to frighten me. And how would they have known where I was? The more I thought about it, the more the old man's explanation seemed the most plausible. Keith and Robert were still snoring in the room next door so I crept out of bed and put on yesterday's clothes. I wrote a quick thank-you note and left it on their dining table, and then tiptoed out of the flat to retrieve my car.

The shattered glass still covered the ground near the passenger door but there was nothing I could do to clear that up. I studied the side of the car where

I'd fallen and I ran my hand over a small indent in the passenger door. "Sorry, Frank," I said out loud, resolving to get it fixed as soon as I had the time. I looked around, but I wasn't really expecting to see anything that might give me a clue as to what it had all been about. Maybe it was nothing. Perhaps it had just been a random occurrence.

When I got home, I gave Sam Charlton a ring. He had previously worked for the Human Trafficking Unit in London and his perspective on Gloria would be really welcome; I was fairly sure there would be a lot of crossover between trafficking and exploitation.

"Verity, hi," he said cheerily down the phone. "How's things?"

"Things are good, Sam," I said

"Enjoying the sunshine?" he asked.

"It's beautiful," I agreed. "Although I'm not sure how long it's going to last."

"The vagaries of the English summer."

"Indeed," I said and I gave him a quick update of where I had got to with trying to find Gloria. I admitted that, although I'd seen lots of people, I didn't seem to be finding much out that was pointing me towards her.

"So, what are your plans?" he asked. He rarely proffered advice unless I directly asked him for it—it was one of the qualities I really liked about him.

"I think I need to find Noah," I said. "I feel like he's important. A link somehow. It seems that it threatened Sarah, and he definitely knew Gloria. Why would he threaten Sarah?"

"Hmm," said Charlton.

I had a mental image of him rubbing his finger along his jaw.

"Yeah, who knows? I guess he could have been working for someone. Doing the heavy work?"

"I just don't know how to track him down. Maybe I'll go back to the home, try Liam again. Or maybe one of the other workers. The manageress was a little guarded about confidentiality. If I can find someone with a loser tongue..." I joked, eschewing any ethics I might have had.

"You mentioned there were some photos?"

"Yeah, both the social worker and Nash mentioned them. Maybe you could have a word with Nash? He might tell you a little more than me."

Nash and Charlton had never physically met, although they had both been involved in 'the incident' and I knew they shared similar police interests. They had spoken a couple of times on cases where children from London had been found dealing drugs in Lincolnshire. Charlton had explained that this was a form of exploitation—drug gangs from the cities sent children, often children in care, to the counties to sell their drugs for them. The gangs knew children were less likely to be arrested, and if they were arrested, less likely to receive a prison sentence.

"I'll ask around, see if there's anything I can dig up that might help you."

"Thanks, Sam. The social worker also mentioned that she thought, at least on one occasion that Gloria was in pain when she got home. Why would that be, do you think? Why would she be hurt?"

"Maybe she resisted. If the social worker's right and she's being exploited, maybe they wanted her to do something she didn't want to do."

"You mean they might have beaten her to make her do something?" I found Gloria's photo on my phone and looked down at her smiling face. Shivers ran down my back.

"It's a possibility. Look, I'll see what I can do to help," Charlton said.

I considered telling him about being pushed over the night before, but I kept quiet. I thought about the elderly neighbour and Robert both saying there had been several incidents recently and decided that I was being paranoid.

"Thanks, Sam," I said, and we disconnected.

I had just walked as far as the kettle when my phone rang. I thought it was Charlton, wanting to tell me something he'd forgotten to say, but it was an unknown number.

It turned out to be PC Deborah Keal. She said that Nash had asked her to give me a call.

"I'm heading into the city on foot," she said. "Part of our 'higher visibility' campaign. But I'll be due for a ten-minute break when I get there. We could meet up for a quick cup of tea?"

We arranged to meet in half an hour, so I abandoned thoughts of a coffee at home, gathered all my things together and set off past the cathedral and down the hill into the city centre. My sunglasses cast a dark hue over the piercing reflections of the sun in the shop windows. People were fanning themselves with whatever they had to hand, to cool themselves as trickles of perspiration ran down their faces. I paused occasionally to look in the shop windows on my way down the hill, not wanting to sweat on my newly washed linen dress. The forecasts kept predicting thunderstorms and I could sense that they would be on their way before too long.

I was meeting PC Keal in Caffé Nero – her choice – and I arrived first, so I bought my coffee and sat down to wait. I glanced at the hordes of shoppers walking by, out for a weekend of leisure on the high street, everyone in shorts and T shirts, and the odd man walking along without a top. I was just thinking unkind thoughts about some of the shapes walking past, when I noticed a policewoman coming through the door. I signalled to PC Keal, who went to join the, thankfully short, queue. She looked to be in her early fifties, with short blonde hair and a plump, friendly face. I could see that Gloria would have felt comfortable with her, she just had that grandmotherly look about her.

"Thanks for meeting me," I said as she sat down opposite, putting a teapot and cup onto the table before returning her tray to the counter.

She took off her hat and laid it down next to the teapot, revealing an inch or two of greying roots in her hair. "Not a problem," she said, shaking out her hair. "I hope I can be of some help. We're all worried about Gloria."

"You often went to pick her up after she'd been found, is that right?" I asked.

"Yes. I went down to Kent a couple of times, other places around the country, Leeds a few times and lots of places around the city."

"And she never said where she'd been or who she'd been with?"

PC Keal pondered that question for a while, pulling her mouth to one side as she thought.

"One time," she said. "I thought she was going to open up. I'd been to a police station somewhere…I think it might have been one of the Kent trips. She'd rung her foster carer and told her she was in a park somewhere and she shared her location on her phone. The local police went round to pick her up and I went off to the nick to fetch her back."

"How was she?"

"Miserable."

"Miserable? How so?"

"She'd obviously been crying. Her face was all puffy. She looked like she was in pain. I thought she was going to say something. She was so close. When she saw me walk in, a familiar face, she crumpled. I took her in my arms and she just sobbed. Great, big sobs. My uniform was soaked." She gave a sad little laugh at the memory. "I asked her what it was. 'What's happened, pet?' I said. 'What's happened?' And she said, 'I thought he loved me, I thought he loved me.' Over and over again. And she sat in the car all the way back, staring glumly out of the window, wincing when she moved and every now and then she would start crying again."

"Who? Who did she think it was who loved her?"

"I never found out. She wouldn't say. But she was never upset like that again. When I picked her up, she was more, well just more resigned I guess. She'd glance up at me with that look, like, 'here we are again Deb'. I wondered if she thought I knew more than I did, you know, understood what was happening. I'm sure young people think you do sometimes. But no, we've not got to the bottom of it yet."

"What do you think was going on?"

"Honestly? I think she was being used for sex. They were moving her around. Taking her further afield. What we've seen with some of the other girls is that once they've got them having sex with different men, then they start photographing it, videoing it. That'll be more lucrative, you get the money for the sex and then money for selling the pictures or videos. And they build it up, get them used to it so it seems more normal."

"Do you think that might be why she had the expensive underwear?"

PC Keal tilted her head back and looked up at the ceiling. "It could be. You mean to spice up the videos?"

I nodded.

"It could be, yes. Look pretty for the camera, that kind of thing."

"How can you break it up? Stop it happening?"

"You have to find a way in. With some of the young people, it's easier to do. Some of them will trust you when you say you can help and they just need someone they can rely on, someone to tell them the truth. But sometimes it's just so hard for them to break free. They don't actually believe the truth. They're frightened, intimidated. Who'll believe them? Some of the stories you hear are so horrific that a lot of people think they can't possibly be true, that the young people are making it up. So it's a believable threat when their abusers say no one will take them seriously."

"Nash said that sometimes the men act like a boyfriend, to gain their trust."

"Yeah. I'm pretty sure that's what happened with Gloria. When she started staying out she was cocky, brash and often drunk when she got home. She'd flirt with the younger policemen and joke about being able to get them drugs. She acted like someone much older, more worldly wise. She was overly confident. Arrogant. But as she started being found further afield she changed, she gradually withdrew and would just sit there saying nothing. When I'd take her home she'd just snap and stomp off to her room."

"That fits the description the teacher gave me. He seems to think it was the young people at the home that were leading her astray. His words," I emphasised quickly.

"I don't think so." The corners of her mouth arched down and she shook her head gently. "Liam's a friend. He's had a few talkings to, but he's not a bad lad."

"Did he ever go missing with her?"

She glanced out of the window. She shook her head again. After a while she said, "No. No, not to my knowledge. There are a couple from there who go missing sometimes. We did have an issue with one of the workers not reporting them when they went missing. An agency worker, can't remember his name though, Spanish I think. We spoke to the manager and I think she sorted it. I don't think it's still an issue. But I don't think Liam has gone missing." She gave a quick shrug as if that had cleared that matter up.

I switched tack. "I think there was a taxi firm involved in taking her places? A Star Taxis?"

"Ah yes. I've had a word with them a few times in the past. They'd take young people to houses, known drug dealers. They took them to nightclubs, and I'm pretty sure they took Gloria further afield at least once. They seem to have stopped now. We threatened them with removing their licence."

"Nightclubs?"

"One time we had a call from one of the drivers. He'd just started working with them. He'd moved here from somewhere else, Manchester or Doncaster, well somewhere north. Said he'd had safeguarding training when he worked as a taxi driver there. He was worried we'd tell his boss he'd talked to us, so we had to be discreet. It was late. After midnight. He said he'd just dropped a young girl and an older man off at the Five Two Two nightclub. The home had reported Gloria missing earlier that night, and the girl fitted her description but when officers went out she wasn't there, so it might have been someone else. Or she could have left before they got there. Or maybe she wasn't going there at all."

I was just weighing this up when PC Keal jumped up, looking at her watch.

"Anyway," she said, picking up her hat and putting it on her head, "I need to get on with being visible." And with that, she bid me a cheery farewell and left.

13

After leaving the café, I decided I might as well wander over to the Five Two Two nightclub. I had nothing else to do and as PC Keal had mentioned it, I figured that I didn't have much to lose by going and seeing if there was someone I could talk to.

The Five Two Two nightclub was located on a side road near the river, behind the post office depot. At least it was out of the town centre, unlike some of the other nightclubs whose drunk attendees tended to spill down Lincoln High Street into the early hours of the morning. I guessed the majority of its clients came from the university, which was not too far from the site. The plain, red brick building stood next to some warehouses and storerooms that serviced one of the retail areas. In the front of the building there were some big black doors that looked like large garage doors, containing a smaller entrance within them. There wasn't much to indicate what was inside, apart from the logo on the wall by the entrance. The name Five Two Two was a play on the Lincoln area phone code, which was 01522 and it also sounded a bit like a dance rhythm, I guessed. The logo consisted of an upside down 5 with the two 2s entwined like snakes around it, and the words Five Two Two detailed around the edge.

I tried the door, and surprised myself when it opened. I walked inside and had to wait a moment for my eyes to adjust it was so dark.

Gradually, the darkness eased and the outlines of a corridor began to take shape. I tapped the carpet ahead with my toe and moved forward, the contours becoming sharper as I went along. The only light came from a dim bulb overhead and my eyes gradually adjusted as I advanced. A plush red carpet led down to the end. Framed and signed vintage posters for bands from the 70s and 80s covered the walls along the right-hand side. I walked towards the opening at the end of the corridor, where a velvet curtain was swept back and hooked against the wall with a gold rope tie. This led through to the main bar and dance floor.

A long bar almost filled one side of a large room. Bottles of liquor glistened and shone on shelves, backlit with different coloured lights. The bar was dark wood with brass fittings and I shuddered as I imagined it three deep in students trying to buy cocktails. I glanced around the room. A few tables randomly littered the edge of the dance floor, and booths with round tables circled the remaining walls. The booths were higher than the dance floor, you had to step-up into them. Although on first glance it appeared relatively plush, the place was actually fading and getting old. Everything, on closer examination, looked as if it needed updating. The velvet on the seats in the booths was fraying, and the brass surrounding the bar was tarnished.

"Hello?" A disembodied voice interrupted my thoughts.

I span round to try to see where it was coming from. A man had appeared behind the bar; I assumed he must have been there when I arrived, but maybe bending down, hidden from view.

"How did you get in?" He scowled over at me. He was tall, maybe six feet, fortyish with a shaved head and he was wearing a tie-dye T shirt. He lifted the door of the bar and came out onto the dance floor, spreading his sandalled feet out wide and puffing out his chest. If he was trying to appear intimidating it was working really well.

I swallowed and, overcompensating, said a cheery, "Hello! The door was open."

"What do you want?" He spread his feet a little wider, making himself look broader.

I was momentarily taken aback, and I hesitated.

"Eh?" He took a step towards me.

"I just wanted to talk to someone," I said, a little too quickly. I hoped I hadn't given away my nervousness. "I've been hired to help try to find someone who's gone missing, and it seems she might have come here. She's a young girl, only fifteen."

"This is a nightclub. No one under eighteen is allowed in." But his voice had quietened somewhat, and he pulled his chest back in a little.

"I've got a photo," I said, rummaging in my bag for my phone. "Maybe you could just take a look and see if you recognise her?" Just as I picked the phone up it started vibrating. It was a number I didn't recognise so I dropped the call and scrolled to my photo album. I found the picture of Gloria and handed my phone to him.

He took the phone, fished out some reading glasses from his pocket, and peered at the picture. He adjusted his stance as he studied the photo, bringing his legs closer to his body, almost becoming smaller. He shook his head.

"I don't recognise her." He looked up. "But we do get hundreds of people in here, as you can imagine. And, obviously I'm not always here." His tone had become much softer. Maybe he was moved by the picture of a missing teenager.

"Do you get many underage drinkers?"

"Not that many. The bouncers are usually quite good at spotting them, and the bar staff are trained to ask for ID if they're in doubt." He paused for a moment, and then said, "Mind you, some of them do have false ID. But no, it's not a big problem here. Maybe in the centre of the city you might find it more, but I guess they don't want to trek out here only to be turned away. Sorry I'm not being much help."

"Okay, thanks anyway," I said. "It was worth checking." Maybe the girl the taxi driver had dropped off had been going somewhere else. Or maybe it wasn't Gloria. I was getting nowhere.

I put my phone away and turned, ready to head for the door, but then he shouted after me, "You might want to come back and see the owner, Aidan. He's almost compulsive about the licensing laws. The doormen are really good at turning people away who are too young, but if anyone does get in and is asked to leave, Aidan'll know about it. He won't let them back."

"Okay." I wasn't sure if it would be worth it, but you never knew. "When is he around?"

"He's usually here in the afternoons, but you're probably more likely to catch him in the evenings, from about nineish, maybe ten, most nights." He glanced at his watch. He turned towards the bar, then added, "Except on Mondays. He has Mondays off."

"Thanks," I shouted. "Who shall I say told me to call by?"

"Mark," he said as he disappeared behind the bar. "Mark Henry."

And with that I headed back down the carpeted corridor and ventured out into the sunshine.

14

Once I was back outside I fished my phone out. Whoever had called had left a message, so I dialled up the voicemail and stood in the shade whilst I listened.

"Uh, hi. Um, this is Liam, you know, from Plumtree House? Yeah, well, you left me your number. Uh…it's just that my friend Aziza, she lives here too, yeah? Uh, she'd like to talk to you. She might be able to help with, uh, Gloria. Okay, yeah we're gonna head into town so let me know if you can meet us. You've got my number now. Well, uh, thanks then, bye."

I could picture Liam fiddling with his hoodie and shuffling in his seat as I listened. I called him straight back and he said that he and Aziza were already in town and having a drink in Café Santos, in the city centre. I said I'd be there in ten minutes and set off along the side of the river to find them.

As I approached the café, I shielded my eyes and scanned the people sitting at the outside tables. Liam was there, still wearing the same hoodie and cargo trousers as yesterday despite the searing heat. He was sitting with a young lady of about fourteen or fifteen, under the shade of a tree. He stood up as he saw me approach, the politeness taking me by surprise, and he introduced me to Aziza. She was a slight, small girl, with olive-coloured skin and a light green scarf draped around her head and shoulders. She remained seated and looked up at me out of the corner of her eyes, her shoulders hunched over slightly. I tried to smile reassuringly, although I wasn't convinced I quite pulled it off. After nipping inside to order a coffee I rejoined them outside on the patio.

Liam jiggled his leg as he spoke. He pulled at the cords of his hoodie, bringing it tight in around his neck, constantly fidgeting. Maybe he had cold blood or something; I was dressed in a thin summer dress and I was sweltering.

He looked at Aziza, and then at me. He gave a light cough and swallowed, then said, "Aziza thought she might be able to help you, you know, with finding Gloria."

"Thank you," I said. I wasn't quite sure where to start—I didn't want to just launch in with this timid-looking young girl, so I said, "Tell me a little bit about yourself, Aziza. Where are you from?"

She hunched her head over, almost as far as she could whilst still maintaining eye contact and whispered, "Afghanistan."

"How long have you lived here?"

"A couple of years, I was fifteen when we left," she said, her voice gradually becoming clearer.

"So you're seventeen? Like Liam?"

"I'm eighteen actually, now," she said. She glanced up at me briefly, seeming to gain a little confidence as we spoke.

I was surprised she was so old. "And you're allowed to stay at Plumtree?" As the words hit the air, I quickly followed that up with, "I'm sorry, I didn't mean to sound rude, but I always assumed children's homes didn't let you stay once you were eighteen."

Liam interjected, "I think they're a bit more, you know, human these days."

Aziza nodded. "I'm starting university this autumn. I can stay there 'till the course starts."

"What was it that made your family come over to England?" I asked.

She leaned her shoulders back so that they were very lightly touching the back of the chair and lifted her head a little. "I'm from a Christian family," she said. "We were persecuted in Afghanistan. We just had to leave in fear of our lives."

"Oh." I must have sounded surprised, and I looked at her scarf.

She touched the fine green material and said, "It's a cultural thing, nothing to do with religion. In Afghanistan you wouldn't probably know someone's religion from the way they dress. Everybody dresses in the same way, more or less."

"So did you leave with your family?"

"Yes," she said, looking directly at me now, losing her inhibitions a little. "The Taliban had killed some of my mother's relatives, and my parents decided we couldn't risk staying any longer."

"How did you get here?"

"We travelled for months. We were in the backs of lorries, the boots of cars sometimes. But we got separated along the way. I'm not sure where, maybe it was in Turkey, I don't know. But I was alone when I arrived here."

"Has anyone tried to help you find them?"

"Yeah, my social worker is in touch with the Red Cross. They did trace my uncle, he was in Germany. I spoke with him on the phone. But they haven't found my mum yet. Or my dad…"

"But they're still trying?"

"Yeah, I guess…"

"And what can you tell me about Gloria?"

She looked down, retreating once more into her shell. I'd pushed it too far too fast. She said nothing.

"Did anything happen to you, Aziza?"

She looked around. She nodded her head slowly, but remained silent.

"Is there anything you can tell me, that will help me?"

She nodded again, but then said, "I can, I will, but not here. There's too many people. Can we meet later, somewhere more private?"

"Of course," I said softly, although really I wanted to jump up, take her by the shoulders, shake her and shout *tell me now!*

I switched to something less personal, "Did you know Noah?"

She looked up again, seemingly relieved that I had moved on. "Yes," she said. "He was at Plumtree House when I moved in."

"And were you friends?"

"To start with, yes, kind of. And we kept in touch for a little while after he left. But he changed.

And then we lost touch." She looked down and started picking at the fingernails on one hand with the nails of the other.

"Do you know where he moved out to?"

"Yeah. There are some flats, council flats, they have people nearby if you need help. He moved into one of them, but I think they threw him out. He was always breaking the rules, stopping out, drinking beer and taking drugs. I think he took people back there, which he wasn't supposed to do. When he got thrown out I don't know where he went."

"I could do with finding him," I said, almost to myself.

Liam became suddenly animated. He sat upright in his chair and stopped jiggling his leg. "I think we might be able to help," he said.

"Oh?" I was curious.

"Yeah, there are files at Plumtree."

"I thought the records were locked away in the office."

"They are." He winked, and a sense of devilment appeared in his eyes that I hadn't seen before. "But I think we can, like, get to them. If you come back with us, to the house?"

"Ok," I said nervously, "that would be fantastic." I was a little wary as to what I might be agreeing to, but I was desperate to find out more about Noah so, for the time being, I put my reservations to one side.

Liam smiled and nodded, rocking in his chair, and rubbing his hands down his trousers. The challenge had brought him to life and I could see for the first time why he might have caused his teachers some grief.

"What did you and Noah do together, when you were friends?"

"We used to play five-a-side football at the leisure centre," Liam said.

I thought about the gym token that Gloria had had, because she was a child in care.

"Did you get that free? Like Gloria's gym membership?"

"Yeah," he said. "We can go to any kind of leisure facility." He shrugged. "I guess there has to be some kind of perk." And he gave an ironic laugh.

"How does that work then? Do you have a free-for-all pass? Or what?"

Aziza answered, "No, we can ask for membership of anywhere, and the council pay for it. Then you get the card, or token, or whatever sent to you. Or you can pick it up. It means that you don't stand out. It's not like a big flashing light over you saying, 'this person is in care', it's just the same as everyone else's membership."

"Did you go to the gym?"

They both shook their heads, then Aziza added, "Noah and I used to go to the swimming pool, in the early days that I was here. That's part of the gym but it's a different membership. We never went to the actual gym though."

I wanted to find out a little more from Aziza; I was desperate for a hint of what she had to tell me, even if the private details were left till later.

Eventually, I asked, "Aziza, did you ever run away from Plumtree House?"

She immediately looked down and clasped her hands in front of her. I'd touched a nerve, *damn.* I hoped I hadn't pushed too far. But she nodded and started picking at her nails again.

"Do you still run away?"

This time she shook her head, but she still said nothing. I was grasping at straws.

"Did something help you? Or was there someone who helped you?"

Very quietly and slowly she said, "There was a guy at Plumtree, he used to work in the evenings sometimes. He was great, we used to chat about all sorts of things. I'd sit on the stairs when I was upset and he'd come and sit with me. We just sat there chatting, you know, about life and stuff." She looked at her hands again. "But he's not there anymore."

"Oh. What happened?"

"He was from one of the agencies. They never have enough staff, and they're always calling in agency workers. He used to be there quite a lot though. Then he suddenly stopped. I don't know why. I don't know what happened, he just suddenly stopped coming there to work. He was really nice too. He put me in touch with HSL and they were great."

"Ah," I said, "Hope, Strength, Lives? Is that right?"

"Yeah. They were amazing. I'm so pleased I went there." She looked up again, her face more open, her brow less furrowed.

"What was the guy's name? The agency worker."

"Francisco," Aziza said. "Francisco Martínez."

We had all finished our drinks by this point, so I went in and paid and then we headed off.

15

On the way to Plumtree House we had hatched a plan. It was a little sketchy, it had several gaps, and was not without its risks, but it was a plan nonetheless. As we hovered just out of sight of the house and revised what we were about to do, I started to have second thoughts. Niggling little doubts were tugging at my chest. If I got caught, the consequences could be serious.

"Let me get this straight," I said to the two of them. "I am about to enter someone's office without their knowledge and rummage through confidential papers?" When I said it out loud I almost lost my nerve.

Aziza and Liam had become quite enthusiastic on the way there and had stated categorically that if I didn't do it, they would break into the office themselves. They were also desperate to find out where Gloria was and although I wasn't sure if I believed that they actually would break in, I didn't want to risk it and have them take the blame. I was the adult here, after all.

"Don't worry," Liam replied, repeating what he had told me earlier. "We're very well practised at creating a disturbance. You'll have plenty of time to escape from the office if needed."

So I pushed my doubts to one side and prepared to break the law. I swallowed, took a deep breath and went and hid, as planned, down the side of the house, on a steep grassy bank, just below the office window.

The windows resembled old-fashioned Victorian sashes, although they had, at some point, been replaced with rather hideous plastic uPVC ones. I crouched down and, although probably entirely unnecessary, held my breath, as I waited.

I waited for what felt like ages. My legs were beginning to shake with the effort of crouching down for so long. Muffled voices drifted down from the room above me, and I desperately wanted to lift my head up to see what was happening. Maybe Liam hadn't been able to lure Amelia out of the office quite as easily as he'd planned. Maybe she was refusing to leave. I was almost at the point of giving up when I heard the window sliding open.

I held my breath again, fearing that it might be Amelia, but when I looked up I saw Liam's head appear through the open window.

"Quick," he shouted in a stage whisper, and he held out his hand.

I slung my handbag crossways over my body and grabbed hold of his hand. Between him pulling, and me pushing, I managed to heave myself over the windowsill and into the office. "You'll have about ten minutes," Liam whispered, then he tiptoed out of the room and quietly closed the door.

I looked at my watch—I had until about quarter to three. *Shit, where to start?*

I tried to take in my surroundings and orient myself as swiftly as I could. A dark wood desk stood immediately in front of me, with an office chair a metre or so away from it, as if someone had recently pushed it back to stand up and leave the room. A small set of drawers sat underneath the desk, to the right of the chair. There was no lock on the drawers, but my guess was that they would be filled with stationery and things you'd need frequently if you were sitting there working. A few photos were scattered on the top of the desk, but I had no time to look at them now.

Various filing cabinets leaned against the walls beneath framed pictures that had clearly been drawn or painted by teenagers. I counted four cabinets, two to my left and two to my right. *Fuck!* I ran over to the ones on the left-hand wall, wondering where to start. One of them had a key in it, so I thought it easiest to start there. I yanked open the top drawer, which was filled with suspension files, each section containing a fat beige folder. I pulled a couple out at random. They were staff records. Each file had personal information, shift patterns, supervision records, appraisals. And they all had a photo clipped to the personal information sheet. I stuffed them back and opened the drawer below. More of the same. The third and fourth drawers were full of blue files, each one brimming with purchase orders, receipts, invoices and so on. Nothing of any help, whatsoever.

I yanked the key ring from the lock, pulling so hard I almost displaced the spider plant that cascaded down the side of the cabinet. There were two keys on the key ring so I tried the second key in the filing cabinet immediately to my left. Nothing. I ran over to the other side of the room and tried it in one of the cabinets there. Nothing. *Fuck!* Sweat poured off my hands, making them slippery and I fumbled with the key and dropped it on the floor. Blood was thumping through my ears, like a drum beating away the seconds of time that I had left. I scooped up the keys and tried the final filing cabinet. *Bingo.*

Muffled noises were worming their way into my consciousness, but I tried to ignore them, although I knew these were not the normal noises of teenagers going about their business. The actual words were inaudible but the high-pitched tone and raised volume told me that an argument was brewing. I quickened my pace.

This cabinet was full of more employees' files. I grabbed at a couple, disappointed. These seemed to be employees who no longer worked here. I was starting to panic, sure that I would run out of time before I managed to find anything of any use. I pulled open the second drawer; this time full of pink files. *Agency staff!* This might be of some use, although I was still no closer to finding a file about Noah. I raked through the files, my fingers slipping every now and again, meaning that I had to go back and recheck, but I could only find agency staff who, apparently, still worked at the home. I closed that drawer, and in my haste I crashed it shut too quickly causing quite a noise. *Shit!* I stopped dead, standing still for a second, listening intently, my chest visibly rising and falling with the effort of staying calm. The voices drifting into the room were becoming louder and more agitated; the argument was heating up. Occasionally a clear shout pierced through the stale, summer air. "What the fuck?" somebody bellowed. They were at the opposite end of the house, but each yell was becoming louder, each raised voice was becoming more distinct. They were gradually getting closer. I silently lowered myself to the floor and opened the bottom drawer as quietly as I could. This contained more files of agency staff, but it seemed that this time, these were people who no longer worked here. They didn't appear to be in any particular order and I rummaged through until I found the file for Francisco Martínez.

I pulled his file out and spread it out on my knees before taking a look at my watch. Four minutes had gone past already—I had to be fast. I scanned the papers, flicking through them as quickly as I could with my clumsy, clammy hands, trying not to get anything out of order. Francisco had apparently worked here until a few months ago, when he'd seemed to stop getting shifts. I flipped through a few more pages until I found some supervision records and I skim read them as fast as my brain would compute what it was seeing. But I found no record of any disciplinary, complaints, or anything suggesting that he hadn't abided by the rules. That didn't sound right. Perhaps I was missing something, or maybe there had been another Spanish agency worker. Maybe the one PC Keal had referred to was a different person to the one who had helped Aziza? I grabbed my phone and took photos of all the supervision records, an appraisal, and a copy of

Francisco's shift schedule from the last month he'd worked here. There was a photo clipped onto the first page, as with all the others, where the personal details were, so I took a picture of that too. Six minutes had passed at that point, so I put the file in order and placed it back in the filing cabinet, exactly where I'd found it.

Expletives pierced the air and rattled through the door; agitated tones clashed and fought, the air filled with desperate cries for calm. Deep thumps punctuated the words, as somebody hit walls, or doors. Hurried footsteps sounded on the stairs as someone came rushing down to see what the noise was about. I was running out of time.

The folders in the drawer in front of me seemed to be a complete jumble, maybe kept by someone different to the others. Desperate to see if there was another Spanish sounding name, I raked through the rest. There was nothing. But then something caught my eye. I flicked back. One of the files was labelled 'Jack Clayton'. Jack Clayton? Wasn't that the name of the trainer at the gym? I snatched the file out, fully aware that I was using precious time and I still hadn't found anything out about Noah. The photo clipped to the personal information showed a man who was younger, and his build was slighter, but there was no doubt that this was the same Jack Clayton I had met at the gym the other day. A large red label had been stuck onto the front of the file and on it, someone had handwritten 'passed to the local authority designated officer'. I had no idea what that meant. I went directly to the supervision records, scanning them for any clues. The last one was dated about four years ago and it seemed that Jack Clayton had been asked not to come back. I tried photoing and reading at the same time, the papers slipping in my hands as I did so. What I did see told me that Jack Clayton had worked here, and that he had been sacked for inappropriate behaviour with one of the young people. That put a new perspective on things.

As I scrambled to get the file back in the cabinet, shouts rang through the air. Liam's voice, and Amelia's voice, clammering over each other. And getting louder. Liam swore, and Amelia raised her voice a notch; they were still halfway down the hallway, but definitely closer than before. My breathing was laboured and loud, my hands unsteady. In my haste, the papers from Jack's file scattered and spilled onto the floor. There was no time to try to put them in order, so I just bundled them back together and stuffed them roughly into the folder.

Two more minutes! Shit. I didn't even know where the keys were to the other filing cabinets. *Think, Verity, think!* Whenever I had worked in an office I'd always kept keys in my desk drawer so I ran across the room, bashing my thigh on the corner of the desk and desperately squashing the urge to shout and swear out loud. I yanked open the drawer, and, yes here were the keys. But my heart dropped, there were about three key rings and all of them contained keys that looked as if they could be for a filing cabinet.

I grabbed them all and ran to the nearest of the two cabinets I had yet to open. I was fumbling with the keys, desperate to get in the drawers. Profanities sliced through the air like knives, getting louder and closer with each second. Punches rained down against the office wall, vibrating through into the room, gradually heading towards the door. Liam was ranting now, incoherent. He was going to be grounded for days for this. I'd have to find some way to thank him. If I didn't get caught and arrested in the meantime, that was.

I knew I only had a couple of minutes left and I scrambled with the keys, wasting precious moment after moment, until eventually one fitted and the drawer opened. I said a silent 'thank you' when I realised this contained the records of young people. They appeared to be in alphabetical order and the top drawer started at 'J'. Liam and Aziza had told me on the way over that Noah's surname was Walker so I went straight for the bottom drawer.

Shouts and screams still punctured the air as Liam and Amelia drew ever closer. I prayed that they would give me a couple more minutes and rummaged through the files until I got to W. Aziza had obviously joined the fray, her strident insults a world away from the timid girl who had sat, head bowed, twirling her scarf through her fingers. An unknown male voice was attempting in vain to calm everyone down. I only had seconds left, I knew it.

I grabbed Noah's file and without reading, I photographed the personal information and then scanned through for any clues as to where he had gone after he had left his council flat. I imagined that the home only kept records for a certain amount of time, and I couldn't see any other addresses. But then, just as the voices crescendoed outside, and fists started banging into the wall and office door, I saw a form detailing whether the young person was in training, education or employment. 'Employment' it said in Noah Walker's file. 'Employer: A Star Taxis'.

The door handle was rattling furiously as someone tried to enter, and Liam's shouts grew even louder, a body thumping into the door, preventing access for another few, precious, seconds. I rammed the file back in the drawer, closed and locked the cabinet, no longer concerned about the noise. I threw my phone into my handbag and snatched up the keys, tossing them all into Amelia's desk drawer, making no effort to put them back how I had found them. Then I launched myself at the open window, flinging my bag onto the grass bank and diving headfirst over the windowsill and onto the ground below just as the office door opened and an explosion of bodies burst into the room.

16

An eruption of pain split through my shoulders as I hit the ground heavily, rolling a couple of feet down the bank and juddering to a halt. Shakes convulsed through my body and I breathed in and out furiously, convinced that the people in the room above would be able to hear me. My lungs burned as they tried to keep up with the capacity of oxygen my brain was demanding and I struggled to slow my breathing down. Suddenly exhausted, I leaned against the wall, listening to the commotion above me, drifting through the still open window. Sweat poured down my face and my legs turned to jelly. As the adrenaline kicked in around my body, I felt compelled to keep shaking out my hands and feet, I was jittering that much. Minutes went past before I was able to sit still.

Sitting in the sunshine was quite relaxing in itself and I leaned my pounding head against the wall, allowing my eyes to droop as I concentrated on slowing my breathing down. In through the nose and out through the mouth. In and out, until gradually my heart rate slowed and the trembling abated.

When I opened my eyes, there was calm. The shouting had stopped and I had missed what had been said whilst I had been trying to slow my breathing. Eventually, I decided I might be able to stand up without my legs collapsing underneath me. Straining my ears, I tried to hear what was happening, but I was rewarded with silence. I picked up my handbag, steadied myself and walked round to the front of the house, placing my feet deliberately and cautiously to make sure that I didn't fall over. I took in a couple of deep breaths and then, in keeping with our plan, I rang the front doorbell as if I had just arrived. I waited, brushing myself down and removing a couple of stray blades of grass from my dress.

A young man in his twenties or thirties answered the door and I asked if Amelia was about. He ushered me in and knocked on the office door. Amelia's disembodied voice called for us to enter, and the young man opened the door and gestured that I should go in.

"Everything okay?" I asked. "You look a little anxious."

Her face was grey, her hair tousled and falling over her face. Amelia smoothed down her hair, lifted up her glasses and ran a hand across her dark, shadowed eyes. She repositioned herself in her chair. "I've just had to deal with an incident among some of our young people," she stuttered, her voice high and thin. Then she quickly added in a matter-of-fact manner, "Nothing out of the ordinary. They kick off sometimes. Par for the course." She drummed her fingers on the desk and shuffled once again in her chair, her body language not chiming with her words.

"I'm really sorry to bother you," I began. "Is this a bad time?"

She shook her head and gestured for me to come further into the room. On our way over from the café, Liam had suggested I call in, just in case anyone saw me, or heard me in the vicinity. To give credence to why I was there. It had seemed sensible at the time, and I now had things I wanted to talk to her about.

"I met PC Deborah Keal this morning," I said, at least starting off with the truth. "And she mentioned that there had been an agency worker here, I think she said his name was Francisco. She said that there were issues with him not reporting young people when they went missing?"

Amelia smoothed down her hair again, to little effect, and took a deep breath. The colour was returning to her face. "Yes, Francisco," she said, her voice lowered as she spread out her hands and placed them on the desk in front of her. "He doesn't work here anymore. We let him go."

"Because he wasn't calling the police when he should?"

"Yes, that's right."

"When young people go missing do you always have to report them?"

"Sometimes we try and keep tabs on them. Follow them to see where they go."

I must have looked quizzical, because she quickly followed that up with, "Well, we can't lock them in. It's a home, not a prison."

"But you often have an idea of where they are?"

"Normally, yes. Usually they go somewhere familiar. To their families, or friends. Or they just stay out a bit longer than they should, like most teenagers. Francisco wasn't following protocol. He'd let them leave, make no effort to follow them, and if we didn't know where they were, or they stayed out past a certain time, he wasn't telling the police. We couldn't have him here anymore."

"Can you tell me which agency he worked for?" I anticipated her answer to that.

"I'm sorry, that's confidential information." And her eyes flicked briefly to the filing cabinet that I now knew held the said confidential information.

"Is it possible to have a quick word with Liam?" I asked.

"I'm sorry, I'm afraid he's in his room at the moment."

"I'll be really quick," I said, and smiled what I hoped was a winning smile. It seemed to work.

"He's currently grounded. Two minutes." She stood up and led me out of the room and up the stairs.

The house was large, and the staircase meandered up, turning twice on the way to the first floor. At the top of the stairs, you could turn either left or right. The landing stretched down the length of the house, and Liam's room was the third door along on the left. Amelia knocked and a grunt emanated from within. Amelia took that to be permission to enter and opened the door, letting me pass in front of her.

I poked my head round the door and flashed a broad smile at Liam. His room was dark, the curtains

124

drawn tight against the sun. He looked to be reading some kind of comic, the sort with those Japanese-style drawings. He gave me the thumbs up sign and winked. He was lying on top of an unmade bed, the duvet spilling off the side and onto the floor. The wardrobe door was open, with clothes leaking out in an untidy heap. The whole room smelled of teenage hormones.

"I hear you're grounded," I said, conscious that Amelia was feet away, and no doubt listening to what I was saying.

Liam grunted again, then silently laughed and, once again, gave me the thumbs up sign.

"I'm hoping to see Aziza again tomorrow," I carried on, although Liam obviously knew this already. "Can you ask her to text me when she knows where she wants to meet?"

"Sure," Liam said, and I closed the door and left him to it.

17

When I got home, I busied myself with household tasks, cleaning and emptying the dishwasher, putting a load of washing in the machine, and ironing a couple of summer dresses. I went into the garden and deadheaded the flowers, watered the tubs and pulled out a few weeds. And then I made myself some pasta and took it into the garden with a glass of red wine and ate it while the garden clung onto the last few shafts of sunlight before it disappeared behind the buildings opposite. I wasn't sure that red wine with pasta wasn't some terrible culinary faux pas, but as I didn't have a Michelin starred chef passing by I carried on without concerning myself too much.

Once the garden was in shadow, the temperature dropped quite significantly and I moved indoors, poured another glass of wine and went and sat on the sofa to peruse the photos I'd taken at Plumtree House.

I started with Noah. I looked at his photo, obviously taken a few years ago but even then he'd looked like a young man you wouldn't want to get on the wrong side of. I knew photos could be deceiving, but his thick set jaw, and scowling brow line just screamed of a fiery, temperamental young man. A tattoo snaked its way across his neck, disappearing behind his left ear. His personal information told me that he had recently turned twenty, and that he had left Plumtree House not long after his eighteenth birthday. He'd moved into the council flat that Aziza had spoken about, but there was no further information about how long he had been there, or where he had gone after he'd been asked to leave.

On the page about employment, there was a contact number for A Star Taxis. There was a name too, Florin Petrescu, so I copied that into my phone with the number and made a note to call them, or go and visit them, tomorrow.

I moved on to the pictures of Jack Clayton's information. He looked quite different in his photo, obviously taken several years' ago. Much more petite, and he had a naïve look about him. He looked nothing like a personal trainer. I read the information about his disciplinary:

'Resident LB was quite distressed. LB alleged JC had touched their genitals, over clothing, when demanding that they went to bed. LB said JC had come into the bedroom and shouted that they get into bed several times. LB said that JC had pushed them onto the bed and grabbed their genitals over their jeans, laughed and walked out the bedroom. LB

127

remained in the bedroom and reported the incident the following morning when JC had left.'

Reading between the lines, it seemed that this was not the first time this had happened. There was no indication from the recording as to how old, or what gender LB was. The end of the recording stated:

'Conclusion: allegation substantiated. Refer to DBS.'

I studied the photo of the front of the file with the big red notice. I quickly Googled Local Authority Designated Officer and discovered that:

'The Local Authority Designated Officer (LADO) is the person who should be notified when it has been alleged that a person who works with children has:

• Behaved in a way that has harmed a child, or may have harmed a child
• Possibly committed a criminal offence against or related to a child
• Behaved towards a child or children in a way that indicates she or he may pose a risk of harm to children.'

That explained the red label then. If LB's account was correct it seemed that Jack Clayton had ticked all three of those conditions. But if that were the case, I wondered, would you be able to work with children again? Jack Clayton was working at the gym and was bound to come into contact with young people. I made another Google search, this time of *DBS*.

This turned out to be the Disclosure and Barring Scheme that regulated people who worked with children and vulnerable adults. I still didn't really understand, so I fired off a short email to Joy, asking her if she had a few minutes to call me, as I had a quick question.

Francisco's information was intriguing. Given what Amelia, and PC Keal, had said about him, there was nothing in his supervision notes, or his appraisal, to suggest that there had been any wrongdoing at all. The appraisal had been quite positive about his contributions to life at Plumtree, there was a recommendation that he accessed some training about trauma-based practice, but nothing negative at all. There was no mention of not reporting young people who had gone missing, or allowing people to leave without checking that they were safe. And there was no record as to why or when he had been asked not to work shifts there anymore.

I was confused.

On the personal information sheet there was a contact phone number, so I rang it but I couldn't get through, my phone informing me it was an unknown number. The agency Francisco had worked for was called AdelaCare and there was an email contact, so I sent off an email asking if they could get him to contact me.

I went to replenish my wine, and then sat back down on the sofa and opened up my laptop. I searched for 'Hope, Strength, Lives' and perused their website. It began by describing the difficulties that unaccompanied young women encountered when they came to Britain – fear of the unknown, language difficulties, not understanding the law to name just a few. It went on to explain that, when these young women were exploited, or taken advantage of in any way, they were at an additional disadvantage in that they dreaded being denied the right to stay in the country. Fearing deportation was an extra string in the bow of the exploiters who often encouraged the girls to break the law, by drinking, taking drugs, stealing, selling drugs and so on, and then threatened to hand them over to the authorities if they didn't comply with certain demands. Most of the young people did not know where to go for advice and many worried that the people looking after them, foster carers or residential staff, would turn against them if they knew what they had been doing. The exploiters were expert at convincing the young women that they were making active choices, whereas in reality they were being terribly manipulated.

The website described different models of exploitation, some of which chimed with what I had been hearing about Gloria, and in my notebook I wrote a whole page of questions to ask Aziza when I met her tomorrow.

Hope, Strength, Lives offered services to all young people who were being exploited but they had a specialism in young women who were alone in the country and seeking asylum.

There was a page that contained stories from young people the service had helped. I read it open-mouthed and in horror at the suffering these young people had experienced. I thought about Gloria, clutching her Little Mermaid and finding a home here, only to be further harmed and traumatised in a country that should have offered her shelter and support. Someone had told me, maybe it had been PC Keal, that often adults didn't believe the young people because what they were saying was too horrific to understand.

One of the stories caught my eye. It was a young girl called Jane:

'When Mary from HSL got in touch, I was at my lowest point ever. I had been badly beaten and the effects of some drugs were wearing off, so I was shaking and feeling the withdrawal. I had no money and I had nowhere to go and no one to turn to. I've never felt so alone. The only people I knew were the people doing this to me. I'd run away after a group of men had arrived at the house. I was locked in a room and told I had to have sex with all these men. I lost count, some came in as a group. They took turns, sometimes two at a time, and someone filmed everything from the corner of the room. When they'd left, I was crying so the people holding me beat me and told me to look more cheerful; they were going to take me to another house where there were more men and they wouldn't want to pay for sex with someone so miserable. I had nowhere to go and no one to turn to. When we got to the new house they put me in a bedroom. I managed to open a window and jump down onto a flat roof. I don't know where I ran, or who helped me find Mary, some kind stranger. Meeting Mary turned my life around. Now I volunteer for HSL and help other

*people to see what is happening to them. I owe my
life to her.'*

It made depressing reading. I was just packing up
my laptop and getting ready for bed when my phone
pinged with a message. It was from Aziza.

*See you tomorrow at the Freedom Café at 4.30?
My friend works there and says it'll be quiet by then.
If ppl in there's a back room we can use. Ok?*

I texted back that I would see her there and then
I locked the door, turned off all the lights and went
to bed.

Sunday

-18-

On Sunday morning, thick black clouds were forming on the horizon although overhead it was still clear. The air was damp and warm, but cooler than the previous few days. I wanted to go over and talk to the taxi firm and I decided it would be better to head off sooner rather than later. My iPhone told me that there were increasing chances of thunderstorms from 2pm onwards. To be on the safe side, I stuffed an umbrella in my handbag and headed out.

The cathedral looked stunning with the blue sky directly overhead and the dark clouds swirling along the horizon behind. A breeze was beginning to move the tips of the trees and I wondered if I should have brought a raincoat. I walked faster, down Steep Hill and along the High Street, past the level crossing until I got to the Magistrates' Court. Nash had said that A Star Taxis was based near there, but it turned out that the shop front was actually a few hundred yards further on, sandwiched between a Polish supermarket and a tattoo parlour.

As I pushed the door open, an old-fashioned bell jingled over my head, and shortly after, a thick-set man appeared through a door at the rear. He looked about fifty. He was combing his hair back over his head, and when he'd finished, he tucked the comb into his shirt pocket. He positioned his stocky frame behind the counter at the far end of the room, and brought a laptop to life, obviously believing I was about to order a taxi.

He looked up. "Can I help?" he said. He had a trace of an Eastern European accent, but I guessed he had lived here for quite a long time. It was mingled with the flat vowel sounds of Lincolnshire.

"I'm looking for Florin," I said.

"Which one?" he asked. Maybe Florin was a more popular name than I'd thought. I had to consult my notes.

"Petrescu."

"That's me," he said, nodding and smiling and spreading his arms as if to indicate I had found what I was looking for.

"I'm trying to find someone," I said. "A young girl. I know she used your firm a few times and she's gone missing. I'm just trying to get any information about where she used to go, who with, that sort of thing. To try and get an idea of where she might have gone to, where she might be now."

"Hmmm. I see." He rubbed his chin. "I will try to help, but…" He trailed off, obviously not that hopeful that he'd be able to do much.

I took out my phone and showed him the picture of Gloria.

"Ah." He nodded. He clearly remembered her. She was stunning—she'd be hard to forget.

"I remember her." He nodded again. "She was always with group, they used to hang around out here." And he indicated the street outside with his hand. "They used to wait around and then go off in taxis, one or two at a time. It wasn't them that paid for taxi, though."

"Do you know who paid?"

"I couldn't give you name. Or even description, I'm sorry." He shook his head and shrugged. "Always cash. Usually paid when they got to other end. I don't think we saw who paid, and the girls would come and say where they wanted to go."

He lifted his hand and wagged his finger at me. "But," he said. "But, pay attention, because we don't have this issue anymore. The police came a few times and told the young ones to scarp it. After a while they came in and told us not to take them. That it was bad people paying for taxis." He thought about this for a while, looking down and rubbing his chin hard as if he might be able to conjure up some information for me. "We had training. When the licence was up for renewal, it's part of council policy now." He shrugged. "All taxi firms have to have the safeguarding training. Now we know what to look for and we don't take the girls now."

"Where did they used to go?"

"Various places. Addresses around town. Always different places."

"Anywhere else?"

"A nightclub, sometimes."

"Which one?" But I already knew the answer.

"The Five Two Two."

I got my phone out again and showed Florin the picture of Noah. "Does this young man work here?"

Florin snorted and held his hands up, palms towards me, like he was trying to stop a train hurtling towards him.

"Not anymore," he said, shaking his head. "Not anymore."

"Why is that?"

"He was not to be trusted, that one. He worked here," he said, pointing to the spot he was currently occupying. "Taking calls and placing orders. Matching callers to available taxis. But he was untrustworthy, believe me." He looked at me imploringly as if he had to convince me he was in the right. "He was stealing from me, right here, right under my nose." And Florin hit the desk, as if to indicate where right under his nose was.

"Taking cash?"

"More often credit cards. He'd take card details and pay money into a different account, one he'd set up so people didn't notice the name was slightly wrong when they got their bills." He looked down, thoughtfully. "He was changing the records on the computer so that it all matched."

"How did you notice?"

"He got greedy. Few fares here and there," he said, moving his hands back and forth, "and I probably wouldn't have noticed, but he gets greedy, taking too much. I noticed nights he was working, takings were low, but drivers were saying they'd been busy."

"So you let him go."

"And told him not to let me catch sight of him again."

138

"Do you know where he is now?"

"No!" He held his hands up and bowed his head. "I do not want to know where this man is."

I thanked him and left, feeling that I was not really getting much further forward. The breeze was getting up and I shivered as I crossed the road so that I could walk in the sunshine.

As I was striding back towards the city centre, my phone rang. It was Charlton, so I answered the phone and found a bench to sit on whilst we spoke.

"Sam, how are you doing?"

"Good, Vee. How's things with you?"

"All good here thanks. It's looking like it's going to rain later, but we still have sun at the moment."

"It's started here," he said. "It must be heading north."

I looked up at the sky and the clouds were, indeed, approaching from the south. "Maybe I have a couple of hours before I get wet, then.

"Listen, Verity, I think I have some news. About Gloria."

"Oh, wow." I sat up, suddenly more aware of everything around me.

"Yeah, I had a call from CEOP—"

I interrupted him, "See what?"

"Sorry, CEOP. It's the Child Exploitation and Online Protection agency. The guy I spoke to there called me back. They might have something. I don't think it's a lot, but he's wanting to meet. He said he'd be okay with you sitting in on the conversation as long as he and I agreed in advance what he was able to say."

"Okay, great. Thanks, Sam. When does he want to meet?"

"Tuesday. He wants to talk to Nash first. I think they have some photos, or something."

"Tuesday? Okay. I'll book a train. I can head down tomorrow." Then I added, "And photos? That sounds intriguing."

"He didn't sound as if he thought they'd be much help, but you never know. It's worth going to talk to him."

"Yeah, sure. And it'll be nice to see you; it's been a month or two now."

"Yeah, it will. And, er, I was wondering…"

"Yes?"

"Well, you know, for ease, 'cause we'll be travelling together and that, if you wanted to stop at my place this time?" He gave an audible sigh down the phone.

I wondered if he'd debated with himself before deciding to ask me that. But it did make sense, so I agreed and said I'd let him know my estimated arrival time when I'd booked my train.

I sat on the bench for quite a while after we'd ended the conversation, staring at my phone as if Sam's presence was still there, and I smiled to myself. It would be nice to go to London for a couple of days, and it would be really great to see Sam again. I opened up the train booking app and booked a train down to King's Cross tomorrow afternoon, and a return on Wednesday lunchtime. I sent Sam a quick text letting him know I'd be arriving about 4pm.

A reply pinged back almost immediately.

Great. I'll come to KX to meet you.

19

I wandered into town and meandered round a couple of the clothes shops, but I didn't see anything that caught my eye. The predicted rain hadn't arrived yet, so I found a sunny spot outside one of the city centre cafes and bought myself a sandwich and a cake. The air crackled with the promise of impending thunder and I wondered if I should head inside, but the clouds seemed to be travelling quite slowly.

I was having an internal competition with myself, judging the outfits that wandered past and awarding imaginary prizes for the most hideous. I had a vision of myself on a podium with a row of trophies and a microphone, handing them out to passers-by.

'And to you, young lady, yes, you in the lacy…errr…"shorts", the prize for wearing the least possible material whilst still, technically, remaining clothed'. Riotous clapping and cheering! 'And to

you, middle aged man, the prize for the most pregnant-like belly on full display, that is not actually a pregnant belly.' Yay!

I hoped no one was being quite as judgemental about my choice of outfit.

It was almost time to meet Aziza, so I started to make my way to the Freedom Café to wait for her. The Freedom Café was so called because all their offerings were free of just about any ingredients at all. Gluten, grains, animal products, dairy, eggs. Heaven knows what they made their cakes and things from. Quinoa I guessed. I ordered a Fairtrade, organic coffee and went and sat in the corner to wait for Aziza. She'd been right about it not being very busy. They closed at 5.30pm on a Sunday and I was the only customer.

I passed the time by reviewing the questions that I had written down last night and deciding which order I should ask them in, so as not to overwhelm her. Then I looked at the photos I'd taken yesterday to see if there was anything I'd missed. And I checked my email to see if AdelaCare had got back to me, but they hadn't.

When I looked at my watch it was 4.45pm. Aziza was late. I sent her a text.

I'm here, sitting at the back in the corner. Do you want me to order you a drink?

There was no response.

I waited a little longer. I double checked the time of the train tomorrow and made a list of what I needed to do before I left the house for a couple of days. A sense of disappointment was creeping its way through my body, as I started to contemplate whether Aziza was going to turn up. I imagined that she had lost her nerve and bailed out. Having read all those stories on the HSL website, I could see how hard it would be to talk about those things to someone who was, practically, a stranger. A heaviness was pulling at my chest as I started losing grip on the hope that she was just late. She wasn't going to show and my questions would go unanswered. I sent her another text.

Hi. So sorry you didn't come to meet me. Understand it must be really hard. Maybe meet soon?

The young lady behind the counter was beginning to clear up, tidying all the cups away, wiping the tables and putting salt and pepper pots to one side, I presumed for a refill. I didn't want to be in her way, but I was reluctant to go home, in case Aziza had been held up and arrived after I'd gone. I picked up all my things one at a time, taking my time to place them in my bag, lingering to make sure I hadn't forgotten anything. Eventually I had to leave and I hovered outside for a while, just in case.

I debated with myself about going to Plumtree House and seeing if Aziza was there, but then I reasoned that if she'd bottled out of meeting me, I wouldn't help my cause by turning up on her doorstep and insisting on seeing her. I had to hope she'd see my text and decide I wasn't so scary after all.

I did think about which way she might be walking through town if she was on her way and running late, and I partially followed that route as I meandered up the hill, keeping a careful watch out in case I bumped into her. But I knew it was hopeless. The thoughts of what she might have told me played about in my mind, and I sighed to myself as I got closer to home.

I spent the rest of the afternoon packing my bag, watering the plants and generally making sure I was ready for a few days away from home. I checked my phone every half an hour or so, each time disappointed when there was no response from Aziza.

20

That evening after I'd eaten dinner, I decided to go to the Five Two Two nightclub. Mark Henry had said that the owner would be around after nine or ten and I really wanted to ask him about any underage girls, or boys for that matter, who had been barred from the club. I couldn't see any point in waiting, I was going to be in London tomorrow and that would mean that the next opportunity I had would be Wednesday.

I picked out a dress that looked more businesswoman than nightclubber; I wanted to be clear about the purpose of my visit. Then to complete the 'serious investigator' look that I was aiming for I spent a little time applying some make-up. I assessed myself in the mirror, and certainly my reflection gave the impression of someone who knew what they were doing. Good job people couldn't see what was in my head, I thought, imagining a brain full of very little other than question marks. A small handbag, just big enough for my phone, keys, credit card and a little cash, complimented the look, and I fished out an old pair of shoes that had heels tall enough to look sophisticated but small enough to be comfortable to walk all the way across town.

The air was damp with the impending rain as I stepped out of the front door, although it wasn't actually raining yet. I looked at the sky and decided it would be better to be safe, so I ran back in and put on a raincoat; it looked as if the promised storm was reasonably imminent.

Steep Hill was busy, mostly it seemed with people moving from pubs at the bottom to pubs at the top, or the other way around. There were a couple of independent pubs towards the bottom of the hill that John and I used to visit quite frequently. He had liked his beer and had been working through their repertoire a pint at a time. I walked past them without looking in.

The High Street was beginning to fill up. At this time of night, it generally attracted young people gearing up for a night out, with its fair share of hen parties and stag dos. But I was surprised at how busy it was for a Sunday night. Did people not have jobs? Or lectures to get to? I bumped headfirst into a group of women, mostly in their thirties and forties, staggering out of one of the bars. They all wore sashes around their shoulders and pink T shirts that announced this was Chantelle's hen night. They were all giggling, swaying uneasily as they spilled across the pavement. The lady I took to be Chantelle had a bridal veil in her hair and was carrying a six-foot inflatable penis. An older lady, zigzagging across the pavement, and wearing a sash that said 'mother of the bride' lurched into me as I tried to step out of their line of progression.

"Watch where you're going, love," she shouted and wagged her finger in my face.

I stood to one side to allow them to pass. A young woman at the front, her hair piled high on the top of her head, consulted a piece of paper. "Right," she shouted. "Next pub is this way." And she pointed further down the street, tottering on high heels and almost falling in her haste to lead the way. I let them all reel slowly past and watched as they filed into the next unsuspecting premises.

A crack of thunder way in the distance split the air, and I picked up my pace. The last glows of sunlight sank below the buildings behind me, leaving the street completely in shadow, dusk taking hold as I scurried along towards my destination. Black clouds were hovering on the horizon, waiting to take over the sky like battleships on the sea biding their time before launching an attack.

It was just after ten when I reached the Five Two Two, and I was hoping I was ahead of the crowd. I didn't want to be there when it was too busy or too noisy. I wanted to be able to have a sensible conversation without having to shout. The door was open when I arrived, with a tall, well-built black bouncer outside. He asked my name and what I was doing there.

"I've actually come to have a word with the owner, Aidan," I replied, and shrugged, wondering why it mattered.

"You're a bit early that's all," the bouncer replied, a little defensively. He jerked his thumb towards the inside and added, "He'll be making sure the bar is in order before the throngs arrive." He swept his hand to indicate a rope barrier, which I guessed was to keep a queue in order. They were clearly expecting a few.

I stepped over the threshold and made my way down the corridor, past the old photos and through the door with the velvet curtain. The place was completely empty. I walked out onto the dance floor and shouted tentatively, "Hello,"

A lilting Irish voice replied from somewhere behind me and I turned to see where it was coming from. Sitting in one of the booths was a gentleman with a full head of sandy hair, nursing what looked to be a whiskey. He was wearing camel-coloured slacks and an open-necked, pink shirt.

"We're not open yet," he said. "Did Bob not tell you?"

"I'm not here for the club," I answered, indicating my carefully put together outfit as if it should have announced that for itself. "I'm looking to have a word with the owner."

"Ah. Well, that'll be me, then," he said. "Just taking a break before getting the bar ready. What can I do you for?"

"I'd like to talk to you about underage people coming to the club."

He wrinkled his nose. "You're not from licensing, are you?"

"No," I laughed.

"Well, then." He got up and walked over. "Why don't you prop up the bar while I get ready?" He held out his hand. "Aidan," he said. "Aidan Dennis."

I took his hand and shook it. "Verity Spencer," I said.

"Well, now, Verity Spencer, how can I help you?" And his face cracked into a broad smile.

I'd have put him in his late forties, but he could have been older. His face was what my mother would have described as 'lived in'. When he smiled his crow's feet creased deeply around his eyes, and his cheeks revealed small dimples. His fair complexion was sprinkled with freckles, and a day's worth of stubble covered his chin. He indicated a stool at the far end of the bar, and I perched on that, while he went behind the bar and began removing glasses from the dishwasher, cleaning them, and placing them on shelves ready for use.

"Can I get you something?" he asked.

"I'll have a gin and tonic, please," I said and put my handbag and coat down on the bar stool next to me.

He moved around the bar, pouring the drink, obviously knowing where everything was without having to look. I got the impression he was a hands-on owner, which tended to indicate either someone with a passion for their business, or someone who micro-managed. A couple of bartenders arrived, a young lady and a man. They walked through to a room behind the bar, chatting as they went. A staff room, or kitchen I assumed. They re-emerged a few minutes later wearing old-fashioned bar uniforms with white shirts, black trousers and aprons.

Aidan placed a coaster, and then the drink, in front of me. He smiled, his dimples appearing either side of his crease lines. "So, what can I tell you about underage drinkers? And why is it that you want to know?"

I told him a little about Gloria, her story and how her foster carer was concerned about her because she'd disappeared about five weeks ago. He busied himself around the bar while I filled him in on the background.

"It's just that the taxi guy said that they'd brought her here. Her and others, I think. And I was wondering if you knew anything about it, or if you knew who they were with." I paused. "Or anything really that might help me track her down." I shrugged my shoulders.

People had started to drift in and were waiting at the bar, the staff busy serving them drinks. Someone had turned on some music, although it wasn't very loud. A young man with a beard and a top knot was hovering near a small stage at the edge of the dance floor. A DJ maybe? I wasn't sure. They were playing the Spice Girls' Wannabe the last time I'd been in a nightclub.

Aidan tilted his head towards one of the booths. "Let's sit down," he said. "It's going to get noisy soon." And he indicated to the bar staff where he would be.

They nodded and carried on serving the customers.

He picked up both drinks and led me to a booth at the far end of the dance floor, and it was surprisingly quiet when we sat down. I was sure it would get noisier later, but the booth certainly shielded you from the ever-growing sounds.

"So, tell me, this young girl…"

"Gloria."

"Yeah, Gloria. She's missing and you are trying to find her?"

"Yes. I have a photo if that would help?"

"Sure." He nodded.

I showed him the picture of Gloria on my phone. He raised his eyebrows and held out his hand. I nodded and handed him the phone. He held it close to his face and studied the photo. After some time, he started to nod and he looked up. He handed me back my phone. Pins and needles tingled down my back in anticipation.

He nodded again. "Yeah, I've seen her in here," he said. He ran his hand through his hair, pushing it back off his face. A forelock of hair instantly flopped back over his forehead. "I rarely forget a face. I've definitely seen her here. She looks over eighteen. She came by a couple of times, but we rumbled her eventually and told her not to bother coming back."

"Your barman said he didn't recognise her."

"He was probably being cagey." He held his glass in his hand and scrutinised it as if it might hold some answers. "Was it Mark?"

I nodded.

He twirled his whiskey in his glass and drank it down in one go. He glanced over to the bar, and the barman seemed to look up instinctively. Aidan indicated our empty glasses and the barman tilted his head in acknowledgement.

He looked back at me, his eyes creasing and his mouth curling into a lopsided smile. He looked around him and then bent across the table towards me, speaking more quietly. "I wouldn't be too sure to trust what Mark says. His days here are numbered and he knows it. He's been my number two for a couple of years, but he's fallen short of the mark, ha, so to speak." He laughed at his own pun. "He'll let anyone in, as long as they have cash in their hands." He rubbed the fingers of his left hand together in the internationally recognised symbol for money. He leaned further across the table, glancing sideways to make sure that no one was too close, and then he looked me directly in the eyes. "And he's not been averse to taking money to turn a blind eye."

Just then, the barman appeared with our drinks. Aidan moved back to allow him space. The barman took the empty glasses and put them on his tray, and then set down the new drinks, without saying a word.

"Thanks, James," Aidan said, as the barman turned away.

"Mark told me that you were the one on top of the underage drinkers."

Aidan contemplated his drink, gave it a swirl and took a swig. "I won't risk my license," he said, his gaze not leaving the glass. "But I'm not here all night. It's really his department." He looked up, "Well, him and the doormen. The doormen are good at turning people away, checking for ID, you know? But sometimes they do get through. Once they've been identified, though, I expect them to stay away. Mark is supposed to make sure of that."

"So, let me get this straight," I said. "Mark has been letting underage people into the nightclub and turning a blind eye."

Aidan was nodding.

"So how does that work? He asks them to leave, and if they create a fuss, he's what? Been taking money to keep quiet about it?"

"To be honest, I don't think he waits until they create a fuss. I think he knows who they are and targets them straight away. Nice little earner."

"But you haven't sacked him yet?"

"I will," he said with conviction. He brushed his hair back. "I need to get my ducks lined up. I think he knows that I'm onto him and he's trying to cover his tracks. He's going to slip up. He's going to get greedy." He sat back and leaned against the velvet back of the booth. "But I'll get him. I value loyalty in my staff." And he glanced over at the bar staff, and nodded.

"Did you see who Gloria came in with?" I asked.

He gazed off to the left and pursed his mouth. Then after a second he once again began to slowly nod.

"Young guy, maybe thirty, late twenties? Dark, short hair. Arms that would shame Popeye."

"Jack Clayton," I mumbled, and I had to fight to stop myself from punching the air. "Jack Clayton, the trainer at the gym."

"You know him?"

"I went to see him to talk about Gloria. She goes to the gym where he works. He wasn't very helpful though." I thought for a minute. "Did you ever see him in here with anyone else?"

Aidan shook his head. "You think your man might know something about where she is?"

"I don't know." I shrugged. "Maybe not. I'm just worried that he was getting her involved in something she didn't really want to do."

The place was really quite busy now. The music was getting louder by the minute and the dance floor was filling up with writhing, sweaty bodies. Aidan explained that a couple of years ago they had installed a special sound system. On the dance floor it would be thumping. But here, especially at this end of the room, it was much quieter. He said that when he had bought the place, about ten years' ago when he came over from Ireland, it had been completely run down. He'd refurbished it and made it into one of the most popular nightclubs in the city. He glanced around, proudly.

"It needs doing again, now," he acknowledged, looking at the state of the velvet in the booth.

"So, where in Ireland are you from?"

"County Donegal."

I shook my head, betraying my ignorance of Irish geography.

"In the north," he said.

"Northern Ireland?" I didn't think his accent sounded like he was from Ulster.

"No, no. It's further north than much of Northern Ireland, but far too poor and Catholic to have been considered part of the UK." He thought for a minute. "Thankfully," he added. "I'm pleased to be part of the republic."

"Do you get back there often?"

"When I can." He smiled. "It's beautiful. Windswept. But beautiful." And he raised one eyebrow. He held his glass up. "To absent family."

We clinked glasses, and I thought of John.

Just then, my phone began to ring and my watch vibrated on my wrist. I looked at the time, it was just coming up to midnight. The call was from Liam. I wondered what on earth he could want at this time of night. I ignored it, thinking I'd call back in the morning. I wasn't ready to interrupt my evening just yet. Not only was I starting to get some answers, but I was having a pleasant time too.

Aidan stood up. "Excuse me for a minute," he said and headed off in the direction of the gents. Immediately my phone started ringing again. This time, a wave of irritation caught me off guard. Whatever Liam wanted would surely wait until the morning? I snatched it up, and pressed answer.

"Yes," I snapped, unable to keep the frustration out of my voice.

A small, scared and barely audible voice replied, "They've got her."

Everything stopped. My body went cold and goosebumps crept up my arms. I had to readjust completely. He sounded frightened and concerned. I wasn't sure if I'd heard him properly.

"What?"

"They've got her."

Suddenly the noise in the nightclub became overwhelming and intrusive.

"Liam? What is it?"

"Aziza. She's gone, they've got her. They've taken her. I don't know what to do. I don't know where they've taken her."

"Are you sure she's gone?"

"Can you come? Please. Can you come? I need help."

"Are you okay? Liam?"

Heavy breaths filtered down the phone, intermingled with soft sobs. Liam was crying.

"Liam, are you okay?"

"Please, come," he begged. "I need help. I can't get home."

"Okay, okay. Where are you?"

There was silence, followed by some crackling.

"Liam?"

"Please. I'm near the football ground."

"Which part? It's huge?"

"I don't know." And he started crying again. "I can see a big Co-op sign. It's the Co-op stand I think."

"Okay, stay there. Liam, I'll get there as soon as I can."

"I'm sorry," he whispered. "I'm so sorry." And then the line went dead.

I stood up. Aidan was just coming back.

"Something I said?" And his face creased up to make way for an enquiring grin.

"I'm sorry, I have to go," I said, flustered.

"Can I call you a taxi?"

"No, it's fine," I said, trying not to sound too tense, but in a rush to get to Liam. I grabbed my things and thanked him, then turned to dash off.

"Come back," he said.

I turned round. He was standing with his right hand in his pocket. His face broke into a broad smile. He pushed his left hand through his hair and then raised it to say goodbye.

"I will," I said and then I squished my way through the sweaty dancers and ran down the corridor and out into the night.

21

A few large drops of rain were falling as I ran back towards the High Street. I put my raincoat on without bothering to take my handbag off my shoulder first, and I zipped it up, pulling the hood up to protect me. I was dithering about whether to get a cab, but I figured it was about 10 minutes to walk, and it seemed that by the time I'd stopped off at a taxi firm, waited for a cab, had to pay the driver and so on, it would be just as quick to walk. I picked up my pace, half running as I scuttled down the road, hugging the shop fronts as the rain pelted the pavement, bouncing back on my legs and soaking my ankles as I went. When I turned into Scorer Street, I broke into a sprint, wishing that I had worn flatter shoes.

The city felt very different at that end of town. The houses were small and tightly packed and most opened straight onto the street. Wheelie bins scattered the pavement, big numbers painted on their sides. Some had messages painted on them. *'Don't touch me thieves'* one announced. I ran past another declaring *'Fuck off Tories!'* I'd have laughed if I hadn't been trying to quell the panic that was beginning to tighten in my chest. I quickened my step, running faster now, and the rain seemed to mirror my pace, falling harder as I ran. Under my coat, my handbag banged against my hip.

I ran over a little bridge across the canal and turned into Sincil Bank, the massive Lincolnshire Co-Op sign, against the end of one of the stands, looming out of the darkness ahead. There was a light just near the turnstiles, and I ran down towards this. The doors to the entrances were all locked. I glanced around; there didn't seem to be anyone else here. The fencing surrounding the grounds was foreboding, with huge spikes on top, a deterrent against people trying to climb over. A road went down past the side of the football ground, between the stand and the canal, and a black wrought-iron fence ran along the other side of the road, preventing anyone from falling into the water. There was nobody about.

"Liam?" I called out, catching my breath and swallowing the falling rain. I paced about, pulling at the cuffs of my raincoat, unsure what to do, the tension in my chest exacerbating the effects of having sprinted for the last quarter of a mile.

I glanced up at the light, spotting a CCTV camera pointing down towards the gates, so I decided to stay within range of this.

"Liam?" I shouted again.

Just then a flash of lightning lit up the entire sky, and for a brief second three figures appeared in the

158

light, walking towards me from the far corner of the stand. I stayed where I was, and the image disappeared once more into the dark. A clap of thunder crashed into the night. I hadn't been counting, but it was a few miles away yet.

I looked up nervously at the camera and stood as if rooted to the ground. The three figures started to take form through the gloom, and I could tell that one of them was Liam, his grey hoodie reflecting the light a little. The other two were clearly men, both well-built. Both had hoods pulled over their heads, and the stockier of the two was pulling Liam along by the arm. They stopped, about twenty yards away, Liam and the stocky man to the right, and the other, taller man to the left. The taller man took a few paces forward.

"Come here," he shouted, his voice almost lost in the pouring rain.

I stayed where I was. I didn't want to leave the reach of the camera.

"Will you come here," he shouted again, like an exasperated father to a recalcitrant child.

When I didn't move, he turned and said something to the man holding Liam. The stocky man kicked at the back of Liam's knees, causing him to collapse to the ground. Before Liam had time to react, the stocky man grabbed his hair and thrust his head sharply into the wet road.

"Stop!" I shouted. "Stop it!"

"Then come here," the taller man said.

I glanced up at the camera and left its sanctuary, walking tentatively towards the tall man. He had a bandana tied around his face, and his hoodie pulled down over his forehead. It was impossible to get a look at him.

"Closer," he said.

And I inched a little closer. "Leave Liam alone!" I shouted and glanced over to see if he was alright.

He looked up at me, a frightened small boy. Blood was trickling from his nose, washing down his face with the rain and dripping onto his grey hoodie. The stocky man behind him also had a bandana covering his face. I had no idea who either of them were.

The tall man suddenly lurched forward and grabbed my wrist, spinning me round so that I was in front of him, my back to his chest. He held my arms above the elbows, squeezing tight and pulling them together, his thumbs digging into my flesh through the coat.

As I struggled to try to break free, he hissed into my ear, "Now you're going to see what happens to snitches." He looked over at the man, still holding Liam by his hair, and shouted into the rain, "Okay?"

And with that, the stocky man pulled his right leg back and kicked Liam with startling force directly into the middle of his back. Liam cried out in pain and fell to the ground, the water splashing with the force as he hit the road. The rain was strong now, battering everything as it fell—trees, weeds, plastic bins. It was bouncing high off the tarmac, hammering down around us and deadening the noise. The stocky man clenched his hand into a fist and slammed it into Liam's cheek, his head snapping sideways with the force.

"Stop it! Stop it!" I screamed. "Leave him alone!"

I struggled and writhed in the tall man's arms. His grip loosened slightly as my raincoat became slippery and less easy to hold. He let go of my right elbow and quickly slung his arm across my throat, squeezing hard, and I forced my mouth above his arm, gasping in air and rain in equal measures. He still had hold of my left arm and I tried to grab at him with my free hand. I made contact with his sodden sleeve, but I couldn't loosen his grasp.

The stocky man was pushing Liam back onto the road, and Liam was pushing back against him, trying desperately to scrabble to his knees. Another flash of lightning lit up the road. Blood was pouring from Liam's nose now and swirling into the puddles on the ground, his hoodie soaked with rain and blood. Drool dripped down his chin and he wiped his face with his sleeve. And then the darkness enveloped us once more, Liam and his attacker pixelated in the dim light.

I grappled and fought, but the tall man's grip was too tight. I drew my arm forward and jabbed my elbow as hard as I could into his chest, but it had little effect. A few feet away, the stocky man took another swipe with his foot, kicking Liam hard on the shin. Liam cried out and his shoulders shook as he lay injured in the rain, curled into the foetal position. The man kicked again, this time at the arms Liam had protecting his stomach, but hardly a sound came from his mouth and he slumped onto the road.

"For God's sake, stop it!" I screeched, panic threatening to overcome me. "For fuck's sake, stop what you're doing. Stop it, now!" My words dissipated into the driving rain, lost as soon as they left my mouth. I gritted my teeth and growled as I fought against the man holding me, stamping my feet and thrashing about in his grip. I clawed at his arm and kicked back with my right foot, aiming for his knee, but catching only the side of his lower leg. I tried again, pulling my knee up to my chest and jabbing my foot hard behind me. A crunching sound, and a searing pain in my heel, told me that I'd made contact with something hard, and his grip loosened a little. The stocky man was punching Liam to the side and back and I redoubled my efforts. As I turned quickly in the tall man's arm, I thrust my knee up again, this time jabbing into his side, just below the ribs.

He drew his arms up, in a gesture that said 'enough!' and he shoved me away from him, hard, with the palms of both hands. As I staggered backwards, I grabbed at him, clawing at his bandana and ripping it from his face. But I wasn't able to steady myself and I stumbled a few paces before falling heavily on my bottom. The bandana was in my hand and the man turned away, but not before I'd seen his face. The face of Mark Henry.

"C'mon," he shouted across to the stocky man, who glanced up at me, and then down at Liam. Liam was shaking, soaking, silent. He took another look at Liam's limp body, and pulled his foot up as if he were about to stamp on Liam's head.

"No!" I screamed. I launched myself across the tarmac and flew at the man, sending him reeling into the railings that ran along the side of the canal. His body folded over and he shouted out.

"Bitch!" he yelled, stomping towards me.

I cowered down, waiting for the blows but Mark span round, grabbed him by the sleeve and dragged him off. They took one last look at Liam and then they ran off into the night.

Liam was moaning softly, lying still on the ground, and I rushed over, falling on my knees beside him. I took his head in my hands and laid it on my lap.

"Liam," I whispered, wiping the rain off his forehead. "Liam. They've gone"

He was breathing shallowly against my body, and I ran my hand gently over his soaking wet hair. The rain whipped across the road, thunder piercing the air as I yanked open my coat and fumbled in my handbag for my phone.

I cradled Liam's face in my arms whilst I called for an ambulance and stroked his head and his cheeks. He mouthed something to me and I leaned in to hear.

"Noah," he murmured. "That was Noah."

"Shhh, shhh," I said softly into his ear. "Shhh"

I wiped a mixture of blood, rain, mucous and spit from his chin with the hem of my dress. I wrapped my arms around him, pulling him in close. "I'm sorry," I whispered. "I'm so sorry."

And I cried softly, as I rocked him gently in the driving rain, lightning and thunder coming almost at the same time now as the storm raged directly above us.

Monday

22

It was gone 4am when I made it home on Monday morning. I went straight up the stairs, tumbled into bed and sobbed; for Liam and what he had been through, and for the guilt I was feeling that it had been my questioning that had got him into this.

I had accompanied Liam in the ambulance, and sat with him whilst he was seen in A&E. Amazingly the worst injury he had sustained appeared to be a broken nose, although he was badly bruised all over his body. His face was swelling and he would definitely develop a pair of black eyes over the next few days. One of the workers from Plumtree House, a young lady called Rachel, who I hadn't met before, had turned up at around 2am and we sat in silence whilst Liam fell in and out of sleep in an A&E bed. Periodically doctors had come and spoken to him, asking him a host of questions, many of them more than once. Where did it hurt? What had happened? Had he lost consciousness? Did he feel nauseous?

They had also asked about the events leading up to the attack; trying to see if he had gaps in his memory.

Liam had told us that he'd been tricked. He wasn't sure who had sent him a message, but he'd received a text from Aziza's phone and had gone out to meet her. When he got to the meeting place she wasn't there. He said he had tried desperately to reach her, calling and texting to no avail. He'd received a series of strange messages taking him on a wild goose chase until he had encountered Noah and Mark Henry with Aziza's phone. They'd forced him to call me, under duress, and get me to go to the football ground. He had a pretty clear memory of everything that had happened before, during and after the attack.

At some point someone must have called the police, because a policeman turned up and asked us a few questions. He was very gentle with Liam. We had told him what we knew.

"There's a CCTV camera there, on the corner of the stadium," I'd said. "Although I think it might be pointed at the turnstiles so it might not have picked them up when they ran away." I'd thought about them with their hoodies pulled up over their faces, and added, "Not that it would tell you much."

"It might tell us something." The policeman had shrugged. "Clothing, and so on."

I agreed that I would go into the station the next day and make a formal statement. Rachel from Plumtree House said she'd talk to Liam's social worker about arranging for him to do the same.

"When he feels up to it," the policeman had said.

Various doctors had felt Liam's head, taken his pulse, taken his temperature and so on and the conclusion appeared to be, as there was no sign of a fracture and no sign of concussion, that he could go home. The worker from Plumtree House was on strict instructions to bring him back immediately if he showed any signs of deterioration and they provided her with an information sheet describing what to look out for.

I lay there in bed, staring at the ceiling, unable to sleep. My head was hurting with different threads of thoughts fighting for space, tumbling and crashing and then dissipating. What was Mark Henry's role? Aidan had been right not to trust him, but what was he doing beyond making a bit of cash from underage drinkers? And how did Liam fit in? And was it really Jack Clayton who had been to the Five Two Two with Gloria? *Agh!*

I turned on the light and grabbed my notebook. It was just after five and the sun was already rising. I wrote down all the questions I had and any thoughts that were doing the rounds in my head so that I didn't forget anything. And then I drifted slowly into a deep, restorative sleep.

I woke with a pain in my arm where I had been laying in the same position for too long when the alarm went off at 9am. Dreams of Gloria dissipated, strands of memories floating up into the air, lost forever.

I examined my arms when I got out of bed; big bruises were appearing above the elbows on both of them. Nothing compared to how I imagined Liam was looking. I resolved to call in and see him before I headed off to London.

The air was cooler and crisper as I walked to the police station to give my statement. It was still sunny, but the temperature was several degrees below the highs of the last few days. I announced my arrival at the desk and sat in the waiting room. My bum was going numb on the hard seat by the time a policeman put his head around the door and called my name. I stood up and followed him. We walked together along the little corridor that Nash had led me down, past the custody suite door and back into the same interview room I'd been in a few days ago. He indicated for me to sit down and then sat opposite me.

He held out his hand. "PC Creasey," he said, and I wondered what fun his coworkers had with that.

We discussed the events of the night before, covering the same ground that Liam and I had done with the policeman at the hospital, and PC Creasey faithfully wrote everything down via a tablet. When I got to the part where I had reached out and pulled Henry's bandana off his face, he paused and looked up.

"How sure are you that it was Mark Henry?" he asked.

"That's definitely who it was."

"But it must have been quite dark?"

I thought hard. He was making me doubt myself now. "Yes," I conceded. "It was fairly dark, although there was some light from the wall of the stadium. And it was lightning, too."

"He had a hoodie, pulled down over his head?"

170

"Well, yes. But I'm convinced that's who it was."

"It may be hard to prove. It'll be easy for a barrister to put doubt in a jury's mind."

I could see that. It had been dark, and rainy, and I had only briefly seen him as I was falling to the ground and he was turning away from me.

"And the other one?"

"Noah Walker. I didn't see him, and I've never met him before."

"How do you know about him?"

"Liam knows him. Liam told me that he used to live at Plumtree House." My mind wandered back to me flicking through Noah's file in Amelia Macdonald's office. Instinctively my hand curled around my phone, which was laying on top of my handbag, holding it down as if it might leap up of its own volition and start showing PC Creasey the pictures I'd taken.

"But you didn't see his face?"

"No."

We were just finishing up when there was a knock on the door, and Mike Nash poked his head into the room.

"Verity," he said. "I heard you were in the building again."

He exchanged pleasantries with PC Creasey, who then left the room, and Nash sat down in the seat that was now vacated.

"How's the young lad, Verity?" Nash enquired.

"Shaken, but luckily only suffered a broken nose and some bad bruising."

"Good to hear, Verity, that is good to hear."

"Has anyone spoken to Mark Henry yet?" I asked.

"Apparently he's not shown up for work this morning. Not at home either. We'll keep trying though."

"And Noah Walker?"

"Absolutely denies any involvement."

I deflated into my unmovable chair. "And no one got sight of his face."

"Disappointing, isn't it?" Nash agreed, lowering his head and looking down at his hands.

"Any news on Aziza yet?" I asked.

He shook his head. "Not a thing, no. Not a single thing."

"When Henry grabbed hold of me, just before the other one started on Liam, he said something like 'this is what happens to snitches'. Do you think Aziza's disappearance is connected to Gloria's?"

"That I can't say, Verity." But he tapped the side of his nose as if he thought it undoubtedly would be.

"I'm off down to London later. Sam and I are going to meet up with a chap from…some agency, I forget the name?"

"Ah yes, CEOP. I have a call scheduled with them later today."

"I think they might have some news on Gloria."

"Yes," said Nash. "It'll be interesting to see what they have to say."

"Let's hope we get somewhere soon."

"Let's hope, indeed. We can but hope."

23

On my way through town, I picked up some chocolates and a card for Liam, and then walked home via Plumtree House to drop them off. Rachel answered the door and I asked how Liam was doing.

"He's okay," she said. "In remarkably good spirits, actually. He's been assessing his eyes in the mirror to see how black they're getting."

I laughed and handed over the chocolates. She said that Liam was resting at the moment, so I agreed to call in when I got back from London.

When I got home, I quickly ran around the house and garden, checking that everything was okay and that the plants would survive without me for a couple of days. Some of the more delicate flowers had been completely beaten down by the rain last night, so I clipped them back and hoped they'd reshoot. Then I picked up my overnight bag and headed to the station.

I grabbed a coffee, a paper and a croissant from the station café, and sat on the platform whilst I waited for the train. I sent Charlton a message, letting him know I was on my way, and that the train was running on time. Almost instantly my phone pinged with a message, but it wasn't a reply it was a message from Collette.

Remember Charlotte's birthday? 5pm Thursday x

Shit! I had forgotten again! I really needed to get her a present. I sent a slightly less than honest reply.

Of course! Was going to text for present suggestions? X

She probably knew I wasn't being completely truthful as a rather unhelpful response came back.

She'll love whatever you choose. See you Thursday x

Great. *Thanks Collette!* The train arrived and I found a seat in a corner, where hopefully no one would come and sit next to me. I had just started to eat my croissant when another message arrived. This time it was from Charlton.

Safe journey. See you later. Hear you had a bit of excitement yesterday.

He must have had a conversation with Nash.

Yeah. Too much. Give me five minutes with that t**t. I'd like to chop all his bits off and string him up by his balls!

A reply came zipping back.

Might I suggest that you'd find it easier if you did that the other way round?

I spent most of the journey completing the sudokus in the paper. They were really tough, but by the time we arrived at King's Cross I had not only finished them but a couple of the other puzzles as well. I grabbed my bag from the overhead shelf and headed off to find Charlton.

As I approached the gates, I spotted him leaning against one of the pillars, just catching the sun's rays. He was looking dashing in a white open-necked shirt with the sleeves rolled up and dark blue jeans, his arms folded across his chest. He'd shaved his head again since the last time I'd seen him and his dark skin was shining in the sunlight. We kissed politely on the cheeks and had a brief hug.

"Do you want to walk back to my place?" he asked. "It's about a twenty-five minute walk."

It was a warm and sunny day, a few degrees warmer than Lincoln but not too humid; perfect for walking, so I agreed that that would be a good idea. He took my overnight bag and slung it over his shoulder, and we headed north towards his apartment. We sauntered along, admiring the many new developments along the canal so it actually took us a lot longer than he'd estimated. It was only a few years since I'd walked behind King's Cross station and the change in that time had been phenomenal. Cafes, bars, shops and residential developments brimmed with life and filled previously barren spaces. The new Gasholder Park was filled with people picnicking, reading the paper and generally taking a break from their busy days. The canal teemed with colourful narrow boats and the tow path was overflowing with fellow walkers. We walked all the way along the canal as far as Camden Lock, adding a few more minutes to our journey, as it was a more pleasant route than the road. And then we decided that, as it was such a beautiful day, we may as well stop for a drink. So we found a table outside one of the pubs and sat there watching the world go by, whilst Charlton drank a pint of beer and I had a red wine.

"I bought some rioja in, specially," he said, glancing at my wine. And he looked up and smiled as if wanting approval.

"Thank you," I said, smiling back, before taking a sip of my wine. "Cheers," I said, and we clinked glasses.

"Cheers," he replied. "Welcome to London."

We finished our drinks, and carried on walking. Charlton lived almost halfway between Kentish Town and Tufnell Park underground stations, in a duplex apartment that took up the top two floors of an old Victorian terrace house. The area had streets of three and four storey houses, almost all of which had now been converted into flats. Flats that no doubt sold for the price of a five-bedroom house in Lincoln.

Charlton's flat had two reasonably sized bedrooms and a bathroom off a cramped hallway, just as you entered the front door. A stairway led you up to the top floor, which was built into the eaves of the house. It was a lovely bright space, with a four-paned dormer window at the back that you could fold off to one side and which overlooked the back gardens of both this street, and the one adjacent to it. A tiny, open-plan kitchen fitted into one corner of the room, and on the opposite side to the dormer window, a sofa, chair and coffee table formed a comfy sitting down area. It was a small but cosy room and, as I would have expected, minimalist and very bachelor-style.

Sam showed me into the spare room. He put my bag down on the bed and left me to sort myself out. When I emerged up the stairs, some delicious cooking smells were emanating across from the kitchen. It was tiny, but that wasn't hindering Charlton's culinary creativity.

"Hope you like curry," he said.

And I answered that I did, although I wondered what he would have said if I'd turned my nose up. Charlton had pulled back the dormer windows and I sat and looked out whilst he cooked, studying the backs of the houses on the next street, and deciding who had extended with good taste and who hadn't.

24

After eating all that I could, and wiping my plate with left over naan bread, I sat back in my chair and held my stomach.

"That was amazing, Sam," I said, and silently clapped in the air. "I don't think I'll need to eat for another week, though."

Our conversation drifted easily from one topic to another. We even touched on politics, and were surprisingly close in our beliefs. He told me that he had been brought up by his divorced mother in South London. "She had a tough time," he said. "Three boys to bring up.

"What are your brothers called?" I asked, interested in his background.

"Joseph and Daniel. Mother was quite religious. I'm in the middle," he added, pointing to his chest.

"The forgotten middle child?"

He raised an eyebrow and nodded. "Yeah, kinda."

"What do they do?"

"One's an architect, that's Joe. And Dan is a pilot for British Airways."

"Wow, she must be really proud of you all."

"Well, she's definitely proud of them. They left their roots behind. Well and truly rising from the dregs and achieving way more than anyone in our family ever before. They got degrees and everything." He rubbed his chin with his hand. "But I'm not sure becoming a policeman was high up on her list of wishes for her children. Being black, living in an area more well known for its riots than anything else. You know." He leaned back and folded his arms.

"But now, she must be proud of what you do?"

He pursed his lips. "Well, I make up for the disappointment with good looks and charm."

"Ah, I knew you must have a saving grace somewhere hidden in your depths."

"Well, there it is."

I looked over at him. I was enjoying his reminiscing. It was nice to share his memories. "Where does your mother live now?"

"Still in the flat where I grew up. In south London. It was almost a slum then, probably worth a fortune now."

"And your father?"

"I haven't seen him since the day he walked out. Dan was a baby, I can't remember how old. Definitely less than a year."

After a couple more glasses of wine, and a move to the sofa, we touched on the topic of holidays. I told him how John and I had loved to go on holiday, that I had often surprised him by taking him to an unknown destination, and that occasionally choosing a holiday location had led to a row when we had both become stubborn with our choices.

"You, digging your heels in?" Charlton asked, opening both eyes wide. "I can't believe that for a second."

I swiped him, playfully, across his knee.

"I haven't been on holiday for just over four years," he went on, glancing at the ceiling and leaning back in his chair "It wasn't a great experience."

"And where was the last place you went?"

"Thessaloniki," he said. "With my ex-girlfriend."

"Oh?" I pulled one of my legs up onto the sofa and wrapped my arms around it, resting my chin on my knee. "How long ago did you split up?"

"Just over four years ago." He smiled. "We'd been there two days. We'd had a plan to go to the White Tower and as we were setting off she said that she had a headache and was going to go back to the hotel for a sleep. 'You carry on,' she said, she knew I really wanted to go and see it. So I walked along for a bit, but then I thought, 'No I'll go back and check she's okay'. I thought we could always do the tower another day. She obviously had miscalculated my interest because when I got back to the hotel she was in the bedroom shagging the porter. She hadn't even bothered to lock the door." He shook his head, laughing. "It's funny now, but it didn't seem very funny at the time."

"Oh my God," I said. "What did you do?"

"I grabbed him by the hair and pulled him out of the bed, mid-coitus, you know, and threw him into the corridor."

"Naked?"

"Absolutely. He banged on the door for a while, but then he gave up and went away."

"And your girlfriend?"

"Ex-girlfriend, Veronica, kept saying she was sorry but I didn't get that. It was obviously a planned encounter. I just went down to the bar and drank myself into a stupor. When I eventually stumbled back into the room she'd gone, all her possessions and everything. She flew back home. We spoke a couple of times after that, you know arranging for friends to pick up possessions from each other's apartments, but there was no real feeling anymore. Funny thing was…"

"Yes?"

"The next morning I was in the bathroom, shaving, and there was a knock at the door." He paused. "And standing there, bold as brass, was the porter asking if he could have his clothes back. Ha! What a cheek." And he leaned his head back and roared with laughter.

"Oh my God," I said, laughing along with him. "Well at least you can see the funny side."

"Yeah, believe me it took a while," he said, standing up and taking our glasses over to the kitchen. He returned with them replenished.

Eventually, the conversation moved to Gloria.

"I'm convinced that Aziza going missing has something to do with Gloria," I said. "And Mark Henry is in the middle of it all somehow."

Charlton cupped his chin with his hand and ran his index finger along his jaw. "And the other guy. The trainer?"

"Jack Clayton. I'm not sure, but I suspect he was the one being 'the boyfriend'. Although you wouldn't think working at a gym would be lucrative enough to be buying designer dresses, underwear and new iPhones."

"Maybe he had a sideline?"

"Selling his girlfriends for sex?"

He nodded. "It's looking probable that somebody was. And, like you say, a gym trainer's wage isn't going to buy all that stuff."

"The other thing is..." I started.

"What?"

"Well, it seems that there are other people that have got involved. PC Keal mentioned houses where young people were given drugs and alcohol and then taxied off to other destinations."

"Yeah? What are you thinking?"

"I'm wondering if it's coincidence that it was Gloria and Aziza that have disappeared? Neither of whom have family here, because they're here unaccompanied. You could make an assumption that there wouldn't be a whole group of people clamouring to find out what had happened to them. It might not ruffle so many feathers. I mean people like Liam, or some of the other young girls in the house might go missing too, but if he disappeared completely, well he does have a family who'd want to find him."

"But Gloria had her foster carer."

"True. But you might not realise how close she'd been to Sarah. If you didn't know her well, I

182

mean." I paused, biting the corner of my lip as I thought. "If Linda Watson hadn't come to see me, Gloria would have just been lost. The police had drawn a blank. She's got no family. If it hadn't been for Sarah everyone would have given up."

Charlton pursed his lips and ran his fingertip across his mouth. "I'm not so sure," he ventured. "Aziza seems to have disappeared as a result of her being on the verge of saying something to you."

"Yeah," I agreed. "Maybe it's just that."

We sat in silence for a few minutes.

"The other thing that's been bothering me…" I trailed off, not sure it really meant anything.

"Yes?" Charlton smiled.

"Well, Gloria's bedroom. It was so tidy."

"Maybe she was just an unusually tidy teenager?"

"No, it wasn't just that," I said, more sure now that I thought about it. "It was as if she didn't belong there. It was like a hotel room. I wonder if she didn't feel as at home as Linda and Sarah liked to think."

"It's possible," he said, nodding and tapping his finger on the end of his nose.

"I wonder if she did worry about what Linda would think of her. If she found out what was going on. Her room just gave the impression of someone who wasn't there to stay. As if she was a visitor in their house, not a family member."

Charlton leaned over and rested his hand on top of mine. I looked across at him.

"We will get to the bottom of this," he said.

"I hope you're right."

It was getting late, so we cleared away our glasses and headed downstairs. He hovered in the bedroom door, and before I had a chance to turn into the room, he leaned down and kissed me lightly on the lips. I gazed down at my feet, and then up to look him in the eyes. His face held a million emotions, none of which were clear to me. He held my gaze for what felt like a lifetime, and I smiled up at him.

"Goodnight, Sam," I whispered, and turned into the bedroom.

"Goodnight," he said and leaned against the wall, his eyes not leaving mine, his mouth curled up in what could have been amusement, or regret, or uncertainty.

I went into the bedroom, closed the door and lay down on the bed. A smile spread across my face and I laughed to myself, feeling unsure of what emotion was rising within me, or indeed, what to do about it.

Tuesday

25

A knock on the bedroom door woke me from a fitful sleep, and Sam appeared with a cup of hot, strong coffee.

"Breakfast will be ready when you are," he said as he turned to leave.

I lay in bed, leaning up to sip my coffee periodically and then hauled myself up the stairs to the kitchen, where Sam was preparing breakfast. I had got out of the habit of eating first thing in the morning, but the smell of freshly heated croissants was too tempting to resist.

As I sat at Sam's dining table looking out of the dormer window and deciding which garden I liked the best, I got a call from Joy.

"Hi," she said. "Sorry I didn't get back to you earlier."

I was impressed that it had only been a day or two. "Not a problem," I said as Sam placed a cafetière of coffee in front of me. I gave him the thumbs-up sign.

"How can I help?" Joy asked.

I certainly didn't want to admit to her, or to a listening-in Charlton, that I had seen Jack Clayton's confidential records, so I just said, "I heard that one of the workers who used to work at Plumtree House had been referred to the Local Authority Designated Officer," I said, almost truthfully. "I was just wondering what that meant?" I had done my initial research online, but I wanted an expert interpretation.

"Oh, yes," she said, her enthusiastic attitude spilling down the phone line.

I could see why she got on so well with teenagers; her positivity was infectious.

"That happens if someone who works with children has had some kind of allegation made against them. It can be anything really, anything that might suggest that they're not suitable to carry on working with children."

"And what happens if they're found guilty?"

"Hmm, well it doesn't quite work like that," she said.

I took the opportunity to have a mouthful of croissant.

"The LADO is there to help decide if the allegation is substantiated or not substantiated."

"And if it is substantiated, would they be prosecuted?"

"Not necessarily. In fact, not often." She paused. "The thing is, the burden of proof is very different for the LADO than it is for a court. We, as professionals, might feel that the allegation has

188

enough credence to make us want to discipline someone, or it might even prevent us wanting to employ this person anymore. But that doesn't mean that there would be enough to take it to court, let alone actually convict someone. To go to court you have to be sure, beyond reasonable doubt, and in most cases we see, it's a child's word against an adult's. We start from believing what children say, but it's not an exact science and you can't always be sure. We might go through disciplinary processes, or we might offer people training. Occasionally we might dismiss someone, or refer them to the police, but it's rare that people get prosecuted."

"And if someone's dismissed, would they be able to work again?"

"It depends. It depends a lot on what the allegation was. If they're referred to the DBS and barred, then obviously they wouldn't be able to work in certain jobs, but the DBS might not bar them. Then it's up to other organisations to check their disciplinary records."

"So, if you were dismissed from one job, but not barred, someone else might decide to employ you?"

"They might," she conceded. "If they're a good employer, they'll check your records and ask previous employers about you. But, even if you've been dismissed they might decide that the risk you present is manageable." She paused, then added, "And some employers don't even check."

"So if you were in contact with children, but there were always other people around, that might be okay?"

"Absolutely," she said. "And don't forget, that we might feel that someone is not appropriate to provide, say, intimate care to someone; bathing or getting them to bed maybe. But other people might not see that there's much risk if they're, I don't know, helping at a football match where there are lots of adults around and they're never actually on their own with children." She paused, then added, "It's a balance that isn't always easy to achieve. Protecting children from potential harm, but allowing people to make mistakes and not ruining their career forever. If you're a foster carer, say, and you're overly harsh with a young person who's kicking off and you hurt them, does that mean that the young person should be removed from your care and you should never be allowed to work with children again?"

"So if a young person in a residential home makes an allegation about a carer, it's not necessarily the end of their career?"

"That's right," she agreed, her pitch rising, and the words coming faster, as she warmed to her theme. "It depends on a lot. Was there another witness? How credible is the story? Are there any injuries? Have there been other incidents? Has the young person made allegations before? It's difficult. Even if what the young person says is believable it might be so hard to prove, that you decide the accusation is not substantiated. Not substantiated isn't the same as saying it didn't happen, that's called unfounded or false, but it means there's not enough evidence to say one way or another."

"And if it is substantiated, there must be evidence?"

"Well, certainly if it's substantiated it means that people genuinely believe what they're being told, yes."

"Great, thanks, Joy. That's been really helpful. Thanks for calling back."

"Glad to be of help." And she laughed down the phone. "Have a fabulous day."

26

Sam had arranged the meeting with CEOP for midday, so after my phone call with Joy, we got ourselves ready and made our way to the tube station. The air was cooler and the sky cloudier than it had been, although glimpses of blue sky promised a clearer afternoon. We took the tube to Euston and then switched to the Victoria line and headed down to Vauxhall. The sky was already brightening a little when we emerged back out into daylight and we walked through a pretty little park on the way to the offices, which were part of the National Crime Agency complex.

I let Charlton announce our arrival to reception, as he had arranged the meeting, and then we sat and waited until a middle-aged man appeared and called out Sam's name. He looked to be in his late fifties, possibly early sixties. He had a full head of wavy grey hair and, although not substantially overweight, could have done with losing a pound or two.

"Peter Williams," he announced as he stretched out his hand, revealing a double-cuffed shirt with silver cufflinks.

I shook his hand, and then he gestured for us to follow him through to a small meeting room.

After the usual pleasantries about the day, the weather, and the trip across London, Charlton kicked off the conversation proper.

"Thanks so much for seeing us," he said. "Now, you said you might have something to tell us about Gloria?"

"Yes," Peter Williams said, glancing across at me. "I will just reiterate that I've shared what we know in relation to this case with the relevant police authorities. In Gloria's case that's Lincolnshire Police and the investigating officer has agreed that you can sit in on this discussion as I'm not going to divulge anything that could hinder the investigation in any way."

"Thanks," I said. "Thanks for letting me be here."

"Now, Gloria we know has been involved in some exploitation activities. I gather some photos were found on her phone that had been sent to and, probably, distributed from another phone."

"They definitely found some pictures on her phone," I agreed. "They'd been sent to just one number. A burner phone, I think. So probably sent on to others from there. Nash said the phone was no longer in use."

"I imagine it would have been decommissioned almost as soon as the pictures were circulated," Williams stated.

"So have you seen those pictures?" I asked. "Or similar ones?"

"Well, first, let me explain a little about what we do here." He clasped his hands together on the table in front of him. He suddenly sat up. "I'm sorry, I'm assuming you don't have too much idea about how we operate? But I don't want to be patronising if you do?"

"No," I agreed. "Not at all patronising. It's all quite new to me."

"Ok," he started. "So, what we do here is try and trace online activity. We track down online paedophile networks and hidden use of the web for exploitation purposes. The main problem we have is that the better we get at tracing usage, the better the networks get at hiding what they're doing."

I nodded, so far so good.

"We're intelligence-led," he continued. "And we get information from across the world."

"How readily do people offer up information?" I asked, thinking that if you were involved in paedophilia you might not be that willing to dob-in other offenders.

He tilted his head in acknowledgement. "Well, much of the intelligence we get is from people posing as paedophiles. Obviously, the Internet doesn't have geographical boundaries and that means that we work very closely with intelligence forces in other countries to try to close the net, so to speak. These networks use sophisticated methods of hiding what they do and ensuring that only like-minded people can access the sites they set up."

"The dark web." Charlton interjected.

"Exactly," said Williams. "There's nothing wrong with the dark web per se, it has many, perfectly legitimate, uses."

"Oh," I said. "Such as?" Adding, "I've heard of the dark web but assumed it was only used for illegal activity, black markets and the like."

"Well." He pursed his lips as he thought. "Things such as governments needing to communicate with each other, citizens from oppressed countries getting messages out, whistleblowing. Spying even. The thing about the dark web is that you can't just access it through a normal search engine like Google. You go through a browser like the onion router, or Tor, and if you use an encrypted VPN tunnel it keeps what you do anonymous. It hides your IP address, meaning that it's easier for people to stay hidden if, say, they're spying and sending information back to their government. Which, as I'm sure you can appreciate, can be a good thing."

"Okay," I said, trying to keep up. I wasn't sure about VPN tunnels or the onion thingy but I didn't think those details interfered with the actual message. I understood the idea of people wanting to hide what they were doing from others.

"But the flip side is that if people are using it for nefarious activities it's harder to follow what they're doing. And much harder to trace people. Plus," he continued, "the URLs are long lists of numbers and letters so you have to have the precise URL address to access sites, you can't just search for 'Paedophiles R Us'."

"So," Charlton suggested, I imagined more for my benefit than anything else, "it's much harder to find people engaged in illegal activity?"

"Exactly," said Williams. "We, and other forces around the world, have people who pose as paedophiles and spend some time chatting, sharing, and generally building confidence with these people, to be allowed access to some of the more troubling sites."

"That can't be an easy job," I ventured.

"No," he agreed. "But the end justifies the means though. Anyway, it's a difficult task, not least because usually the people trading and sharing images are not the same people that are making the images in the first place. But—" He paused before adding, "We have had some success in interrupting and arresting people involved, although these sites are not always easy to completely shut down."

"Even though they're illegal?" I asked.

"Well, what's illegal in one country isn't always illegal in another," he explained. "And if you only shut the site down in one country, that's not enough. We work really closely with other taskforces around the world. In Europe we have the European Cybercrime Centre, but we work with countries across the globe as you can imagine."

Charlton and I both nodded.

"Just a few months ago," Williams continued, "we managed to shut down a massive site on the dark web, selling and sharing horrific images of child abuse, but it was after many, many months of coordinated work from agencies across the world."

"Making lots of money for the owners of the website, I imagine?" Charlton asked.

"Yes," Williams agreed, "it's a lucrative business. That particular guy had made just shy of £3 million selling videos and images. His model, which is not that uncommon, was that sometimes people could pay by uploading their own images. There were strict rules about what was and wasn't allowed, which I won't go into. Let's just say they were quite specific about the cruel forms of abuse that their clientele were interested in. But as a result, people who entered the site had access to thousands of videos and images."

"Did you arrest any of the people accessing the images?" I asked.

"We did, actually," he said puffing out his chest proudly. "People's use of the Internet is all encrypted and anonymised, if they access the right way, but on many occasions there's a trail. Some bits aren't always quite as anonymous as they think. People often forget something, like their payment. In this case people had used cryptocurrency to pay, thinking it would protect them but with many cases we were able to trace it back to the person making the payment."

"Wow," I said. "There are some clever people around."

"Indeed," he agreed. "And we have to try to stay one step ahead of them."

I had meant the taskforces, but he was in full flow so I didn't interrupt.

"The thing is that sometimes we are investigating one thing and it leads to another, through one of the subscribers perhaps. Many times when their laptops are seized they're accessing more than one of these sites and although they try their best to anonymise and cover up what they're doing, something like using the same payment method can help us to make the links we need."

"And has this helped to find something relating to Gloria?" Charlton asked, typically on task.

"It has," Williams affirmed. "We came across some images on a laptop. They hadn't been downloaded from the website that had led us to them, and we still haven't traced exactly where they originated from. There were five different young people in the images and they all looked like they'd been taken in the same place."

"And Gloria was one of them?" My heart skipped a beat. Were we about to get closer to finding her?

"Yes, she was," he stated. "But we have no idea where they were taken. Or indeed when." He reached into a laptop bag and pulled out a photograph. "I do apologise," he said. "This is the least worst, but you get the drift."

Charlton and I pored over the photo. It had been pixelated to blur out Gloria's face, and to give her some dignity but even through the pixilation I could tell it was her. I couldn't see the exact expression on her face, obviously, but I could see her mouth was open and I could only assume that this was in pain. Gloria was spread-eagled, naked on a bed. Her wrists and ankles chained heavily to the bedstead. The bed had what looked like a sheet on it, but it had been pulled off the edges of the bed and was ruckled up around Gloria's lithe body. The sheet was stained with what I took to be blood and, out of shot, someone was holding up a whip as if they were halfway to landing it across Gloria's exposed tummy.

A low whistle from Charlton coincided with a sharp intake of breath from me.

"Oh my God," I said, and looked up at him. "Oh my God."

Charlton just nodded in agreement, both of us utterly lost for anything more eloquent to say.

I glanced back down, unwillingly, at the photo. There was nothing to give away where it had been taken. Behind the bed was an exposed red brick wall, but beyond that there was nothing. Nothing at all.

"You said the images were of five young people?" I asked. "Including Gloria."

"Yes," Williams said. "Although we're not sure on the identities of the others yet. We've asked forces for details of missing young people but we haven't made any matches yet."

Williams took the photo back and placed it carefully once again in his laptop bag.

"The interesting thing is," he said. "This, and the other photos were stills taken from a video."

"A video?" I echoed.

"Yes. But again we have no idea where the video was taken or when. But there is one thing."

We both looked up. Charlton raised his eyebrows, questioningly.

"Our guys think the videos, well at least some of them, may have been streamed live."

"Wouldn't that be risky?" I asked. "Wouldn't they be in danger of giving away their location?"

"Well," he explained, "they use similar methods to hide their IP addresses. And on top of that they'll misuse a satellite ISP, and that allows them to anonymously broadcast large amounts of data without giving away their location. It's very clever."

I didn't really understand the explanation, so I clarified what he meant. "You mean they're streaming abuse, live via the dark web."

"That's the theory we're working on, yes. People are paying to log in and watch it live. They'll be able to access it from all over the world."

"And you have nothing to go on?" Charlton asked.

"The only thing we know is that the user who posts the images and videos uses the name @Nadiasinned. We just don't have a clue who is running it, where from or whether it is still operational, that's all."

That was all, then. Just a minor omission. We knew that Gloria had been horrifically abused, possibly live on air but we had no idea where this was happening, who was responsible or when it had happened. After feeling an initial rush of excitement to get some news that might lead us somewhere, I sank back in my chair and heaved a sigh of disappointment.

"I would suspect," said Williams, adding to my disillusionment, "that they will have switched location, changed the name and started using different ways of routing the signal by now." He paused, then added for final emphasis, "If they are still operational at all, that is."

27

An air of disappointment hung between Charlton and myself as we left the building and headed back towards Vauxhall station. We sat in silence on the tube train, and then when we got to Euston we decided to walk the rest of the way.

We surfaced back into the daylight. Shafts of sun were breaking through the clouds and casting dancing shadows on the pavement. The afternoon was warming up. Charlton said he knew a nice pub with a small beer garden which was almost on our way, so we agreed to go and sit there and think about what we might be able to do next. As we upped our pace, Charlton reached down and took my hand and we walked hand-in-hand along the busy street.

The beer garden was hidden out the back of the pub and it was quiet. People wouldn't have finished work yet, so we made the most of the tranquillity and sat down in the corner of a lovely walled garden and nursed our drinks.

"We have to do something, Sam," I said, almost to myself as I cupped my glass of wine in my hand.

He leaned his elbow on the table and ran his fingers over his chin. He clearly hadn't shaved for a day or two and a greying stubble freckled his jawline.

"What do we know so far?" he asked.

"We know Gloria was being exploited."

"Yes, we know that. What else?"

"Well." I thought for a moment. "We know Mark Henry is involved somehow."

Charlton rubbed his chin again. "We don't know that, though, do we?"

"Well, why else would he be beating Liam up?"

"He didn't do that either, did he?"

I sighed, and rephrased, "We know that Mark Henry was there when Liam was beaten up." I paused. "And we know he was letting underage drinkers in the Five Two Two…" I hesitated. "Actually, we don't know that, do we?"

Charlton shook his head. "We only have the owner's word for that."

I leaned back in my chair. "Shit!" I said. "What *do* we actually know?"

We sat there deep in thought for a while.

I sipped at my wine. "We know that Jack Clayton was dismissed from Plumtree House," I ventured at length. "And there's something fishy about what I've been told about Francisco Martínez. That definitely doesn't add up."

"And someone didn't want Aziza to talk to you," Charlton added. "Any ideas? Who have you talked to?"

"God, everyone," I said. "The school, the social worker, the home, the taxi firm, the nightclub, the gym, the foster carer. In fact, there's barely anyone who knew Gloria that I haven't spoken to!"

We sat there glumly for a while, and then Charlton suggested that maybe, to cheer ourselves up a bit, we should eat out that night and talk about other stuff. I thought that sounded like a great idea. We were getting nowhere and there was little that I could do until I got back to Lincoln the next day, so we spent the next half an hour poring over TripAdvisor and deciding what we wanted to eat.

In the end we plumped for a nice sounding family-run Italian. We lingered over our drinks, and then left the pub and sauntered through the early evening sun to the restaurant. After taking our time over dinner, we wandered back to Charlton's place, meandering through the streets in the balmy light of dusk. As we reached the front door, he took me by the hand, turned me to face him and then leaned down and gently kissed me on the lips.

This time, I kissed him back, heady with the effects of a few glasses of wine and the warm summer evening. He held me briefly by the shoulders, and then wrapped his arms around me.

He lifted his head, and I opened my eyes. I reached up and held his face in my hands. He looked down at me, his dark brown eyes twinkling in the twilight sun.

"Want to sleep in my room tonight?"

And I touched his lips lightly with my finger and nodded.

I was glad we were in Charlton's flat and not my house. I didn't know what memories this place held for him, but I wasn't ready to share my bedroom with anyone just yet.

I looked at myself in the bathroom mirror. I had removed my make-up and cleaned my teeth, but I was taking my time. Eventually I walked through to the bedroom. Sam's trousers were folded neatly on a chair and his pants were folded on top. I noticed that there was a small hole by the elastic of his pants which amused me and, for some reason, made me feel calmer. I looked over at the bed, him lying there with the duvet halfway down his chest, his dark skin glistening in the light of the moon streaming through the window. He was in shape, that was for sure.

"Hi," he said, and smiled at me as I stood in the corner of the room.

I said nothing, just slowly removed my clothes. I kept on my pants and my 'secret-support' vest and slipped into the bed next to him.

I swallowed. It had been a while since I'd been in bed with anyone; with John, the night before he'd driven off to his death. I didn't want to banish the thought of John from my mind, but it seemed somehow inappropriate to be thinking about him whilst lying next to someone else. I had a mental image of John, looking at me from wherever. In my mind he turned and walked away; not from anger or jealousy, but because he knew that I was moving on and he knew that I needed some privacy.

I turned back to Sam. He was lying on his side, his head resting in his hand, as he looked down at me. He touched my cheek with his finger and leaned in to kiss me. I watched his hand run over my body and I loved the look of his dark, black skin against my pale, white skin. He took the bottom of my vest and started to pull it slowly up my body and over my shoulders.

Afterwards, he lay above me. He was leaning up on one elbow and moving the hair out of my face with his free hand.

He smiled down at me. "That was nice."

"Yes," I agreed. "It was."

He rolled over and flopped down beside me. I twisted round and snuggled my back into his tummy, his large body completely enveloping me. He arched his arm over my side and took my hand in his, entwining his fingers through mine as he kissed my hair and whispered something in my ear that was too quiet for me to hear.

Wednesday

-29

I jerked instantly from sleep to wide awake. It was just after 5am and for a brief moment I forgot what had gone on the night before. I turned to look at Sam sleeping next to me and, along with the memories came a wave of nausea rippling through me. I pulled the sheet off me and got out of the bed. I tiptoed across the floor and went into the bathroom, thinking that I might actually be physically sick. Guilt and regret were mixing in my brain and I stared at my reflection in the mirror, overcome with grief for John. The urge to give in to the tears welling up in my eyes was competing with the urge to flee. I wiped my eyes with the back of my hand and took a few deep breaths. The urge to flee won.

I crept into the spare bedroom and gathered all my things together, stuffing them higgledy-piggledy in the overnight bag. Sam's quiet breathing told me that he was still in a deep sleep and I needed to get away from this place before he woke up. What had I been thinking? My husband was barely cold and there I was sharing another man's bed. I took my bag into the bathroom and picked up my things, zipping the bag up an inch at a time. It had all seemed so straightforward last night, there I'd been conjuring up images of John as if he was giving me a blessing to sleep with someone else. My brain had been playing tricks on me, my brain and the wine combining to convince me it had been okay.

I sneaked out of the front door and down the stairs, hoping that Charlton would stay asleep for some time. I wanted to get as far away as possible before he woke up and realised that I'd gone. I gave little thought to how he might feel when he found out that I had fled; I just needed to get away. I walked the nearby streets, heading vaguely south towards London city centre, although unsure of the exact direction I needed. I was almost at St Pancras before I found a café that was opening up for early breakfasts and I went in and ordered a strong coffee.

I had just sat down to drink my coffee when my wrist vibrated with a calendar reminder.

Buy a present for Charlotte!

That was all I needed now, but actually it was a welcome distraction and I thought for a moment about what she would like. She was a real bookworm, so I searched on my phone for the nearest bookshop. It would be an hour or so before it opened so I left the café and wandered around the streets nearby. I found myself at St Pancras old church, walking through its gardens, the early morning sunlight dappling pale shadows of the leaves, dancing through the trees and onto the grass. Behind the church was a large tree, its massive roots enveloping hundreds of gravestones as if it were eating them. The gravestones huddled together around the bottom of the tree and a plaque told me that Thomas Hardy, before he'd found success as an author, had been involved in clearing the graveyard of the church to make way for the railway. Not wanting to throw the gravestones away, and in respect for the dead, he had arranged them around the bottom of the tree, which, over more than a hundred and fifty years, had gradually subsumed the stones. Life eating death. As I stood looking at it, I felt for the gravestones. The roots were like my guilt, crawling over me, consuming me, overwhelming me.

I headed to the nearest Waterstones and bought Charlotte some of my favourite books from my childhood, *Black Beauty* by Anna Sewell and *Anne of Green Gables* by L.M. Montgomery. I knew she'd worked her way through the Narnia series already and I didn't think she'd have read these two.

I was perusing the bookshelves when my wrist vibrated again. A text from Charlton.

Where are you? x

He'd never put a kiss at the end of a message before and it sent a wave of anger through me. I ignored it. I paid for the books and set off for King's Cross. I bought an expensive ticket home to replace the one I already had booked for later that day. I really didn't want to be hanging around.

I boarded the train and found a seat. The carriage was almost empty as it was past rush hour and I was heading out of London. Eventually a few travellers came into the carriage and spaced themselves out across the seats. Another message pinged through from Charlton.

Are you ok? Verity, where are you?

No kiss this time. I couldn't decide if that was better or worse.

And then, ten minutes later a phone call. I dropped the call and put my phone in my handbag.

After only a couple of minutes another text came through.

Verity, talk to me. Please?

I shook my head and sighed. I really was not in the mood to talk to him at the moment. I considered turning my phone off, but then it started ringing again. I grabbed at it and glared down as if it was the phone's fault I was feeling this way. It was an unknown number. I imagined Charlton, back in the office, ringing from a work landline. I gave a long, slow outward breath and stabbed at the screen.

"What?" I snapped into the phone.

An unknown male voice came back at me, "Oh, I'm sorry."

"I beg your pardon," I said hurriedly. "Sorry, who is this?"

"Francisco. Francisco Martínez. The agency asked me if I would give you a call."

I breathed in silently and tried to calm myself as quickly as I could.

"Oh, yes, thanks so much for calling me back."

"No problem, how can I help?"

I could hear the Spanish accent now.

I looked around the carriage, there were quite a few seats occupied by that point, and I really didn't want to talk about Gloria, or Aziza in front of these people even if they'd have no idea who I was talking about.

"Look," I said. "I'm on a train at the moment, but I wanted to talk to you a little about when you worked at Plumtree House, if that's okay?"

"I was not treated well there," he said.

"Yeah, I kind of figured that," I ventured. "I'm heading back to Lincoln now. I could meet you when I get there? The train is due to arrive in around an hour or so."

There was a rustling of papers, maybe him flicking through a diary or something. "I don't have a shift until seven," he said. "So I could meet you later, yes. You want to come to my flat? Or you want to meet somewhere else?"

After some debate, we arranged to meet at Café Santos, Francisco's flat being some way out of the city centre. The sun was shining, it should be lovely sitting outside on the patio and it would be a little more discreet than having a conversation on the train. It was also always useful to be able to observe people's faces, their body language and so on. I was starting to realise that as much could be learnt from what people didn't say as from what they did say.

30

By the time I ended the call with Francisco, I'd had a couple of missed calls from Charlton. I really didn't want to face him yet, so I threw my phone into my handbag and glared out of the window, glowering at the passing fields as if the countryside was to blame for my predicament.

When he rang again, a few minutes later, I snatched at the phone and pressed answer. Holding it to my ear, I was suddenly unsure what to say.

"Are you okay?" Charlton's voice crackled cautiously across the airways. He sounded a little tentative to say the least.

I said nothing. I stared down at my knees.

"Verity, what is it? Are you okay?"

Something snapped inside me. "No," I shouted down the phone, causing a couple of people at the far end of the carriage to turn round and look in my direction. "No," I hissed. "I'm not okay." I paused. "I don't know what you were thinking of last night."

I knew I was being unfair but I didn't care. Guilt was weaving a net around my heart, a devil sitting on my shoulder, whispers in my mind telling me I'd been unfaithful to John. I needed someone to blame. Someone to absolve me of any responsibility.

Charlton was clearly taken aback. "What was *I* thinking of?" He gave a little laugh. "From what I recall I didn't force you to do anything." He was right, of course, and that made me angrier.

"You took advantage, Charlton," I spat down the phone. "I'd had three glasses of wine."

"You weren't drunk, Verity."

I clenched my fist. I wasn't going to admit to myself, or him, that I had made a rational decision. That I had actually wanted to be unfaithful to my husband.

"We should have discussed it before. When we were sober," I said.

"That sounds romantic."

"Oh, fuck off," I spluttered. I wiped a tear away from my eye with the back of my hand. I wanted to sob; in grief for John, in guilt for having started to move on, and in self-reproach for having enjoyed being in bed with another man. I wanted Sam to put his arms around me and tell me that everything was going to be okay.

"We can talk now. We can talk about it now and what we're going to do," Charlton suggested, calmly, down the phone.

I looked out of the window at the countryside hurtling past. I leaned my head against the window and closed my eyes.

"Verity?"

"I don't want to talk about it," I said. I shook my head and ended the call. Then I turned my phone onto silent, turned off notifications for my watch, and buried it deep inside my handbag, as if the extra distance would keep Charlton at bay. I spent most of the rest of the journey glumly looking out of the window and trying not to think about John, or Sam.

As the train got closer to home, I took out my notebook and reviewed what I had written about Francisco Martínez. I swept my guilt to one side and concentrated on the job in hand. I needed to find out what I could about young people going missing from Plumtree House and I needed to find out where Gloria was, for Linda and for Sarah.

31

Francisco was there when I arrived at Café Santos. I recognized him from the photo I'd taken of his file. Although he was easy to spot. His black hair and tanned skin giving his Spanish ancestry away. We greeted each other and I asked him what he'd like, but at that moment the waitress came out with a cup and placed it down in front of him. I nipped in to order a coffee and then returned to the heat of the day, joining him in the sun at the same table I had sat with Liam and Aziza just a couple of days ago.

I started by explaining a little bit about what I was looking into, and why.

"I didn't work there when Gloria was there," he said. "I think she had just moved, because many of the young people talked about her."

"But you worked with Aziza?"

"Oh yes, a lovely young lady," he said smiling.

"Did you know that she's gone missing too, like Gloria. She hasn't been seen since Sunday, and the police don't seem to have a clue. Just like Gloria." I wrinkled my brow. Saying it out loud seemed to make it sound even more worrying.

"That is strange," Francisco said, although with his Spanish accent it sounded more like e-strange.

The waitress appeared with my coffee, and I waited until she'd gone back inside before I carried on.

"Aziza told me that she used to run away sometimes, but that she stopped. She said you put her in touch with HSL?"

"Ah, yes. The thing with Aziza was that she was struggling with her identity. She didn't really know from where she came. She had no family, no one. All this made her vulnerable, very vulnerable." He shook his head. "And, yes, she did leave at night. She stayed out sometimes, very late."

"Did she stay out overnight?"

"One or two times, yes I think she did."

"Where was she found?"

"Well." He thought for a moment. "She just would turn up. Sometimes the police brought her back." He shrugged. "I don't know where she had been. She would never say. And the police would find her outside, in the open spaces."

Just like Gloria, I thought, not for the first time. "She told me that she used to talk to you sometimes. That you would sit on the stairs and chat."

"We did." He nodded. "Sometimes she would get quite sad. She would just sit there. She clearly wanted to talk so I would go and sit next to her. I think she felt safe there, on the stairs. I don't know why."

"What did you talk about?"

218

"Everything. Her family, a lot. She had lost touch when they were making their way here. They were heading to England. She always hoped that they would turn up and find her. She wanted, so much, that her family would come and she would have a proper home with them. She spoke about her mother often. I think they had been very close."

"So, as you said, very vulnerable."

"She was desperate to be loved. To have someone to love her. Someone that was hers, like family." He cupped his hands around his drink and stared into it. "But it wasn't good. What was happening was not good for her."

"Tell me about it?" I said.

"Well, she had a boyfriend. He was no good."

"Did you meet him?"

"No, but I know he was no good. He bought her things, a phone, a dress."

"Like Gloria," I said. "That's what happened with Gloria."

"But I think he gave her these things to trick her, to make her feel that she had to do things for him."

"What made you think that?"

"To start it was just a feeling that this was not right. But she got upset. One day we sat on the stairs, and she said that she thought he was special. He had bought her a dress to wear and taken her on a night out. He told her not to wear her headscarf. And then, after they had had lots to drink, they went to his friend's house and he told her to have sex with his friend."

"What did she do?"

"I think she did. Have sex with the friend. I think it was that he told her he had bought her expensive things and that she owed him. She was very upset."

"I'm not surprised," I said, feeling the pressure Aziza must have felt.

"She didn't know what to do. He was bullying her over the phone. I do not think it was the first time she'd done it. He had photos and he was threatening to send them to her friends."

"But you helped her get away from it?"

"I put her in touch with HSL. It was lucky, I had just completed a course, only a week or two before, and HSL had done a presentation. Very interesting. But I remembered it when Aziza was talking to me, and I told her she should talk to them. Yes, they helped. They are very skilled."

"Did she ever tell you who the boyfriend was?"

"No, never. Even after she went to HSL. I think she was frightened, even though she had got help. I think she was still frightened."

I thought it might be time to throw in the information that PC Keal had given me. "Francisco, Amelia Macdonald said they had to let you go from Plumtree House because you weren't reporting young people to the police when they went missing."

He pressed his lips together and clenched his fists beneath the table.

"*Joder!*" he whispered.

"I'm sorry?" I said

"That woman." He paused and wrinkled up his nose. "She instructed me a few times not to call the police. She said she was keeping tabs on people. Aziza too."

"So, she told you *not* to call the police?"

"Yes, I wanted to. That is what we need to do, so the police can try and find the young people."

"She actually told you not to do it?"

He looked up, nodding. "She would say a worker was following and they knew where they were, the young person I mean. I don't think she was being honest though. I know Aziza was off the radar a couple of times and I am very sure that no one was following her. Or that they knew where she was."

"Why would Amelia not want the police to find the young people?"

"I have no idea," he emphasised the point by shaking his head. "But it's her that needs investigating, not me."

"Why did you stop working at Plumtree House?"

"Amelia told the agency not to give me more shifts. I was the, what do you call it? Escapegoat?"

"Scapegoat," I corrected.

"The police had realised that the young people were not being reported all the time, and I got the blame." He stabbed at his chest with his finger. "I think she picked on me because I helped Aziza, and I talked to her. I do not think Amelia liked it. I don't know why." He shrugged his shoulders and lifted up his hands.

32

I left Francisco sitting in the sun outside Café Santos. I hurried through town, nipping into a corner shop to buy some chocolates, and then I made my way over to Plumtree House.

It was Rachel who let me in, and showed me up to Liam's bedroom. I knocked on the door and peeked around. A waft of unwashed clothes, and unwashed teenager hit my senses. Liam was lying on the bed, playing with a handheld games console. He was nursing two shiny black eyes. He'd obviously had a new splint on his nose since I had seen him last and he said that he'd returned to the hospital a couple of days ago.

"Have you heard anything from Aziza?" I asked hopefully.

He shook his head. "Do you have any news?"

I shook mine. "No. And I don't feel like I'm much closer to finding Gloria either." I thought about the picture I'd seen and tried my best to shake the worry from my brain about where Aziza might be right now.

I smiled at Liam. "Those black eyes are impressive," I said.

"I know." He grinned. "It's great, isn't it?"

"Well, great isn't quite the word I'd have used, but…"

"Look at these bruises, too," he said and he yanked up his T shirt and showed me his torso. It looked like a patchwork quilt of blues and greens.

"Oh my God, Liam!" I exclaimed. "That looks horrific."

"Want to see my shins?"

"No!" I exclaimed. "I think I get the idea. Lots of impressive bruising."

Liam winked one swollen, blackened eye and, pointing to the worst of it, said, "Don't worry, this has got me out of loads of work. And they've said I'm not grounded anymore!" He laughed, "This has got me so much sympathy."

I gave him the chocolates. He opened them straight away, offering me first choice, and I picked a coffee cream.

"I hate those," he said, wrinkling his nose. "Good choice!"

I sat down on the end of the bed. "Liam, listen, I need to get back in the office."

He sat up. "Great."

"But look, I don't think we need to create any more arguments or loud distractions like the last time."

He sank back down onto the bed.

"It worked really well," I added quickly. "But I think we need to be careful. And you don't want to be grounded again."

He tilted his head in acknowledgement. "I think I can lure Amelia out of the office for a while," he said, nodding and smiling.

"What are you thinking?"

"Oh, don't worry, nothing bad. I won't shout, I promise. I'll get her down to the kitchen. Might only be a couple of minutes though."

I wasn't sure that would be enough. I had no idea what I was looking for.

"What do you need from there?" Liam asked.

"I don't know. I honestly don't know, but I need to have another look. I need to try and find something. I just think that Amelia is hiding something."

"Hmmm." Liam pulled his mouth to one side and hoisted himself slowly off the bed. He was clearly still in some pain, despite his bravado. He thought for a minute and then said, "Okay. I'll go first. I'll make sure the office is open. But I can't guarantee how long I can keep her occupied."

"Don't get yourself into any more trouble," I said. "Just get me what time you can."

He shuffled towards the door and poked his head out. He turned back and gave me the thumbs up, which I took to mean it was all clear. "Give me two minutes start," he whispered, and then he was gone.

I stood in his room and listened to his heavy footsteps heading slowly down the stairs, the creaking Victorian wood signalling to anyone who could hear them that someone was en route to the ground floor.

I made a note to tiptoe when it was my turn. I looked at my watch; I wanted to give him long enough so that I didn't run the risk of running into Amelia on my way downstairs, but not too long to eat into the time I'd have to look around. I paced the floor a couple of times and then I couldn't bear the waiting any longer so I crept down the stairs on tiptoes, treading on the edges of each step and trying to make as little noise as I could.

Cautiously, I opened the office door. I had an excuse prepared in case Amelia was still there, but the room was empty. I nipped in quickly, glancing around to make sure that nobody had seen me enter, then shut the door, keeping the handle pulled down until the last minute to make as little noise as possible. I ran over to Amelia's desk and grabbed hold of the filing cabinet keys that I now knew were in the drawer. I remembered which cabinet had previous residents' files and headed straight for that one. It took me a moment to find the right key but once I had the cabinet opened, I went straight for the bottom draw and the 'W' section. But Noah's file wasn't there. I looked through the entire drawer in case it had been put back in the wrong section, but it definitely wasn't there anymore. I pulled open the drawer above, and the one above that, but his file was nowhere to be seen. *Shit!* What did that mean? But I didn't have time to stop and think about that.

I headed over to one of the other cabinets—if I remembered right it was the one that contained all the receipts and invoices. Maybe there'd be something in there about the agencies that Plumtree House used. Some clue about why Francisco was let go. I knelt down on the floor and pulled open the bottom drawer. The first few files I looked at were each for particular companies that sent supplies to the house. Stationery, linen and so on. Nothing there. The next couple were for firms that obviously did work for the house; gardeners, builders, plumbers. Then, in amongst these official files, I pulled out a file labelled 'sundries'. I was expecting more receipts and invoices, but this one was different. This one contained Amelia's personal financial accounts. I pulled it out and spread it over my knees. There were several months', probably over a year's worth, of bank statements. I rifled through them, glancing through the transactions. Every month there were the normal outgoings you would expect from a personal bank account, mortgage payments, credit card payments, utilities and day-to-day expenses. But also, every month, there was a deposit. £500 a month. From an account named J. Clayton. That amounted to six thousand pounds a year. *Jesus!*

I sat back on my heels and whistled silently into the air. I was just about to start contemplating why Jack Clayton would be paying Amelia that amount of money when the office door opened. I quickly scrabbled to get the file back together, but I didn't have the chance before Amelia walked in, catching me with her personal banking details open in my lap. Her eyes opened wide and her mouth dropped as she saw me sitting there on her office floor.

33

"What the hell is this…" she tailed off.

I leapt to my feet, the contents of the file spilling onto the floor next to the open filing cabinet.

"Why is Jack—"

But I didn't get to finish the sentence because she'd dashed out of the door and was headed down the hallway. I ran after her. She threw herself towards the stairs, galloping up, and disappeared round the first corner. I bounded after her, taking the stairs two at a time to try and catch her. She was just about to turn the next corner towards the landing, when I caught up with her and managed to grab her arm and halt her run.

"Why is Jack Clayton giving you—"

But once again I didn't get to finish what I was saying because she lifted up her free arm and shoved me towards the stairs. I staggered backwards, my arms flailing, my feet grappling for ground but finding only empty space. My stomach lurched as I fell through the air, and my arms clutched in vain at the bannister rail. I was tumbling out of control, and I rolled down several steps before thumping into the corner of the stairwell. The wall broke my fall with such a force that all the breath was knocked out of my lungs. Amelia took advantage and, leapfrogging over my crumpled body, she hurtled down the stairs and out of the front door, leaving the door open in her wake.

I picked myself up and gave chase, just as a startled Liam came hobbling down the hall. I had no time to stop, or to explain, I just scurried out of the door after Amelia. She was tearing down Carline Road, away from the city centre and I hurried after her, trying to recover some ground. She was a good ten yards ahead, and she wasn't slow either.

And then Amelia disappeared, turning sharply left into Liquorice Park. I tried to up my speed and raced towards the park. Steps descended steeply down through the park to the road below, and I took them as quickly as I could without tripping over my own feet. About halfway down the steps, Amelia turned left again, emerging out the side of the park. She darted up the road, doubling back on herself along a street that ran parallel to Carline Road. I'd lost a bit of ground on the steps and she was about fifteen yards ahead of me now. I gave it everything I had and started to gain on her. I pounded the road, my breath coming in heavy gulps now, but I was closing in progressively with each step. It was a sunny day, not as hot as it had been the week before, but enough to have me sweating as I ran after her at full tilt. I wiped my forehead with the back of my hand. We were approaching the corner of the road and she would need to make a choice there—whether to turn right, and run further downhill away from Plumtree House, or whether to run up a little cut through and head up the steep incline of Motherby Hill back towards where we had come from. She momentarily hesitated, only for a split second, but it gave me enough time to get within feet of her.

She was heading back towards Plumtree House, and I careered up the little lane, reaching out and grabbing her arm as she raced along. I couldn't quite hold on to her, but I unbalanced her and she fell sideways, crashing briefly into the red brick wall that ran along the left hand side of the cut through. She regained her composure almost instantly and scampered towards the little set of about four steps that connected the path to Motherby Hill. But I was too close for her to get away now. I snatched at her back, not quite getting hold of her, but managing to push her. She fell hard, hitting her knee on one of the stone steps. Her glasses flew off, landing a few feet ahead of her and smashing onto the steps. She let out a cry, and tried to stand up, but I was on top of her now. I couldn't let her get away, I needed to know what part this woman had played in Gloria's disappearance.

My anger at this woman, who was supposed to care for vulnerable children, was bubbling to the surface and I growled through gritted teeth as I pushed her back down onto the steps with my foot. But then, she whipped herself round, causing me to unbalance. I staggered backwards, just about managing to stay upright and she turned round to face me. She scrabbled to her feet and made as if to run up the steps, but I lurched forward, reaching out and clutching her ankle, and I pulled her back down towards me. She was on her tummy and trying to claw her way up the steps away from me. I used her ankle as a lever and pulled myself up, then I straddled her and sat on her back. I grasped her hair and leaned into her ear.

"Why is Jack Clayton paying you money every month?" I hissed at her.

She was stronger than she looked, and through clenched teeth she strained, groaning loudly as she did so, and pushed her body upwards. Then she jerked her back and threw me to one side, like a bucking horse. I still had hold of her hair and I landed on the steps with several strands clutched in my hand. She bellowed and held onto her head where she'd lost a small clump of hair. She pushed herself onto her feet and scrambled up another couple of steps before I managed to snatch at her blouse. This time, I succeeded in grabbing a handful of the material. I yanked her back with more force than I'd intended and she rolled down the steps and onto the tarmac of the path. I turned towards her and bent down to grab her once again. But, from her lying position, she kicked up as I got close and knocked me hard on my left shoulder. I fell against the wall again. And by the time I'd recovered she had made it up the four steps.

I was exhausted but I hurtled after her, crushing her already shattered glasses under my feet as I did so, and caught her just as she rounded the corner into Motherby Hill. Throwing myself at her, I shoved her to the floor, landing on top of her. I was half sitting, half lying on her and I pushed myself so that I was fully sitting up, with a leg either side of her back. I decided to go for her arms rather than her hair; I gripped onto them both and pulled them hard behind her.

"Why is Jack Clayton paying you money every month?" I hissed at her again.

A man appeared at the top of the path. I thought I was thwarted, but as he looked down the hill at me sitting on top of Amelia, holding her down and yanking her arms behind her, his eyebrows shot up, and his eyes and mouth all opened at the same time. He stretched his arms out as if applying brakes and doubled back up the hill and around the corner without saying a word. He clearly didn't want to get involved.

"Tell me," I shouted at her, and shook her by the arms.

She turned her head towards me and shrieked, "I'm not telling you anything. I'm not telling you anything at all. So let me go!" She wriggled underneath me, but I had a strong grip on her now. Sunlight glinted on the beads of perspiration forming on her brow and she blinked as droplets trickled into her eyes.

"Why were you telling Francisco to turn a blind eye when young people went missing?"

She stopped squirming. She obviously hadn't realised I knew this piece of information. But she said nothing.

"I know you were, Amelia. I've seen his records, there's nothing in them to back up what you've said about him not following procedures."

She thrashed around, trying to headbutt me with the back of her skull.

I bent down close to her ear, taking care to keep my head to one side of hers. "If you're not prepared to tell me, then I think I'm going to have to tell the police about the money you're getting from Jack Clayton. I'm sure you'll feel more inclined to tell them all about it once you're in an interrogation room."

"Okay, okay!" she yelled. "Let me go, and I'll tell you."

I loosened my grip on her arms and moved to one side, but as soon as she was free, she span round and slapped me hard across the face. And then she turned and ran up the hill.

I scrabbled to my feet, my cheek stinging, and I launched myself after her. My anger was fuelling me and I caught up with her in no time, clutching at her and dragging her back to the ground. I pushed her hard into the cobbles and restrained her again.

"Right, talk," I demanded. "Talk to me, or talk to the police. The choice is yours. Why is Jack Clayton giving you money?"

She deflated a little, and rested her head on the path. "He just wanted me to turn a blind eye," she said, eventually.

"To the fact that he was taking children out to nightclubs. Plying them with alcohol and drugs? Buying them fancy clothes and phones?" I screeched at her, not caring who was listening or about to come round the corner. "How could you turn a blind eye to that? You're supposed to be in loco parentis."

She shook her head. "I didn't realise to start with, what was going on. I needed the money," she said in a shrill, high voice. She was still struggling in my grip, wriggling and pulling to try to release her arms from my hands. She turned her head to the side. "He just said he wanted to take one of the girls out, and I didn't see the harm, he was giving her a nice time."

"A man who'd been previously dismissed from Plumtree for inappropriate behaviour?"

She stopped struggling, turning right round to try to look me in the eye. "I needed the money. To start with it was just about the money."

"You do realise he was prostituting them to his friends?" I gave her a shove, pushing her head so that she was facing forwards again. This wasn't about her feeling sorry for herself, however much she needed the money.

She nodded and leaned her forehead on the ground. "Once I realised what was going on, it was too late." She pulled her chest up, as far as I would allow.

I wasn't going to let her go again. Not until I had more information, anyway.

"I told him a year or so ago that I was suspicious about what he was doing. He just laughed and said, 'And what are you going to do about it?' He said he'd get me fired. He said he'd go to the police with proof that I hadn't been following procedures. Then I threatened to go to the police myself, and he offered to increase the money. The longer it went on, the harder it was to do anything about it."

I let her arms go, but I stayed firmly sitting on her back. She pushed herself up a little with her hands, but made no attempt to get free. Her shoulders deflated and she hung her head. Maybe she was experiencing some relief at having told someone what was going on.

"He knew who to target. He knew who the most vulnerable young people were, didn't he?"

She nodded. "He seemed to yes. He took some of the others out, but he always ended up sticking with the girls who had no family here."

"Before Gloria, was there anyone else?"

She nodded again, and then she flopped onto the floor and started to cry. *Oh, Jesus, give me strength.* That was all I needed, sobbing.

"Oh for fuck's sake, stop crying," I spat. "This is not about you. Two girls from Plumtree have disappeared. Are you telling me there are others as well?"

"Not here, not from Plumtree. I went to work for a while in a home in Derby. It must have been about eighteen months ago, maybe two years. It was an exchange, I was helping them learn a particular approach to nurturing young people." She gave an ironic laugh. "We had a young girl called Habiba," she said between tears. "A girl from Iraq. She'd come here with her brother. Her brother moved somewhere else, Birmingham I think."

"Where is she now?"

"I don't know," Amelia said, and she started to sob with renewed vigour. "She started going missing, and staying out. She started staying away for longer and longer periods. And then she never came back."

Amelia sank fully into the ground and leaned on her arms, crying into the crook of her elbow.

"Was Clayton involved with Habiba?"

She nodded.

"And had he been involved with any other young people before that?"

She nodded again.

234

"Who?" I couldn't believe what I was hearing. How many young people had these monsters exploited?

She leaned up a little. "Before I moved to Derby, there was a young girl at Plumtree. She was the first I think. The first after he started to pay me. But he just used to take her out. She stayed out late sometimes, but she didn't go missing."

"Where was she from?"

"She was local. She had family in the south of the county."

"And where is she now?"

"She left Plumtree a while ago. She went back to live with her mum when she was about seventeen. I think they moved away, though, they were a travelling family."

"He moved on to people who had no family to care about them. How did he know who to target? How did he know who the most vulnerable ones were?"

She slumped back down on the ground. "I don't know. But I suspect it was Noah Walker. He got Gloria started at the gym, and he used to go swimming with Aziza. He'd have had plenty of opportunity to introduce them to Jack."

"Was he involved with any boys?"

She shook her head. "Not that I can think of, no."

"Have you been keeping in touch with Jack? Does he know that I've been to see you? That I've spoken to Liam?"

She nodded.

"Is Jack at the gym now?"

"No. I don't think so, no"

"Where is he?"

She shook her head violently.

I grabbed her hair and yanked her head back. "Where is he?" I demanded, leaning close to her ear.

"I can't…" she began, tears and mascara streaking her face.

"You fucking can," I shouted at her. "You've let these young girls be sold for sex and you've turned a blind eye for the sake of a few hundred pounds a month? You can tell me now where he is." I punctuated my words with sharp tugs of her hair, her head jerking back and forth with the rhythm of what I was saying. When I had finished, I pushed her head forward with force, and she slumped it down towards the cobbles.

She said nothing, just continued to shake her head. She pressed her lips tightly together and I got the impression she was scared of Jack and what he might do.

"You do realise, I am going to have to tell the police about this, don't you?"

"Yes," she said in a barely audible voice.

"And social services?"

She nodded, clenching her teeth.

"And, in all likelihood you're going to lose your job and, hopefully, never be allowed to work with children ever again?"

She nodded again, screwing up her eyes tightly and pursing her lips.

"Yeah, it's not looking very good for you. But, if you tell me where he is I might skip over some of the details about your bank account." I turned the corners of my mouth down and tilted my head from side to side. "Obviously I can't guarantee that they won't find that out for themselves, but maybe I won't help them with that point. Perhaps adding accepting bribes to your list of crimes won't affect the outcome too much for kids, but it might save you from jail? Who knows." And I shrugged. "But I do need to find Jack, and fast. He needs to be stopped."

She sunk to the ground. "Okay, okay," she said. "I'll give you the address."

I knew the name of the road, it was to the south west of where we were, beyond the council offices. I let her go, and she just lay on the ground, slumped forward on her arms. After a while she pulled herself up and sat, her arms clasped around her knees.

I wagged my finger at her. "If you let him know I'm on my way, the offer's off. I'll tell the police everything."

Slowly, she stood up. She hugged herself around her chest, the torn blouse hanging loosely from her arm. Her shoulders slouched and she hung her head low into her neck; the gravity of what she had done appearing to be weighing her down physically. I stood back, my head up high and my arms folded defiantly across my body and I watched her as she sloped off up the hill back towards Plumtree House, glancing back at me but without saying another word.

-34-

I headed off down the steep incline that is Motherby Hill and emerged onto the main road just next to the old police station, which was standing empty. It was one of the ugliest buildings in the city and known locally as the Ryvita building because it looked as if it had been constructed from giant Ryvitas.

I fished my phone out of my handbag. I needed to time this right. I needed the police to arrive early enough that Jack Clayton had no time to run, but not too early that I couldn't extract a little bit of information from him first. But then, what if the police didn't care? What if there was no one available? What if they didn't believe me? I stopped walking and stood in the middle of the pavement trying to think about what to do. As I looked at my phone, I noticed that I had several missed calls from Sam Charlton. I ignored them, now was not the time to be discussing last night's bedtime activities. I decided that the best thing to do would be to call

Mike Nash and give him the tip off. I'd have to brazen it out with Clayton and see if I could persuade him to tell me anything.

I rang Nash's phone and waited. He didn't answer, which was thwarting my back-up plan. I left a message for Nash as I walked a few paces further on. And then I stopped again whilst I dithered about what to do next. My face was burning, more from the exertion of the last half an hour than the heat of the sun but I sought the shade of a nearby wall. I decided I might as well try someone else who I knew would be interested. I scrolled through my phone to find the number of PC Keal, but just as I was about to press 'call', the phone rang. It was Nash.

"Mike," I said, "thanks for ringing me back."

"Not a problem, Verity, not a problem at all. You said you had some information that might help."

"I've just been having a chat with Amelia Macdonald, the manager from Plumtree House," I said, completely truthfully. "It's just that she told me that it was definitely a guy called Jack Clayton who was taking Gloria out. You know, playing the boyfriend role?"

"Oh yes?"

"I'm not sure she won't tell him that I'm passing this information on to you, so it might be an idea to get someone round there fairly quickly. I wouldn't be surprised if he doesn't do a runner."

"And the manager from Plumtree House told you this?"

"She's known it for some time. She's been turning a blind eye."

"Why on earth would she do that?"

"I don't know," I lied. Then added, "Maybe he has some hold over her? Maybe he has some dirt on her, there must be something." I wasn't sure I sounded very convincing. Surely Nash would figure out that Amelia wouldn't just turn a blind eye for no reason whatsoever, and my suggestions didn't sound that credible. But I had kept to my side of the bargain and not spelt it out for them. Maybe they wouldn't dig that far if they got Clayton in their grip. Maybe they'd find it out for themselves. I shook my head; I didn't really care. Amelia had allowed children in her charge to be hurt and, truthfully, she had what was coming to her.

"Hmmm…" Nash mused.

"He took Gloria to nightclubs, encouraged other people to have sex with her. And apparently she wasn't the first. There was a young girl from Derby, and Amelia thinks that she's still missing, too."

"What's her name?"

"Um, I don't think I wrote it down." Not with my hands occupied holding Amelia flat against the cobbles. *Shit! What was the name?* "Let me see." I wracked my brain. Hamira? Haniba? Something like that. And then it came to me. "Oh yes, here it is," I said. "Habiba. I don't know the surname though."

"When would that have been?"

"About a year and a half to two years ago, I think."

"I'll get someone to contact Derby and see what they can find out."

"And Clayton," I said. "Will you send someone out to see him?"

"I will, yes, I definitely will. We'll need to investigate what's been going on. Although I'm not sure how soon we'll have someone available."

I gave Nash the address. "Well, thanks, Mike," I said. And I ended the call.

35

The address that Amelia had given me was only a five or ten minute walk, and as I walked I thought about how to approach Jack Clayton. I would need to be careful, he was huge. He was built like a body builder and could certainly cause someone some serious damage if he felt so inclined. I turned into the road, both sides lined with terraced houses stretching down a slight incline. Each house had a bay window at the front and some had a tiny yard, just big enough to fit a couple of wheelie bins in.

Jack Clayton was allegedly in number 16, which was at the far end of the street on the right. Each pair of houses shared a door, which led through to a passageway with their actual front doors opposite each other, halfway down the passage. We had always called this arrangement a 'ginnel' and it had never occurred to me that this wasn't a real English word until I'd met John, who'd had absolutely no idea what I was talking about the first time I'd used it

242

in his company. Number 16 shared a ginnel with number 14, and I pushed open the door and went into the dark little passageway. I walked past the front door and down to the end where a gate led into a garden. The gate was partially open and I peered through to see what the layout was. I was worried that the minute Jack Clayton saw that it was me calling at his door, he'd make a run for it. Not only did I not want to lose him, but I was also concerned about the good relationship I had with Nash. He'd be none too impressed if I managed to cause one of his main witnesses to flee. I carefully checked out the surroundings.

The house had a small, paved garden. More of a yard, really. It was surrounded by a wall that looked at least six feet tall and seemed to back onto the garden of the house behind. An overgrown honeysuckle clambered over the side and back wall, and weeds had pushed themselves up through the gaps between the paving stones. A couple of cardboard boxes had been discarded in one corner near the house. There was nothing that would give him a leg up to get over the wall, although I supposed he might have been able to grab the honeysuckle and leverage himself over. I wasn't sure it would hold him, but I quickly fished out my phone and looked at Google Maps. The adjacent road was open ended at both ends, so if he managed to climb over the wall and get through the ginnel on that side I'd have lost him by the time I got round to that street. I pushed the gate a little, so that it was open wide enough that I would be able to run straight into the yard and try to stop him if he tried to escape out of the back door.

As I got to the door, I hesitated. My hands were shaking, and my mouth was dry. But I had to do this. I couldn't wait for the police. For one thing, I had no idea how long they might take to get here. But more importantly, I needed to hear what Clayton had to say for myself. I was getting closer to Gloria and now I had a little leverage to extract some information from him.

I swallowed and took a deep breath, then knocked on the door and waited. After a moment or two, muffled sounds come from within, and then there was a lock turning. I tucked my handbag behind me, and stood back, filling the passageway so that if he tried to push past me I'd have a chance to trip him up before he could escape. I was alert and ready to run after him, as the door slowly opened. But when he saw it was me, he just shrugged, stepped back into the house and jerked his head to indicate that I should follow him inside.

The front door opened opposite the stairs. To the right was a small dining room that gave onto a little kitchen. An old wooden table stood in the middle of the room, brimming over with what looked like car boot sale junk—toasters, lamps, kettles, old brass ornaments, ceramics. There were no chairs visible. The room was clearly not currently used for dining. To the left of the front door was a small living room, and this was where we were headed.

Jack pointed to a faded sofa that filled one wall and I sat down on that. Opposite me, in the corner of the room, was a large TV on a stand, surrounded by DVDs, game consoles and several sets of rather hefty-looking dumbbells. As he sat down in a chair at a right angle to me, he raised both his left eyebrow and the fingers on his left hand, seeking an explanation as to why I was there.

"I've called the police," I blurted out. "They should be here soon."

He looked over towards the television and then back to me, but didn't say anything.

"It's just that, I wanted to talk to you first, before they get here." I paused and looked down at my hands. I held them up to Jack in what I hoped looked like a gesture of reconciliation. "Look, I know you've been bribing Amelia Macdonald to keep quiet."

"I—" he started to say.

But I cut him off, "I've seen her bank statements, and she admitted what you've been doing. The thing is, well I said this to Amelia too and she seemed to think it was a good arrangement, I might forget to mention to the police that I've seen that evidence"—*and that I had been breaking and entering and illegally rummaging through her office*—"if you help me before they arrive." I rubbed my hands together and took a deep breath, trying to sound more confident than I felt. "Now," I added, "I can't obviously guarantee that they won't find that out for themselves, but I won't point them in that direction."

He spread his hands and tilted his head back as if to ask what I wanted to know.

"Where do you get the money to buy the clothes and the gifts?"

"I earn enough." He shrugged.

"At the gym? To buy all those fancy clothes and phones? And to pay Amelia £500 a month? I don't believe you."

"You don't have to believe me."

I changed direction, "Why did you take them out? Those young girls?"

He pursed his lips, clearly thinking for a moment. "Maybe I like foreign girls?" he suggested.

"You made them think you were their boyfriend?"

He laughed. "And what makes you think I wasn't? I took them out, wined them, dined them, treated them nice. They liked a bit of care and attention."

"And then sold them for sex."

"I never made them do anything." He rubbed his hands on his jeans. "They were willing participants. They liked the rewards," he added as if he was trying to inject a little devil-may-care into his attitude.

"So they were happy to sleep around in return for labelled clothes and fancy underwear?"

"Uh-huh."

"I don't believe you."

"Look," he said, gesticulating with his arms. "It was just a game, okay? Just a bit of fun." His eyes opened wide. "I got them to trust me. Took them out...nice places...gave them a little bit of wine, sometimes something stronger. And then introduced them to people."

"Did you keep the money from prostituting them? Is that where your extra cash is coming from?"

"Prostituting them? Fuck!" He stood up and paced over to the television, then turned to face me.

"They come here, expecting an education, expecting to be housed and supported. They need to give something back." He rocked back and forth on the balls of his feet.

"By being dragged around the country to be abused?"

He shrugged and sat back down in his chair. "I didn't take them," he said as if that might absolve him of responsibility. "Not out of Lincoln."

"But you persuaded them to go?"

He nodded. "Like I say. It was a bit of fun, a game."

"And you took them around houses in Lincoln? To give them alcohol or drugs? Or to force them to have sex with other men?"

"I told you"—an arc of saliva caught the sunshine as it left his mouth—"I never forced them to do anything."

"It doesn't sound like a very fun game to me."

He shrugged.

"Do you know what was happening to Gloria when she was being taken around?"

He paused for a moment and licked his lips. "Why should I care?" He jerked his head back. I think he was trying to portray a certain cockiness, but he didn't quite pull it off.

"She's a child, that's why."

He hung his head low, but said nothing. The veneer of arrogance was beginning to drop off.

"Do you know where she is now?"

He shook his head.

"And Aziza?"

Another shake. He stood up again and looked out of the window to the street beyond. Some ancient lace curtains obscured his view. They didn't look as if they'd been taken down and washed since they'd been put up.

"How did you know which girls to target?" I asked his back.

He turned his head round to look at me. "I told you, I like foreign girls."

I ignored that. "They came to the gym, didn't they. Gloria used the gym, and Aziza used the pool."

He looked round again and nodded. "That was part of the deal with Amelia. She told me who the lonely ones were."

"And Noah Walker would come with them?"

"He was at the home too."

"He'd come with them, so you knew who they were," I mused out loud. "Is he involved now, more than just introducing you to lonely girls?"

"That little thug, I wouldn't be surprised. He'll do anything for cash."

"Do you know where he is?"

"No. I try my best not to cross paths with him if I can help it. He's a sadistic bastard."

"I've seen him first hand."

He thought about it for a second and then sighed, "I don't know, I don't really know Noah. Like I say, our paths don't really cross."

"But you know of him?"

"He used to drive the taxi sometimes. The thing is, he always seemed to be looking for trouble. Always complaining about something, winding himself up. He has a reputation; if you need someone beaten until they're unrecognisable, he's your man."

I remembered how he'd laid into Liam. "Hang on a minute, though. I thought he only worked taking bookings for the taxis."

"He'd moonlight sometimes."

He looked back round and gazed out of the window again.

"Jack, where are you getting the money from for this?"

"I told you, I make it myself." He looked down and shuffled his feet.

"From working at a gym and a little pimping on the side? Come on, I'm not that stupid. Besides, you said it wasn't you taking Gloria beyond Lincoln, so someone must have taken over once you'd gained her trust. And then betrayed it."

"I don't know about that, I just do my bit."

"Well then maybe I will have to tell the police about your bribery. I mean, it's a shame because at the moment, what have they got? You going out with girls you really should have left alone. But if you're the main man, well that's more serious. And bribery can see you in prison for quite some time." I was winging it, I had no clue how serious what he had been doing was, or whether jail might be involved. "C'mon, Jack, the police'll be here any minute now. Where were you getting your money from?"

He pulled his mouth to one side and then turned to peruse the street outside for a minute or two, staring through the grimy lace curtain. He seemed to be weighing it up. I guess, in the end, he decided that he'd take his chances with the police having to do their own digging and the possibility that they might not uncover the bribery. He turned round to face me. "Henry," he said. "Mark Henry pays me."

36

When I got home, I stood in the bathroom, twisting this way and that to look in the mirror at the bruises and grazes I'd sustained when chasing Amelia. Nothing more than superficial, thankfully. I pottered about the garden for a bit and then remembered that I'd turned my phone onto silent earlier, so I went into the house and fished it out of my handbag.

There were a couple more missed calls from Charlton, and two texts - one from my phone company telling me my monthly bill was available online, the other from Sam.

Can we talk later?

I stood and looked at the text for ages. I wasn't sure I was ready to talk. I put the phone down and wandered over to my bookcase where there were a couple of pictures of me and John. I just gazed at them, mesmerised. Each photo held memories of a good time. Of holidays, parties, celebrations. Of conversations that had gone on before or after the photos had been taken; conversations about hopes and dreams for the future, about the life we'd planned out for ourselves. The places we'd wanted to visit. I picked up one of my favourites; John and I on holiday in Spain, the sky beyond us crystal blue. John was nursing a beer and I had an enormous gin and tonic. I remembered the day well. We'd walked along the sea front, chosen a bar and then spent most of the afternoon there, watching the world go by with every passing drink. Then we'd stayed by the beach to eat dinner and had been quite tipsy by the time we'd climbed the steep stairs back up to our hotel.

A tear landed on the glass, and I realised I was crying. I missed John so much. Of course I was coping, but I missed him every day. I grieved for the life we'd thought we would have and I hated feeling that I was being forced to move on and discard all the plans we'd made. I ran my finger down his face and wondered what he would say to me if he could. *Be happy, live your life.* Something along those lines. He often used to say, '*You only have one life, but if you do it right once is enough!*' A sudden flash of anger took hold of my chest. I didn't want to be a widow. I didn't want to be here alone, thinking about plans that would never see the light of day.

"You abandoned me!" I shouted at the picture. "You left me to cope here, all on my own. And now look what a mess I'm in."

And the tears flowed faster, dripping down onto the photo and the frame, covering John and I as we smiled happily, sitting there with our half-empty glasses. I felt like I'd been unfaithful to him, but the truth was that he was never coming back and he couldn't expect my fidelity forever. I put the photo in its place and wiped my cheeks with my hands.

I turned back into the room, grabbed my laptop and sat on the sofa. I needed a distraction. I Googled 'NadiaSinned' but nothing came up. I tried it with capitals, without, with a space, without. I tried it on Twitter and other social platforms but there was absolutely nobody out there with that name. I debated downloading the onion router that the CEOP man had talked about, but I didn't really want to be rummaging around on the dark web. I threw the laptop to one side, went into the kitchen and started to heat up some soup. Whilst I was waiting for it to cook, I picked up my phone and sent Sam a text.

Sorry. Feeling confused. Trying to sort things in my head.

Almost immediately my phone rang, but I dropped the call. I really didn't want to talk to him. Then a text came through.

You'll need to talk to me eventually!

I guessed I probably would; I didn't want to avoid him forever more. Just for a little while longer.

I'm not ready to talk right now

I knew it wasn't the answer he was hoping for. I pictured him in his flat in London, looking out of the window into the gardens beyond, or maybe sitting on the sofa, reading my text.

This is crazy!

I closed my eyes and rested my head on the kitchen counter for a second. Then I took the lid off the saucepan and gave my soup a stir. I couldn't be dealing with his emotions right now, I had enough of my own swirling round my brain to keep me occupied. He was trying to force me to talk, and I really didn't want to. I dug my heals in.

Leave me alone for a bit

I just wanted to try to get my head in order, to sort out all the thoughts and feelings fighting for prominence in my brain. But then his next text arrived.

I can't deal with you if you're going to behave like this

"Oh, Charlton stop blaming me!" I shouted at my phone and tossed it onto the counter, feeling the irony in my words as I did so. Then I snatched it back up and stabbed a reply, taking out my frustration on the phone.

Fine. Then leave me alone and we'll all feel better, won't we?

I wasn't sure how I felt when he didn't respond, though.

After I'd eaten dinner, I called Joy Mahoney.

"Hi Verity," she said.

I could almost hear her smiling down the phone.

"Hi, Joy. I need to bring something up with you in relation to Plumtree House."

"Oh, yes?"

I gave her a brief resume of the conversation I'd had with Amelia that afternoon, failing to mention the fact that I'd actually been sitting on her back at the time. "I've passed the information to the police," I said. "But I just thought you would need to let the person know, the one that deals with allegations. Is it the LAD?"

"LADO," She corrected. "Gosh, yes, it does sound like I'll need to. I'll get on to it first thing. Have the police been to talk to her, do you know?"

"I'm not sure, sorry."

"Hmmm," she mused. "I just don't think she should be there at all. I'll call them and check."

Next, I decided it was time to call Linda Watson and give her an update.

"How are you getting on?" she asked. "Do you need any more money?"

"No," I said, "I'm fine. I just wanted to let you know how I was getting on." I told her a little about Gloria going out with Jack Clayton, although I didn't mention his name. I said that she'd been given some of the clothes and the phone by him. And then I told her that she was getting them in exchange for sex. Linda took a sharp intake of breath. I decided mentioning the picture I'd seen at CEOP might be a step too far for her at the moment, so I bit my tongue on that piece of information.

"She got in with some people who aren't very nice," I said, sensing the understatement as the words left my lips. "I'm fairly sure that she didn't want to do most of the things that they were asking her to do."

"I wish she'd told me," Linda said, her sadness palpable down the phone.

"She wouldn't talk to anyone. I think there must have been some threats. I don't know what, but she clearly didn't dare say anything to anyone."

"Do you have any idea where she is yet?"

"No," I said. "But I think we might be getting closer. I know some of the people that she was involved with and, well, that's the trail I'm following at the moment."

"Okay." She sounded a bit doubtful.

"There's another young girl who's gone missing and obviously the police are looking into that. I think it might be connected to wherever Gloria is, so that might help us too."

"I see." Her tone became a little brighter at that.

"I'm sorry," I said. "As soon as I know anything more, I'll call you."

"Thank you."

37

Later that evening I stood outside the Five Two Two, hoping that Aidan would be there. I'd got there earlier than last time and the bouncer hadn't yet taken up his post by the door. I'd been perusing the information I had and the notes I'd taken, and thought it would be good to go and see if I could get any more information about Mark Henry. I'd plumped for wearing something less business-like than the last time and had paired a summer dress with some higher heeled shoes, hoping that this time I wouldn't be required to sprint in them. On the way over, in the taxi, I'd sent a quick text to Liam asking if he had a picture of Aziza and one had arrived a couple of minutes later.

I smoothed down my dress and tried the door. It opened, so I manoeuvred my way down the dark entrance hall, past the velvet curtain and onto the dance floor. I was relieved to see that Aidan was there, standing behind the bar with his back towards me. I walked across the room, my heels clip-clopping on the wooden dance floor as I went, and he turned around, raising his eyebrows in surprise as he did so. His face relaxed when he saw that it was me, his mouth transforming into a broad smile, the dimples appearing in his cheeks.

"I ran off without paying the other day," I said. "I thought I should come back and buy you a couple of drinks in return."

"Did you now." He smiled again. "Well I hadn't noticed, so don't be troubling yourself about that. But welcome back." And he indicated that I should sit down.

I leaned against the bar with my elbows, but soon realised that I wasn't going to be able to stand for very long in those shoes, so I perched on the nearest bar stool.

"Will I get you a drink?" he asked. "Gin and tonic, wasn't it?"

I nodded. He moved around the bar mixing the drink, and then put it down in front of me. He poured himself a healthy measure of Jameson's and stood facing me on the opposite side of the bar. He held the whiskey up to the light. "There's nothing quite like an Irish whiskey to set things right whenever it's needed."

"I've never been a whiskey drinker," I said, and he stood back and raised his hands in mock horror. "It's a bit too sharp. Too…" I struggled for the right description. "Too…stingy on the back of my throat."

He lifted one eyebrow. "Too stingy on your throat?"

"You know what I mean."

"You're just not drinking the right whiskey," he stated.

"Well, I have tried a few."

"You normally drink G&T?" he asked.

"Well, no, actually, I normally drink red wine but it can be a bit heavy this time of year. It's not so much of a summer drink, really, although to be fair I do drink it in all weathers."

"Ah," he said, nodding knowingly. "What kind of red do you like?"

"I like the full-bodied reds, like rioja or merlot."

He walked along behind the bar, studying the shelves along the back wall, obviously unable to locate what he was looking for. Then he bent down, looking underneath the bar. After a moment or two, he resurfaced clutching a bottle and brought it over to show me. It was called Redbreast 12 and had a drawing of quite a cute little robin above the name. "This," Aidan said, pointing to the bottle, "is not for consumption by your average customer who comes here, but I think you might like it." And he poured a small amount into a tumbler and handed it over. "It's triple distilled, like most Irish whiskeys, and they use unmalted barley as well so this one has a nice smooth taste. Shouldn't be so stingy on the throat."

I tried a sip. The anticipated sting didn't arrive, and the whiskey went down a treat. Definitely much smoother than anything I'd tried before. "That is actually, really quite palatable," I said, surprised, before taking another sip.

Aidan laughed and asked if I'd like a full measure.

"Well, you've just made me the gin and tonic," I said.

259

He scooped the gin up and took it to the other side of the bar.

"Not a worry," he said. "If I've made a convert to Irish whiskey then it's worth the cost of a gin and tonic."

"Well, I'm not sure I'm going to be giving up the red wine, just yet," I said, "but this is definitely more pleasant than any whiskey I've had before."

After we'd finished our drinks, Aidan suggested we go and sit in one of the booths and pointed to the one we'd sat in the other night. By then, the bar staff had arrived and were busy getting ready for the first arrivals. "I doubt we'll be too busy tonight," he said, "but let's get out the way anyway. Can I get you another whiskey?"

"Why not," I said. I had quite enjoyed the first one and the taste was in my mouth now.

When we got comfortable in the booth I said, "Have you heard anything from Mark Henry? I hear he's gone into hiding."

"That he has," he said smiling. His crows' feet bunched together around his eyes. He ran his fingers through his hair. "And I hear that after you ran off the other evening you bumped into him?"

"He beat up a friend of mine. Well, he watched on whilst someone else beat him up."

"Is he okay? Your friend."

"He's got some smashing black eyes that he's quite proud of, and a broken nose, but other than that he came out of it reasonably well."

"What was Mark Henry doing beating up a friend of yours?"

"I was about to ask you the same question." I reached for my phone and showed him the picture of

Aziza. "This young girl is now missing too, like Gloria, and I'm thinking that Henry might know something about it. I'm convinced there's a link. She's a friend of the lad that was beaten up. I wondered if you'd seen her in here? Whether she'd been one of the underage drinkers that Mark was turning a blind eye to? She's eighteen now, but only just."

He took the phone and studied the picture, wrinkling up his forehead as he did so. He shook his head. "Sorry, no I don't recognise her at all." He looked up. "Has it been reported to the police?"

"Yeah, they're investigating obviously and they've got some leads, but I thought that there might be a link there to Gloria, so I wondered if she'd been in here."

"And the police think that Mark might have something to do with it?" He leaned forward and took a swig of whiskey, rolling it round in his mouth before swallowing it down.

"There's certainly a trail that seems to lead to him. And some pretty dirty dealings happening along the way."

"More than just letting youngsters drink in here?" He lifted his arm and waved his hand around vaguely to indicate the nightclub.

"It seems that way, yes. It looks like it's got a lot to do with pornography and prostitution. Gloria was being driven around and prostituted. And there are pictures on the Internet, too. And videos too, possibly."

He leaned back and gave a short laugh, presumably in disbelief at what he had just heard. He started rubbing the back of his neck. "Wow," he

261

said, shaking his head. "And you really think Mark is involved in this?"

"Do you think he's capable of that?"

"I wouldn't have said so, before, but…" He sighed. "Maybe that's why he wasn't bothered about the underage drinkers. If that's what was happening to them after he'd let them carry on drinking here."

James, the barman, appeared as if by magic with new drinks. A single for me and a double for Aidan. They must have communicated by telepathy, or something, because he always seemed to know exactly when was the right time to arrive. The conversation moved away from Mark Henry and we meandered through a range of current affairs.

Later in the evening Aidan asked, "So are you a Lincolnshire native?"

"I am," I said. "Born and raised. I grew up on the coast in a place called Sutton on Sea, do you know it?"

"Ah, I do." He nodded. "I grew up by the sea in Ireland, and I do miss it, being here in the city. So every now and again I head on out to the coast." He shrugged. "You know, I close my eyes and listen to the waves. You have to imagine the rocks and pretend that the North Sea is the Atlantic, but it does as a replacement. Both places are good for surfing though."

"When I was a child it was much smaller, quieter. There's been lots of building since then, lots of bungalows, which always strikes me as odd given that it's predicted to be overcome by the sea before too many more years have passed."

"Ah, it's a shame," he agreed. "It's the same with my home town. The building, I mean, not the rising sea level. New housing estates and caravan parks have popped up every time I go back to see my family."

"Whereabouts do they live? Did you say you were from Donegal?"

"The county, not the town. I grew up in a place called Bundoran, it's a seaside resort on the West coast. Think Skegness with Irish accents and cliffs. And worse weather."

"Worse than Skegness?"

"Well, changeable. They do say 'if you don't like the weather in Ireland, wait an hour'. The sun does shine. Just not for long."

As the time headed for midnight, James brought over another round of drinks. I had lost count by this point. I giggled as he put the glass in front of me and I cradled the glass in my hand.

"Just this one," I said. "And then I really should be going."

"I'll order you a cab." He raised an eyebrow at the barman just as he was leaving the table.

James nodded and disappeared back to the bar, and I assumed phoned for a taxi because about twenty minutes later he returned and said that the taxi was waiting outside.

I stood up, wobbling a little on my heels, and Aidan said, "I'll see you out, but just wait one second." He scurried off across the almost empty dancefloor and returned a few moments later carrying an unopened bottle of Redbreast 12. "Here," he said, handing it over. "Take this home with you."

"I can't," I said. "I've already drunk half a bottle and not paid you a penny."

"It's been an enjoyable evening, that's payment enough," he said. "It's not often I have company here."

I wasn't sure how accurate that was, given how intuitive the barman was to his every need, but I nodded graciously and accepted the whiskey. I took his arm as we walked to the door. He paused as we headed down the hallway and pointed to the photos on the wall.

"These all came from an old dance hall in Bundoran," he said. "It was knocked down years ago. I rescued the pictures; they were just going to throw them away. Some of these bands I went to see there." He shook his head. "How the time flies."

Thursday

-38-

A drum beating a persistent rhythm in my head woke me up the following morning. I opened one eye and a hail of light assaulted my eyeball. I snapped it shut. After a minute or two, I tried again, this time opening both eyes gingerly, allowing them to accustom themselves to the daylight. I reached for a glass of water; my mouth was dry like sandpaper and I thought the water might diminish the drumming a little. I glanced around the room; my clothes lay in a heap by the bed, with my shoes plonked on top of them. Tentatively, I slid to the edge of the bed, and without sitting up I rested my toes on the floor, trying to remember the move for getting out of bed. I steadied myself as I sat up, with the room starting to spin around me.

"Urgh," I said to the empty room, and lay my head back down on the pillow.

A few minutes later, and motivated by a strong desire to lay my hands on some painkillers, I made a more successful attempt to get out of bed, and I padded down to the kitchen to see what I could find. I had to rummage around in the drawers as I didn't take painkillers very often, but eventually I came across an old packet of paracetamol. The sell by date had long past, but I took my chances and threw a couple down my neck, followed by a large glass of water.

The bottle of whiskey stood in the middle of the counter with my handbag next to it. Although I couldn't recollect it with any detail at all, I imagined myself arriving home last night. I must have fallen through the door and plonked them on the first available space before heading upstairs, where I had clearly stripped fairly quickly and flopped into bed. I looked at myself in the mirror. I'd obviously had enough of my wits about me to wash my face, but struggle as I might, I could not recall doing so. I groaned again, and went back upstairs to get showered and dressed.

I was feeling a little better after having a shower and cleaning myself up, and just as I walked back into the bedroom a text message pinged through. It was from Keith.

Working from home. Bored. Fancy a coffee? X

Keith did freelance work advising entertainment venues, local radio stations, theatres and so on about increasing their reach. Although it generally meant a lot of travelling and meeting people, often he'd be working at home writing up reports or studying audience figures and other data. I texted back saying that coffee was exactly what I needed, and we agreed to meet at Café Santos in half an hour.

"Why were you out so late?" Keith asked, after I'd explained why I was feeling a little the worse for wear.

"I was at the Five Two Two," I said.

He put his cup down and raised his eyebrows. "The nightclub? I didn't think you were a nightclub person."

"Generally, I'm not," I agreed. "I was doing some research for this job I'm working on."

"I could cope with that," he laughed. "Research that involves drinking half a bottle of whiskey. Let me know next time if you need any help."

We'd almost finished our coffees, and had put most of the world to rights when the conversation turned to Sam Charlton, and I gave Keith an abridged version of what had happened in London.

"Then, when I woke up in the morning, I just panicked," I explained. "I crept out the house and left him there, sleeping."

"Where did you go at that time of the morning?"

"I wandered towards the city centre and eventually came across a café that was open. There were a few people in there, coming off their night shifts, I assume. So I sat there and wallowed in my misery for a while. Until the city started waking up around me."

"And when he tried to track you down?"

"I'd gone by then. I got the first train home that I could. He kept ringing though."

"Did you actually answer his calls?"

I nodded. "Yeah, I did after about ten of them. But I blamed him. I told him he took advantage of me."

He frowned into his almost-empty coffee cup. "To be honest, it doesn't sound like you were trying to fight him off."

I hung my head. "I wasn't," I sighed. "That's what's doing my head in. I wanted to do it. I enjoyed it. And now I can't shake this feeling of guilt. And regret. I feel like I've been unfaithful to John and it's all Charlton's fault."

"Have you spoken to him about how you're feeling?"

"No." I shook my head. "He keeps texting and ringing, and I keep ignoring him. He said he couldn't deal with me behaving like this so I told him to leave me alone."

"And?"

"Well, he has left me alone. And now I'm not so sure that that hasn't made me even crosser."

"You know, you probably do need to talk to him."

I looked down and pursed my lips. "Yeah, I guess. I just wish I knew what to say to him."

He put his hand on my knee. "You know, sweetheart, liking someone else doesn't mean you need to stop loving John."

"I don't know if I'm ready to like someone else yet, though."

He sat back. "Bloody hell, Verity, he's only shagged you. He's not demanding life-long commitment. Just enjoy it."

I nodded. Although whatever 'it' was I didn't know. And it certainly wasn't feeling enjoyable right now.

-39-

I was walking back through town when my wrist buzzed with a text. I'm not sure who I had been expecting, but my watch told me that it was from Liam so I took out my phone to read it.

Call by here? Think I know where to find Noah.

My heart skipped a beat. I still hadn't managed to track down Noah, and he was the best hope to bringing me a step closer to Mark Henry. I sent a text back saying that I was on my way, and changed my course towards Plumtree House. When I arrived, a woman I had never seen before answered the door and declared that she was the manager. Obviously, Amelia had been replaced. Whether it was temporarily, or permanently I wasn't sure, but it was good to know that Joy had pushed things into action fairly quickly.

Liam was in his bedroom, in his normal position lying on the bed playing with a games console. He was wearing his grey hoodie again, nicely clean from being laundered. His eyes had taken on a greeny yellow colour and the bruising had spread around his face and down his cheeks. The splint on his nose looked like it could do with replacing, the tape was curling up at the edges, and I asked him if he'd been back to the hospital yet to have it checked.

He shook his head. "I have got an appointment," he said. "But I can't remember when." He shrugged.

"Is it hurting?" I asked.

He touched it tentatively. "It's not too bad," he said.

"So you think you know where Noah is? How did you do that?"

He took out his phone. "I was talking to someone on Facebook," he said. "Someone I go to school with. Well, did, before they kicked me out. I put a picture on there of my bruises. Anyway, this guy is okay, one of the not-too-annoying people from that school. And he asked me what had happened, so I told him. Then we got chatting, you can do that private, like, so nobody else can see."

"I'm old, Liam, but I do know how Facebook works," I laughed.

"Yeah, well. Then I said I'd like to get my hands on him and this guy told me that he knew where he lived, if I was interested."

"Wow, that's great. Good job."

"So, then," he said, sitting himself up to get off the bed, "when are we going?"

"Liam," I said, taken aback. "I really don't think—"

"Hey!" He pointed to his face. "I've got some payback due to me."

"But you've seen what he's like. He can be vicious. And you're not recovered yet. I saw you yesterday, struggling to walk."

"I can walk fine," he said, standing up to demonstrate by walking across the room.

I had to acknowledge that he was walking a good deal better than the day before, but I didn't want him to get involved again. "What if he gets worked up again? What if he has another go at you? It could well end up worse than before."

"I'll have you to cover my back this time," he joked.

"I don't think so, Liam. It's really not a good idea."

"Maybe not," he acknowledged. "But I'm coming with you. I need to face him down. I need to look into his eyes."

I set my mouth firm and shook my head.

"Fine, then," he said. "I'll go by myself. It actually being me who has the address." And he smiled, pointing to his phone.

After another couple of minutes of me trying in vain to persuade him that it was actually quite a bad idea for him to come with me, I held up my hands and said, "Okay. Okay, I give in. You can come, but you have to promise me you won't do anything to wind him up."

"I won't," he said indignantly.

"Or react if he tries to wind you up."

"Scout's honour," he said, holding up three fingers.

I shook my head. "Honestly, what am I doing."

"You never know, I may be some help. If he starts punching you in the head at least I'll be able to call the police."

"Thanks," I laughed. "That's something to be grateful for, then."

I didn't recognise the address that Liam had and we had to look it up on Google Maps. It turned out to be on the outskirts of town, in the corner of the A46 and Riseholme Road. Normally, I'd have walked, it probably would have taken me half an hour or so, but I thought Liam would struggle to get there, so I suggested that we called in at my house and picked up my car.

"Nice house," Liam said when we got there. "Husband rich, is he?"

"Dead," I said.

"Oh." He shuffled his feet, and looked down at the ground. He clearly didn't know how to respond to that.

"Don't worry," I said, "It was over a year ago now. I'm good." I reached into my handbag and got out the car keys, before pressing the fob to open the doors. I threw my handbag into the back of the car, and indicated to Liam that he should get in. I was halfway to sitting down in the driver's seat, when I had a sudden thought. "Hang on. Wait here a minute," I said then ran into the house.

I leapt up the stairs two at a time and into my bedroom. After rummaging around on top of the wardrobe, I eventually found what I was looking for.

A backpack. It was the one I'd used when I'd had to go to London during 'the incident'. I'd taken almost everything out of it now, but lying at the bottom was a pair of handcuffs. I grabbed them, checked that the keys fitted and ran back down to the car.

Liam raised his eyebrows when he saw what I was putting in my handbag. "Believe me," I said, "you never know when these might come in handy."

"I really do not want to know why you have a pair of those in your house," he said, wrinkling his nose and pulling his lips in tight.

As the engine sparked into action, Lincs FM started broadcasting to the car.

Liam rocked his head back, laughing. "You are so old, man," he said.

"I like it for the traffic," I said in my defence. And anyway, I quite liked the afternoon presenter, but I didn't tell him that. I turned the radio off and backed out of the drive.

40

We pulled up a couple of hundred yards down the road from the address that Liam had given me and sat in the car for a minute in silence. Eventually, I said, "We have to make sure that he can't make a run for it. We need to position ourselves so that it isn't easy for him to get away. Block the doorway, you know. And if he tries to run, trip him up."

I took in a deep breath; I had butterflies flying around my lungs. My nerves were getting to me, heightened by the fact that I had an observer this time. And I didn't want him to get hurt again. We got out of the car. I slung my handbag across my body, and we headed towards the house. It was an end of terrace council house. Or social housing house. A makeshift paving-slab path led over the gravel to the front door, and a discarded fold-up bed lay on its side just under the window of the front room. I knocked on the door, not quite sure whether I was hoping for no response, or for Noah to answer the door. I didn't have long to think about it, because a couple of seconds later the front door opened. I had never seen Noah's face in person, but I recognised him from his picture. His heavy brow ruckled in confusion when he saw me and Liam standing there. He went to close the door, but I anticipated his action and as speedily as I could lifted up my leg and kicked at the door. It caught Noah's arm as it swung open.

"Fuck!" he shouted, clutching at his arm.

"Then let us in," I shouted back. "All we want is to talk to you." And I barged through the door, pushing it against Noah as I did so.

Liam followed behind, and Noah glared at him as he walked into the hallway.

"What the fuck are you two idiots doing here?" Noah barked as we all stood in the hallway, Liam careful to be standing in front of the door so that Noah couldn't make a quick exit.

"Want some more bruises?" He sneered at Liam, his lip curling up to one side. Then he leered at me. "Or maybe you'd like some of your facial features altered? Might make an improvement."

"We just want to talk to you about Gloria," I said calmly, not rising to his provocation.

"Don't know what you're talking about." He puffed out his chest.

"Look, shall we go in? Or do you want to stay out here?"

He shrugged and led us into the front room. I followed him, nodding for Liam to pass me and then I closed the door behind us. Liam once again hovered nearby to slow any attempt at a getaway. Noah stood in the centre of the sparsely furnished room with his hands in his trouser pockets, and jerked his chin upwards, as if to say, 'go on then, what's it all about?'.

"Tell us about your involvement with Gloria," I said.

"Who?"

"Oh, come on, Noah, you know who I'm talking about. Why else did you feel the need to lure me out to see you beating Liam up the other night? You were trying to scare me off."

A smile spread across his face as he said, "Because I wanted to see the little shit in a pulp?"

I felt Liam twitch beside me, thankfully resisting the urge to throw himself across the room at Noah.

"How were you involved with Gloria?" I asked again.

He rubbed his chin with his hand. "Hmm, let me see," he said. "We were friends?"

I let out a long sigh and moved towards Noah. He took a step back towards the window, puffing his chest out a little more.

"Friends?" I asked. "Nothing more?"

"Yeah, just friends," he said, taking another step back.

I took another one forward; he was almost up against the window now. Then he smiled and added, "Friends, like I say. Friends with…" And he tilted his head to one side. "How shall we say. Friends with benefits."

Almost before I even knew what I was doing, I swung my leg hard at the side of his knee. I'd taken him by surprise and he had no time to react. His legs buckled underneath him and he fell sideways, landing against the sofa. Whilst he was struggling to get back on his feet, I kicked him again, knocking his arm from underneath him and he fell onto the floor. I stood back and let him sit up. He glanced from me to Liam and obviously decided that now was not the time to retaliate. As he leaned back against the sofa, he pulled his knees up towards his chest. Looking up at me, he whistled in through his teeth and then laughed. "Fucking bitch." And he laughed again. "Not bad," he said. "Not bad for an old bird."

"So tell me about Gloria," I said.

"Go take a fucking hike," he spat. "You and the boy wonder." And he jerked his head towards Liam. "Fucking piss off and leave me alone."

I decided to call his bluff. "Look, we know you were driving Gloria around. Probably without a licence. Or tax. Or insurance, I would imagine." I glanced over at Liam—his raised eyebrows betraying his surprise. I wasn't sure if he thought I was telling the truth and was surprised I hadn't told him, or if he knew I was bluffing and was surprised that I sounded convincing.

"And so?" Noah tilted his head to one side.

I was on a roll, my bluff was working so I carried on with it. "We know that you were driving her around. We know you were taking her to Leeds. To Kent. To other places."

He rested his forearms on his knees, he didn't dispute what I was saying. I obviously sounded more convincing than I thought.

"Like I say," he retorted, "so what? Driving someone places, as far as I know, isn't a crime. Is it?" He sneered up at me.

"As far as I know filming people having sex with children and distributing the videos online is, though."

He opened his mouth, and then got to his feet. "You don't know what the fuck you're talking about, you stupid, interfering bitch." And he pushed me in the chest, making me stagger back a couple of steps.

I saw Liam out of the corner of my eye, making a move, and I held my hand up at my side to tell him to stay where he was.

"I've seen the videos," I lied. "I've seen what was happening to Gloria. I know what you were doing." And I poked my finger into his chest to try to stop him advancing towards me.

He glanced over at Liam, and then back at me. He tightened his jaw, looking like he was trying to weigh up exactly how much I did know. I was obviously close enough to the truth for him to believe me.

"You were taking that poor girl places and allowing grown men to abuse her, whilst you stood in a corner filming her and then distributed the videos on some obnoxious, filthy, website."

He clenched his teeth and raised his hands up. "Not me," he said, curling his lip again. "Not me. I was just the driver."

"I don't believe you, Noah," I lied again, jabbing my finger towards him in the air between us. "I don't believe you. So far, all the fingers are pointing at you and you're in the frame for this."

He bent down towards me and shouted, opening his mouth wide, spit showering out with every word, "Then you have it wrong. Your information is wrong. Whoever has told you that is a *fucking liar."* He threw his hands in the air to emphasise the point.

I moved away from him, leaning my head to one side, as if I was contemplating what he was saying. As I tilted my head I wriggled my hand, in a gesture of weighing things up. "Hmm," I said. "But you knew what was happening. You're not going to pretend you just sat in the car and waited, blissfully unaware of what was happening inside."

"Oh, give it a rest," he said, taking another step towards me. "So I drove a car. So I sat on a sofa and what." He twirled his hand upwards as he leaned his face closer to mine. "Drank coffee? You need more than that, sweetheart." He was shifting his weight from one foot to the other, his body language not as assured as his words.

"It appears to me that you knew very well why you were driving Gloria around. Even if it wasn't you filming, you're complicit."

"Look, why don't you both just fuck right off and leave me alone?" He turned away from me.

I needed to push him harder. I had no doubt that he was telling the truth. I didn't for one minute think that he was filming, or that he was distributing the videos. He was a thug and I thought it stopped there, but I wanted to prod him into giving me something.

I made as if to be thinking about what he'd said. I tilted my head and then frowned for a second. "The thing is, Noah, I have it on fairly good authority that you are the brains behind this. That you are the one who decided filming was a good idea. That you were the one who set up the website and uploaded the videos." I paused for dramatic effect, and then opened my mouth and held up a finger. "Unless…" I paused again as if I was formulating an idea in my head. "Unless they want to make you a scapegoat and let you take the blame? You think that could be it?"

He rocked backwards and forwards on his feet, not wanting to believe what I was saying. "You're a fucking liar," he said, but he paced back and forth, running both hands through his hair. He clearly believed he could be about to be held out to dry. He stopped pacing and turned to me. "Who told you this? Who's told you this crap?"

Instead of answering the question, I stayed silent for a moment, and then said, "Where is Mark Henry?"

For a split second his eyes shot upwards, and I hesitated, trying to unravel the meaning of that gesture.

"What the fuck…?" he said, open mouthed, my intention that he'd think Mark was betraying him obviously working.

But then, the significance of the flicked glance upwards took form in my head. He'd been glancing up towards one of the bedrooms. He was here. Mark Henry was here. But before I had time to process that fully, a clattering on the stairs and a slamming door indicated that there had been someone else in the house and that that someone was making a run for it.

41

"Don't let him leave," I yelled at Liam, pointing at Noah, and I ran out of the room, crashing the door closed behind me. I hurried down the hallway following the sound of the slammed door, into the kitchen and out of the back door. I looked around. There was no one in the back yard. The garden gave onto other back gardens separated by small fences to the side and back that he could have easily jumped. I scoured the adjacent properties, but there was no sign of anyone running in any direction, just a neighbour a few properties on gathering in her washing.

Then the sounds of a car revving its engine drifted into my consciousness, and I sprinted down the side of the house, grabbing my car keys from my handbag. As I ran towards the road, a small car screeched off, its wheels spinning, leaving a cloud of dust behind it. I couldn't see the driver, but the back of a bald head left me in no doubt that this was Mark Henry getting away and I tore along the pavement to my car, cursing the fact that I'd parked it so far away. And facing in the wrong direction.

When I reached my car I looked up to see the trail of smoke disappearing around the far corner of the road. I knew that this estate was like a maze. There were so many different routes Henry could be taking, and by the time I'd turned my car around and given chase I wouldn't have a clue where he was. I stamped my foot on the ground, "Shit!" I shouted out loud.

A mother wheeling a buggy and holding the hand of a toddler glared across the road in disapproval.

I stamped both feet repeatedly. "Shit, fuck, shit!"

I stood there for a second, watching the dust settle back onto the road, before remembering that I had left Liam and Noah alone. I ran back to the house, going in through the open kitchen door and walking into the hallway towards the front room. Groans and shouts, interspersed with crashes and bangs, radiated out of the front room, which at least indicated that Noah was still here. I looked around for any kind of weapon. Something that would mean I didn't have to go back into the room completely unarmed. In the space under the stairs there was a pile of discarded clothes, bedding, children's games and toys. Fallen to one side lay a yellow child's baseball bat. I grabbed that, ran down the hall, and burst into the front room.

I wasn't quite sure what had happened since I'd left but Noah was now attempting to crawl towards the door, on his hands and knees, one foot outstretched behind him. Liam lay prone behind him, clinging onto the outstretched foot and growling with the effort of preventing him from leaving. As I took a step further into the room, Noah reached for my ankles, pulling them from underneath me, and I fell heavily to the side of him, dropping the toy baseball bat and rolling over onto my back. At the same time, Noah kicked his foot backwards into Liam's face. Liam reeled away, clutching at his chin, and releasing his grip on Noah's foot.

Noah leapt to his feet and before I had time to sit up, he grabbed one of my arms, yanking me into a sitting position. I swung at him with my free arm, but he blocked me with his forearm, a jabbing pain searing through my wrist as it clashed with his bone. Liam had managed to get to his feet and he moved behind Noah, thrusting his hands around Noah's throat and squeezing hard. Liam's face contorted with the effort, twisting and stretching with determination. Noah let go of my arm and thrust his elbows into Liam's already heavily bruised ribs. Liam clutched at his side and cried out in pain, reeling back into the wall.

Taking advantage of not being held down, I scrabbled upright and kicked at Noah's chest but it had little effect. He lunged for me, grabbing me round both of my legs and forcing me back to the floor. Liam was resting against the wall, trying to regain his composure, clearly in pain. Noah leaned above me. He grabbed my throat with one hand and drew back his other. I closed my eyes, every muscle tensing up, but nothing came. I opened my eyes to see Liam grasping at Noah's hair, jerking his head back, forcing Noah to let go of my throat. Noah swung his body round and sprang at Liam, pushing him to the floor, raising his fist ready to land a punch.

I snatched up the toy bat and swung it hard at Noah's back. It hit him with a good deal more force than I had intended and he fell on top of Liam, shouting out in pain. Pushing himself onto all fours, he turned to face me, a look of fury spreading across his face. His mouth contorted into a grimace and his jaw shook. I swung the bat again, this time hitting him on his left upper arm, and again hitting his right arm with a backhand swing. He was still getting up, still advancing and I swung the bat once more, this time hitting him on the side of the neck. The blow momentarily incapacitated him and I threw the bat to Liam whilst I grabbed the handcuffs from my handbag. Catching the bat with his left hand, Liam swiped at Noah's head, hitting him sharply to the side. Noah grabbed at his head, grunting as he fell to the floor. I slapped one of the handcuffs around Noah's wrist.

Liam stood over us both, threatening Noah with the baseball bat. Noah was weakened, but still struggling and I clung onto the spare end of the handcuffs with both hands. The only fixture I could see was a radiator a few feet away and I yanked the handcuffs hard towards it. They wouldn't quite reach and I pulled harder. "Move!" I shouted at Noah.

But he reached with his spare hand and clutched at the bat that Liam was holding above his head. He didn't quite get hold of it, but it was enough to send the bat spinning across the room. As Liam turned to retrieve it, Noah kicked at his back forcing him to the floor. He yanked his hand free from my grasp, wrenching the handcuff from my hands. I let out a yell as the metal ripped at my fingers.

Noah made once more for Liam. I shot across the room, picked up the bat and brought it down on the back of Noah's head. He fell, poleaxed, onto the carpet. He was still conscious, but weakened, moaning lightly and blinking his eyes as if trying to focus.

"Quick," I said to Liam, "we need to get him to that radiator before he recovers."

Together, we dragged his heavy body across the carpet. I attached the handcuff to the bottom pipe of the radiator and snapped it shut. I stood back and watched as Noah grew more alert, his expression changing as he became aware of his predicament. His eyes opened wider and his mouth moved as if he was about to say something but didn't quite know what to say.

"Which is Henry's bedroom?" I asked him as he stared about the room.

"Uh?"

"He's just done a runner, leaving you to pick up the shit, Noah."

He thought about it for a second or two, saw that I was holding the bat again and sighed. "The one at the back," he said, looking at the floor.

"Right, follow me," I said to Liam, and we headed out of the door leaving Noah alone in the front room. "Are you okay?" I whispered to Liam when we were in the hallway.

He nodded, the splint on his nose almost falling completely off with the motion, and a trickle of blood fell from his right nostril.

I crept up the stairs, Liam following closely behind. His breath was laboured—I could tell he was in some pain. We tiptoed up to the landing, unsure if there was anyone else in the house. At the top of the stairs, a bathroom and separate toilet both had wide open doors and I peered into the two rooms before moving onto the bedrooms. I went to the one at the front first, just to check that it was empty. On the far side of the bedroom, by the window, was an unmade bed with a greying sheet that looked as though it had, at one time, been white. A few empty crisp packets and take-away containers littered the floor. The side wall had a built-in wardrobe. I walked into the room and peered inside but its only contents were a few clothes. On the opposite wall a bookshelf held a few old ornaments that appeared as if they might have been left there by the previous resident, and an overflowing ashtray. I jerked my head at Liam and we walked back down the hall to the other bedroom.

There was no one in there either, but it was clear that someone had left in a haste. A couple of the drawers were open. Underwear and socks spilled out where Mark Henry had obviously grabbed a few items of clothing before he'd run. The wardrobe door was flapping on its hinges, the inside almost empty. In one corner of the room a neatly made single bed sported a Lincoln City football club duvet and pillowcase and at the foot of the bed was a desk. It was actually more like a home office, with a proper office chair and a large curved desk. Three laptops sat on top of it, with some wires hanging next to a gap from where a fourth had clearly been removed. Shelves along the wall next to the window were buried under boxes, and I went over to examine them. They all contained cameras, microphones, headphones—all the equipment you needed to make videos. I turned to the desk and looked at the laptops, pressing the enter key on them all. They were all, obviously, password protected.

"I don't suppose you're a secret hacking genius are you?" I laughed and looked up hopefully at Liam.

"I couldn't even pass computer science GCSE, sorry." He shrugged.

"If we were in a film we'd sit down for five minutes and figure out the passwords." I screwed up my mouth and chewed on my bottom lip.

We both stared at the screens as if something might leap out at us and give us the answer. We stood there, silently, staring pointlessly at the laptops until the screensavers kicked in again. And then bounding across the screens, tumbling and twisting, sprang the word @NadiaSinned.

"Fuck!" I said to nobody in particular. "We were so close. If I'd realised straight away that he was staying here when Noah flicked that gaze upwards I'd have caught him coming down the stairs." I kicked the table. "Fuck! Ow!"

And Liam laughed. "What is that?" he said, pointing to the screen.

"You know the website I was talking about? The videos?"

He nodded.

"That's what it's called."

"Do you really think all that was happening to Gloria?" Liam said, looking crestfallen. He sat on the edge of the bed and stared at his hands.

I'd forgotten that he'd had a sweet spot for her. I sat down next to him.

"I thought you were pulling his leg."

"Well, I was mixing truth and fiction," I said. "But, the thing is, Liam, that I'm absolutely certain that she was being taken around the country, under duress, and they were making her have sex with, well, who knows who or how many people? I think they convinced her that she was doing it for…well, love maybe, I don't know. I'm pretty sure they convinced her she was choosing to do it. And when she tried to resist…" I looked across at him, his brow furrowed in anguish. "I think she might have tried to say no. But they frightened her."

Liam stared down at his hands. "She could have said something to me. I'd have helped her."

I patted him on the knee, and he turned to look at me.

"For whatever reason, she couldn't talk to anyone," I said. "I don't know if she was ashamed, or if she'd been threatened, or bribed, or blackmailed, or a combination of everything."

He looked back down at his hands, wringing his fingers together, and heaved a sigh.

I crouched down in front of him and took his hands in mine. "We will find out where she is. I'm not giving up. C'mon."

42

We went back down to the front room. Noah was leaning against the radiator, his hands resting on the ground.

"So," I said, "Henry's done a runner and left all the equipment in your house."

"They won't find anything incriminating on those laptops. He'll have taken his main one with him."

"And all the cameras, microphones and stuff?"

"He does YouTube videos. So what? Is that a crime now, too?" And he gave a snort.

I moved closer, but took care to stay out of reach of his free arm. "What do you think the police will make of your involvement?"

"I drove a car," he said and shrugged. "They'll be more likely to do you for wasting police time." He put on a whiney voice, "Oh, oh officer, that man over there was driving a car. Arrest the bastard now!" He threw his head back and laughed. "You already have form pointing the finger at me for numbnuts here getting beaten up." He nodded towards Liam. "There's no proof, nothing to implicate me. They've dropped that one. You're going to look like you've got some kind of vendetta if you're not careful."

"You were driving without insurance. Or tax."

"Says who?"

"And taking Gloria around so she could be raped on film," I snapped at him.

He looked up at me, raising the top corner of his mouth in a sneer, clearly feeling that he had the upper hand. "And your proof of this is?"

I looked down. I didn't have any proof whatsoever. He'd more or less admitted his involvement, up to a point, but what proof was there? If he denied it to the police, which he would, there was nothing to prove he was culpable. There was nothing to prove he was involved in the filming, or photography. And even if he had driven Gloria around, even if he had had his own 'benefits', I had nothing to suggest he'd been involved in anything further at all.

"Fine," I said. "Come on, Liam, let's go." And we turned to leave.

"Hey!" Noah shouted, indicating the handcuff.

"Oh, yeah, sorry," I said, fishing out the keys and tossing them towards him. They landed just out of his reach.

"How am I meant to get free? My phone's over there." He pointed to the other side of the room.

"I'm sure you'll figure it out," I said, and we closed the door and left him there.

Sitting in the car, I looked at myself in the mirror. My hair was all over the place, and I had little scratches on my face. My clothes were torn, and my knee was bleeding from a carpet burn. I looked over at Liam. "How are you holding up?" I asked.

He touched his nose. "This is okay," he said. "It's my ribs that hurt again."

I sank into the car seat. "I'm going to be banned from going to Plumtree House ever again," I said.

"Don't worry. Do you really think I'm going to tell them what I've been up to?" He smiled. "And besides," he added, "you were awesome!"

We drove back mostly in silence, and I stopped the car just up the road from Plumtree.

"Are you sure you're okay?" I asked.

"I'm fine," he said. "Don't fuss. You sound like somebody's mother."

"I'll leave you alone for a bit. Hopefully your ribs will have time to recover."

"Yeah, but keep me up to date about Gloria," he said.

"I will, and if you hear anything from Aziza, let me know won't you?"

He nodded and got out of the car. I could tell by the way he was walking that he was in more pain than he was letting on, and I sighed at having got him into a scrape for a second time.

I was a mess and I was looking forward to getting in the shower. As I drove home I thought I ought to let Mike Nash know what I'd found out at Noah's place. And what my suspicions were about his and Mark Henry's involvement, even though the only solid evidence I had was a screensaver on Henry's laptops. I'd have to think about how I phrased it so that I didn't sound like a deranged vigilante trying to make things fit with my own theories. Maybe that was it; maybe I was trying to make things fit. As I pulled into the drive, I looked at my watch. I would call Nash, but not right now. A couple of hours wouldn't make any difference and right now I had a children's birthday party to get to.

43

I ran into the house and straight upstairs. I showered and changed into a pair of cropped trousers and a short-sleeved knitted top. Charlotte's present was still in my overnight bag and I took it downstairs and rummaged through the cupboards until I found some wrapping paper. I made a passable job of wrapping it up. I hadn't got round to buying a card, so I searched through my stack of stand-bys. There was nothing really suitable for a small girl, but as Charlotte was quite a bookish child, and as I had bought her books as a present, I selected one with an arty photo of a bookcase. It would have to do.

Thoughts were tumbling over each other in my head, and I couldn't stop pacing about, despite having showered and had a cup of tea. I looked at my watch; I'd have time to walk over to Collette's if I went briskly and it would give my body some time to relax. She lived over to the south of the city and it was probably about a forty minute walk, but I needed the fresh air.

Collette and Marcus lived in a smart three-bedroom detached house just off Boultham Park Road. They'd bought it not long after Charlotte had been born and it suited a family. The large garden gave the girls space to run around, and over the years, with the benefit of Marcus's promotions, they'd changed the kitchen, put in bifold patio doors and several smaller improvements. It was a running joke that they'd just have it how they wanted when it was time for the girls to leave home and for them to downsize.

I arrived just a few minutes after 5pm, trying my best to appear calm and presentable, having covered a few small scratches on my face with make-up and the walk having helped my body to rid itself of excess adrenaline. I quickly turned my phone onto silent and switched off notifications, so that I could give my full, uninterrupted, attention to my goddaughter. I didn't want a buzzing wrist to interfere with a couple of hours of purgatory. I arranged my face into what I thought looked like an expression of joy, and let myself in, looking round for any sign of Collette. Emily saw me first and came running over.

"Hello, gorgeous," I said, lifting her up and giving her a big hug. "How are you?" I gave her a kiss on the top of her soft head. "Where's the birthday girl?"

She pointed out into the garden. A small group of children clambered over the climbing frame, hurling themselves down the slide. Laughter filled the air, mingling with the cries of parents exhorting their children to be careful. Emily ran to join them, her shouts ringing out across the garden, even though she was two years younger than all the guests. She was such a vivacious, outgoing child. How the same two parents could produce such different children was a mystery to me.

Inside, Collette had extended the dining room table and buried it under paper tablecloths covered with dancing unicorns, princesses, rainbows and hearts. Some of the children were swarming around the table, grabbing sandwiches and miniature sausages; the little girls in their party dresses and the boys in posh shorts. In the centre of the table was a magnificent cake creation that must have taken Collette hours. It was a fairy castle with turrets made from upturned ice cream cones and pink walls with ivy growing up them. She had the patience of a saint. Especially considering fifteen hungry kids would devour it in the space of about ten minutes. And they would probably have been just as happy with a mass-produced caterpillar from Tesco. It crossed my mind that she'd made it more for the mothers' benefit than the children's.

The parents—there was one dad other than Marcus—stood around chatting, patting their little darlings on the head, sipping glasses of wine. But every now and again, one of them would sneak a look around them. You could almost see their thoughts as they glanced round mentally weighing up the quality of the food, the decorations, the house, the prizes. I shuddered and put on my best smile; Collette would need a little moral support. We had known each other since just after I'd finished university, before husbands and children had come on the scene, and she had supported me through some very dark times. It was the least I could do.

I went out, through the doors and found Charlotte in the garden. "Happy birthday, sweetie pie!" I shouted before bending down to give her a kiss.

I handed over her present, and she carefully opened it up. She wasn't like me as a child, ripping off the paper as quickly as I could. Charlotte loved her present and it was all Collette could do to persuade her to carry on playing with her friends rather than go and curl up on her bed and start reading.

"How are you?" I said to Collette when Charlotte eventually returned to her group of friends.

"I'm good, I'm good," she answered, nodding a little too energetically and smiling a smile that didn't reach her eyes.

"Mummy, mummy, Issac found the golden egg! He needs a prize!" Emily ran over and tugged at her mother's legs.

"I better go," Collette said, pursing her lips and raising her eyes to the sky. And with that, she bounced across the lawn shouting, "Who wants another game of pass the parcel?"

She spent most of the time running around giving out little presents for prizes and generally appearing as if she was having a fantastic time, although it was quite clearly an act. She was trying really hard to look like mother earth and was probably convincing those who didn't know her quite as well as I did. I hovered in the patio doorway, watching the games and periodically nibbling something from the table that didn't look as if it had already been mauled by some small, grubby fingers. Every now and again a parent would wander over and ask me which child was mine. When I replied that I didn't have a child, that I was here because I was Charlotte's godmother, they generally lost interest fairly quickly and sauntered off.

After standing there for quite a while on my own, Collette's husband Marcus ambled over. His face was telling me all I needed to know. With his downturned eyebrows and firm set mouth and jaw he looked like a middle-aged nun who had just woken up and found herself in the middle of an orgy.

"Hi," I ventured. "Having fun?"

"No," he said. "You?"

"Not really." I looked out at the garden. "I'm not sure she is either, if truth be told." I nodded in the direction of Collette, who was animatedly leading a group of children on a chocolate hunt, taking exaggerated steps, arms aloft, and opening her eyes and mouth wide with faux-excitement. She'd have put any children's TV presenter to shame.

"You don't host birthday parties to have fun, you know," Marcus observed. "You host them to demonstrate what a marvellous parent you are." He tilted his head towards his wife. "We've been meticulously planning this for weeks. I had to book the day off months ago. Jesus, thank God the kids' birthdays are six months apart."

He went off to do his duty of presenting a 'good image' to the other mothers, smiling as he charmed them, whilst they fluttered over their beloveds and told them to 'go slowly' as they threw themselves headfirst down the slide. It's a wonder people of my age had survived until adulthood, out all day on our bikes, fishing eels from ditches to take home for dinner, eating packed lunches on grass verges and not getting home until almost bedtime. I didn't remember anyone telling me to go slowly, or be careful. I didn't remember ever thinking about danger. Perhaps I'd had particularly negligent parents. Yet, miraculously, here I was.

A few moments later, a stunning, blonde lady came and stood nearby. She must have been nearly six feet tall, with a figure that wouldn't have looked out of place on the pages of a glossy magazine. She wore pale yellow pedal-pushers and a blouse that was decorated with lemons. Her hair was pulled into an up-do that had the perfect amount of hair floating loose to make it look effortless, but not messy.

She held up a hand by way of a greeting. "Gretel," she said with a heavy German accent, and she leaned against the opposite patio door.

Oh, blimey, this was the mother who most intimidated Collette, and I could see why.

"Verity," I said. "I'm here in the capacity of being Charlotte's godmother. I don't have any children myself."

"Ah, well," she said, "that's not so bad. I have three girls. Triplets." And she pointed to three little children dressed in picture-perfect outfits, their hair plaited and tied with bows that matched their dresses. I remembered now that Collette was in awe of how unperturbed Gretel always was, how perfect her children always looked and how effortlessly she seemed to parent the girls. Collette would arrive at school late and flustered, make-up free and red-faced, to be confronted by an immaculately tailored Gretel leaving the school, having arrived in plenty of time. Despite having three children to get ready.

"How do you cope?" I asked, genuinely amazed that she could achieve anything other than getting them dressed by the end of the day. "How do you even manage to give them breakfast in the morning?"

Gretel waved a dismissive hand, raised her perfectly plucked eyebrows and cocked her head. "I cheat," she said.

I looked over at her and giggled.

"I put them to bed in their school uniforms and feed them crisps on the way to school," she added. "But I wouldn't tell another mother that."

"Your secret is safe with me," I said, and Gretel sashayed off.

I stood and watched all the party antics, getting more convinced by the minute that I would have failed horribly as a parent. I must have been there for quite a while when a high-pitched squeal interrupted my thoughts. I'd been in another world completely. Charlotte had rushed up to me, and was tugging at my top.

"Look! Look! Come over here," she shouted excitedly.

She dragged me over to the play table where a group of children were drawing and writing with different coloured pens.

"We're writing our names backwards!" Charlotte exclaimed. "My name is Ettolrahc, backwards. What's yours, Verity?"

I picked up a piece of paper and wrote it down. "Ytirev," I read it out. "It sounds Russian, doesn't it?"

Charlotte giggled.

I pointed at her. "And you sound like a Viking!"

"I like sounding like a Viking," she exclaimed, and jumped up and down. "I'm a Viking! I'm a Viking!" she shouted excitedly. "It's funny, but it's not as funny as Issac. He sounds like a girl backwards."

And the other children started to laugh. I looked down at the name written backwards, Cassi, and then scoured the faces of the parents to see which of them had thought it was a good idea to mess around with the generally accepted spelling of a name. Maybe I should start spelling mine more exotically, Verrietee, or something.

"We're going to call him Cassi from now on," Charlotte laughed.

"Well, that's not very nice," I started to say but I stopped mid sentence.

I stood there, open mouthed as the whole room whooshed away from me and I thought I was going to fall over. I steadied myself against the table. The children's laughter faded into the distance, replaced by the intense thumping of my heart. I leaned against the table, the beating in my ears getting faster, sweat starting to pour down my face, and I struggled to bring the room back into focus.

"I, I have to go," I stammered, reaching over and grabbing my handbag. I looked around to find Collette but I couldn't see her. I bent down to give Charlotte a kiss on the top of her head then dashed off. "Tell Mummy I have to go," I shouted to Charlotte as I ran out of the room. "And thank Issac for me." And then, as an afterthought, "Oh and happy birthday!"

I ran out of the front door, slamming it behind me. I ran as fast as I could, cursing myself for not having seen it before. It was there all the time, staring me in the face and I hadn't noticed it. @NadiaSinned. It was so obvious I could have wept. Nadia Sinned backwards spelled Aidan Dennis.

As I ran, I grabbed the phone from my bag. I needed to let someone know where I was going. I paused to glance down at the screen. *Shit, twelve missed calls from Charlton!* What was wrong with the man? I scrolled to Nash's number and dialled, but there was no answer. I'd have to call Charlton, I needed to tell someone where I was. I threw the phone back in my bag and started running again. I'd call when I was closer. I ran as fast as my legs would let me, up Boultham Park Road, along the side of the river and over the bridge towards the Five Two Two. People turned as I ran past them, clearly not wearing running gear, but I didn't care. I barely saw them. I had one thing in mind, and that was to get to Aidan Dennis as soon as I could.

My heart pounded against my chest and I couldn't decide if it was nerves or exhaustion. I wasn't even sure that he would be at the club, although he'd indicated that he was most afternoons. How could I believe that though? Just about everything else he'd told me must have been a lie. Unless…unless it was Mark Henry using his name?

I was almost outside the nightclub, and I slowed to get my phone out. Much as I didn't want to talk to Charlton I really needed to let someone know where I was and with Nash being unavailable he seemed the most likely. It would also give me time to get my breath and think about what I was going to say when I got inside. I'd been in such a hurry to get there that I hadn't thought about what I was actually going to do when I arrived. I fished out my phone and at that exact moment a text came in from Charlton. I clicked on it.

Will you answer the fucking phone! Think we have the venue.

But before I had the chance to reply a voice from behind shouted, "I wondered when you'd be back."

I span round, and as I did so the phone was knocked from my hands onto the ground. It started to ring, and Charlton's smiling face appeared on the screen. I stretched out a hand, but I couldn't reach it. I was being dragged by the wrist into the dark corridor of the nightclub. Music pounded away from inside, and as I was pulled onto the dance floor it became deafening. House music beat into my brain, thumping into my ears. It was impossible to think. And then, a hard blow on the back of my head turned everything black.

44

I couldn't recall how I got there, but the next thing I was aware of was waking up in that vast, dank, warehouse strapped to the chair. The two men, Steve and the other, gruff and gap-toothed man, had dragged me, kicking and struggling to the room at the end of that cavernous space. What greeted me there suddenly, vividly, brought sense to everything. And I had never felt so frightened or alone in my life.

Strapped to a bed in the middle of the room was a naked Aziza, her furrowed brow and wild eyes screaming terror. A glimmer of hope flickered across her face as her gaze met mine, soon to be replaced by despair as she no doubt saw that I, too, was incapacitated. Aziza's hands were pulled directly above her head, stretching her torso, and secured tightly to the bedframe. Her legs were spread apart and each ankle was chained to a bed post at the bottom of the bed. I ached for this timid and religious young girl, exposed in such a sickening way.

A red ball gag filled her mouth. Welts, cuts, bruises and burns covered her torso as well as her arms and legs, and on her breasts traces of what looked like hardened candle wax had dripped down her side and onto the sheet beneath her. Some bulldog clips, pegs and a massive dildo had been left on the bed, which was streaked with blood and bodily fluids, alongside a half-used candle and, *oh my God,* a pair of pliers. Vomit rose into my mouth and I fought against it, knowing the gag could render it lethal.

A massive hook, like a meat hook, swung above the bed and all sorts of implements hung from the walls; paddles, whips, canes, wooden clamps, masks, gags, leather straps and suits, dildos, animal tails and ears. There were a whole host of items I had no idea what they could be used for, but I wasn't going to let my brain stop to think about that right now.

Opposite the bed a big row of blank television screens covered the wall. Several large stage lights overhead, provided the only light, creating a stark and austere atmosphere. Cameras had been positioned around the room, most of them covering, from numerous different angles, the bed that stood in the centre of the concrete floor.

Steve and his companion hauled me further into the room. Steve fastened thick cuffs around my wrists, connected by a chain that was about ten or twelve inches long. Yanking my arms high above my head, he lifted me up so that he could attach the chain onto a hook that was just too high to allow me to comfortably put my feet on the floor. The restraints holding me were pulled tight, my body weight pulling down on my arms, and I tugged on them in the hope that I might be able to free myself, but it was useless. The two men briefly left Aziza and I alone in the room as fear and tension built in my chest with each passing second. I glanced over at her, tears now mingling with the candle wax on the sheet, and I didn't dare to think about what had been happening to her during the last few days. Her face was contorted in a mixture of terror and awful anticipation and she began frantically shaking her head. Even though I knew it was futile, I rattled my wrists once more against the shackles holding them on the wall. My body hung heavily on the constraints and I reached down with my feet to try to alleviate the weight. If I stretched with one foot, I could just about lift myself up for a few moments on the ball of my foot and then switch to the other foot. It gave a few seconds relief each time.

A movement beyond the little window in the door caught my attention. The door flung open, and Aidan Dennis strode into the room, one hand in his pocket. He looked around, as if weighing things up, walked to the far side of the bed then glanced over at me.

"The merry widow!" he exclaimed. "Welcome to our pleasure palace." And he stretched his arms wide and surveyed the room.

I must have raised an eyebrow or something, because he went on, "Don't look so surprised, Verity, my darling. You need to be more discreet when you're snooping into other people's businesses. It was so easy to keep tabs on you." And then he added, for good measure, "Come on, sweetheart, you didn't seriously think Mark Henry had the intelligence to organise this all by himself, did you? No"—and he shook his head and glanced at the floor—"his talent was in keeping the young ones quiet. Selecting the right kids, gradually building up the pressure, all the time getting them accustomed to the fact that they were good for only one thing."

Aidan started walking about the room, touching some of the implements hanging from the red brick wall. Every now and then he fetched down a whip or a paddle and inspected it before replacing it with precision back in its allocated space. He glanced around at the room, as if admiring his work. It was the size of a small classroom and had a distinctive brick zigzag pattern that ran around the wall near the ceiling. Aidan continued pacing the floor, picking imaginary fluff off the edge of the bed and checking the cameras. He walked over to Aziza and stroked her hair. She flinched and cried out around her gag.

Aidan looked up at me. "Apart from this one," he said, looking back at Aziza and touching her breast lightly. "We'd given up on her until she decided she might spill the beans and we were left with no choice but to bring her here."

He came over and stood in front of me. I tried to take a swing at him with my bare foot, but he simply caught my ankle and held it in his hand. "Shame you won't get to let that lovely family know where Gloria is now." And he stroked my foot before letting it fall back down against the wall. "Well," he carried on, walking back over to the bed, and then glancing across at me from the other side of the room, "it is going to be a bit unusual having our next piece of entertainment in the room watching, but it'll be fun, Verity. You'll be able to see what you have to look forward to." He looked down at Aziza and ran his hand over her breast and stomach.

She shuddered beneath his touch.

"We've been having fun, haven't we, my lovely?"

I twisted and turned uselessly against the wall, and he laughed.

"Anyway," he announced, clapping his hands together. "It's about time for you to meet our sponsors." And he returned to the far side of the room, where he stood in front of a small table that held a laptop and various other items. He tapped on the keyboard and then picked up a remote control and flicked it towards the bank of television screens. He turned towards me. "We've had a rest for an hour or so, time to see who's still around." He looked me up and down, nodding to himself, and then carried on, "We might have some new faces. Who knows?" He shrugged before turning back to the laptop.

There were a dozen television screens, arranged in three rows of four along the wall opposite the bed. The @NadiaSinned logo wandered across each screen until they gradually started to spark into life.

"Let's see who's about this evening," Aidan said, watching intently as a couple of the screens filled with the faces of men. They were obviously joining in from their homes, like some kind of Skype meeting. Behind them was evidence of their everyday lives—bookcases, plants, family photos, pictures on the walls. Scenes of normality looking down on a scene that was as far from normal as you would wish to get.

"Phil! Welcome back," Aidan said, as the first face appeared, and he waved towards a camera that was mounted directly above the televisions. "And, Rory. Hi!"

"Afternoon," said Phil.

I wasn't sure what they could see—they were obviously logging in on computers somewhere through the whatever router it was. The camera that Aidan was talking to was focused directly on him, so I imagined that, at the moment, he was all they could see. There was a red light shining on the top of it, presumably to indicate that it was active.

By now, a few more of the screens had lit up with faces. All men. All white. Mostly puffy faced and middle aged. Aidan greeted them all.

"Paul. It's been a while, greetings to you in Bangkok. What's the weather like?"

"Humid," said Paul. "Same as ever." Sweat poured off Paul's round and pallid face as he lifted a pudgy hand to wipe his forehead.

"And, Justin," he said switching focus to one of the other recently enlivened screens. "Are you still in Norway?"

"Still here," replied Justin before he smacked his lips together and smiled from somewhere in Norway.

After a while, all the screens were filled. Aidan brought the laptop back to life and clicked on a few keys. He stood back, hands in his pockets, and looked up at the screens.

"Welcome, everyone," he said, smiling broadly into the camera. "Or should I say, welcome back. There doesn't seem to be any new faces this evening, so you all know the form." He ran his hand through his hair and then indicated the laptop. "Just to remind you all. Don't forget to pay for all the time you want to be here," he instructed them. "We have…" He scanned the open page on the laptop. "Five, six, no seven people outside our private room, in the hallway, waiting to join. As soon as your payment runs out, the highest bidder in the queue will take your place, and if you want to rejoin you'll have to join the queue and re-enter another bid. Okay?"

The heads all nodded and murmured their approval.

"Okay." Aidan nodded towards the camera above the screens.

Immediately the red light went out and he switched his focus to a different camera. Someone was clearly controlling the cameras from another room.

"This evening, we have a special guest with us. Don't worry, chaps, she'll be entertaining us before too long, but all in good time. We've still got lots of fun to be having with this one yet." And he pointed towards Aziza. "I just thought it would be…" He paused, his hand resting lightly on his chin, as if he was thinking carefully about his words. "…educational for her to see what she has to look forward to."

The terror was mounting in Aziza's face, and she struggled futilely on the bed. Across the room, a red light appeared above a camera pointing straight at me. The faces on the screens leered. Some of the men licked their lips and one of them made movements that clearly indicated he had started to masturbate. I was sickened, and turned away. But where could I look? There was horror everywhere in this room.

45

Aidan clapped his hands together. "Right, let's get bidding," he said. "Many of you were here earlier this afternoon, so let's have some creativity from you, yes? Ha! You've two minutes." He looked at his watch, then down at the laptop. "Starting from...now." And he clicked what I took to be a timer on the laptop.

All the images on the screens were replaced by clocks counting down two minutes; the hands moving at a snail's pace as they indicated the time remaining. I looked over at Aziza who gazed back at me, pleading, her eyes open wide and her brows knitted together. She was breathing heavily around the gag and moving her head wildly from side to side. This process was obviously not new to her and she was already anticipating what would happen next. I could hardly bare to look over at her, the mixture of hope and disappointment in her face sending convulsions of guilt through every fibre of my body.

And whatever was about to happen, I was powerless to prevent it.

I looked back up at the televisions as they counted down the last few seconds, the anticipation creating new waves of nausea to pulse through my body. Suddenly all the clocks disappeared for a brief second. Then the screens came back to life displaying a padlock sign, presumably to indicate that bidding time was now finished. A green flashing sign came up on one of the screens on the second row *'HIGHEST BIDDER!'* it announced in capital letters. It was the screen that had previously been occupied by Paul in Bangkok. And then, one by one, words and phrases appeared on each of the screens in turn. *'Fat dildo'*, *'shag with Steve'*, *'candle wax'*.

Tension pulled hard at my chest, a heavy weight dragging at my lungs. I curled myself in, lifting my feet up off the floor, hanging painfully by my wrists, trying to alleviate the pressure. Words kept appearing, each one adding to the sense of dread, and overwhelming me with an unbearable, agonising apprehension. Every screen showed what the person behind it had bid to happen next. *'Whip'*, *'paddle'*, *'tit torture'*, *'strip the bitch on the wall'*.

The fear, the tension, and the pain swirled through my body mixing to form a horrific combination of physical reactions. My lungs heaved, fighting to get enough air into my body as I breathed through the cloth that was stuffed into my mouth. A burning pain tore through my chest as the pressure inside my lungs built, forcing my heart to pump even harder and creating a devastating sense of trepidation.

Gradually all but two screens were left. It seemed that they were counting down from lowest to highest bidder. The second to last screen came to life. *'Death'* it pronounced. Aziza whimpered from the bed. And finally the *'HIGHEST BIDDER!'* sign disappeared to be replaced with *'caning arse'.* Then all the words vanished and the faces of the men returned. The smiling victor, Paul, was punching the air, and the man who had bid for death looked crushingly disappointed.

Steve and the gruff man appeared in the room, seemingly unbidden. In what was clearly a practised manoeuvre, they unchained Aziza, flipped her onto her front and rechained her ankles and wrists to the bed. Aidan stood back behind the laptop and leaned against the wall, one arm folded over his stomach and the other rested on it with his hand placed on his chin. He looked for all the world as if he was about to watch someone undertake a three-point-turn in the road. Steve went over to join him, tapping keys on the laptop. I assumed controlling the cameras from there.

"Dave," Aidan said, finally giving the gruff man a name. "Over to you."

Dave went over to the wall, studying a row of canes. He lifted one off the wall and held it up to the winning bidder.

Paul shook his head and said, "No, thinner." He was standing up now, peering closely into the camera, his cheeks reddening, his tongue in the corner of his mouth, clamped between his thick lips.

Dave surveyed the canes again and selected another. This one met with Paul's approval, and Dave held it in his hand while slowly circling the bed.

I wasn't sure if he was teasing the watching men or Aziza but as he paced around he began to touch her body with the end of the cane. As he did so, Aziza sobbed uncontrollably around her gag, squirming her body away in an attempt to avoid the touch of the cane. Dave ran the cane across the sole of Aziza's left foot, causing her to jerk her leg against the chain. With the very tip of the cane, he traced it along the back of her thigh, and then up the curve of her back, her muscles twitching as he did so. He brushed it through her hair, and down the top of her arm, her sobbing growing louder, and her shaking more violent, every time the cane touched her skin.

And then, without warning, Dave drew the cane up high and brought it down, with a resounding crack on Aziza's bottom. Her whole body bucked in response, the chains clattering against the bed frame. A pool of urine spread across the sheet and Aziza let out a deafening cry around the gag. I growled in defiance around my own gag, furious that I was unable to stop this torture, frustrated at my helplessness and I kicked back against the wall. A fiery red stripe was beginning to appear where the cane had landed, and Aziza was burying her head deep into the mattress as if it might help her to escape. Several of the men were now openly masturbating, some not appearing to be ashamed at all to be making noises.

Dave circled the bed again, and he ran the tip of the cane over the angry red line that the first strike had left. He drew it up again, this time from a different angle and brought it down with force across the top of Aziza's thighs. A muffled scream emanated from Aziza's lips and her body contorted with the pain, rattling the chains again and shaking the whole bed. The man on the right of the top row finished masturbating and, soon after, his screen went blank, before being replaced by the eager face of someone new.

Dave was gearing up for another hit, this time across Aziza's lower back. And then again across her bottom. Blow after blow, the cane rained down leaving red wheals across her bottom, thighs and lower back. Aziza's body jolted horribly with each thwack of the cane, her distressed cries becoming more tortured with each strike. Little drops of blood bubbled up along some of the red lines, slowly growing in size and then dripping down the side of her body and onto the bed to mingle with the other fluids already soaked into the sheet. One or two of the men were standing up, their erections on show as they grunted along with the rhythm of Dave's strikes.

I thrashed pointlessly against the restraints holding me there on the wall. There was nothing I could do. It seemed as if my stomach was filled with a cannon ball, weighing me down, pulling me into despair. I lashed out with my feet and cried out in frustration, but nobody paid any attention. I was determined not to give in to my terror, that would be failure. I was determined not to resign myself to the inevitable, determined that they would not forget that I was there screaming, if not fighting, for Aziza. I screeched out again, with all the force I could muster and glared furiously over at Aidan. A brief smile played at the edge of his lips as he turned away, returning his attention to what was happening to Aziza.

Eventually, Dave stood away from the bed. He looked Aziza up and down as if he were admiring his work before stroking her legs. A visible tremble ran through her body. Then he turned to the televisions, looked at the faces of the men, and gave a bow.

46

Aidan took centre stage once more. The red light on the camera above the screens lit up again as he turned to address them. He spread his arms wide, nodding and smiling.

"Enjoy that?" he asked the screens.

A dozen heads nodded and made appreciative noises.

"Sure then, that's a good thing because there's more to come."

I shifted in my restraints. Piercing pains forced their way up my arms, which were weary from carrying the weight of my body for so long. There wasn't an inch of me that didn't ache. I reached down with the toes of my left foot and rested my weight on them for a few seconds, and then switched to my right toes. I couldn't keep it up for too long and had to revert to hanging from my wrists. Apart from being a huge strain on my toes, my feet were still in pain from being tied to the chair in the warehouse. I tried to heave myself up a little, to relieve the muscles and let a different set take the strain for a while. I looked over at Aziza, her body covered in angry red lines, blood dripping down her side, and thought that my suffering was nothing compared to what she had been through.

Aidan put his hands in his pockets and paced slowly up and down in front of the foot of the bed, Aziza's spread-eagled body behind him. He looked up at the screens and gave a quick clap. "Well now, it must be time for the next bid." And he walked over to the laptop and set the timer going once again.

After two minutes, the padlocks reappeared, and the *'HIGHEST BIDDER!'* sign returned, this time on the screen that was on the left of the top row. As the bids were revealed, there were a few more of the screens that said *'death'*. I held my breath and gripped onto the shackles holding my arms above my head. There was a palpable tension in the room. Aziza had been missing for four days now and maybe her death was what they were gearing up to. I stared at the screens as each bid was revealed, unable to tear my eyes away whilst simultaneously not wanting to see what was coming next. Eventually, the *'HIGHEST BIDDER!'* notice disappeared.

'Steve and Dave together' appeared on the screen, and an initial wave of relief ran through me, to be quickly replaced by revulsion at what I had just read. I glanced over at Aidan, pleading with my eyes for him to do something to stop this madness, knowing it was useless, knowing he was choreographing the whole show like a conductor in charge of an orchestra. He looked back at me, a smile spreading across his face as he held up a hand. A

patronising, smug gesture. A signal you would give someone to calm them down. I growled around my gag, flailing my feet back at the wall. Aidan gave a short laugh, and turned to Steve, raising one eyebrow.

Without batting an eyelid, Steve reached up and brought some kind of a frame down from the wall. He and Dave didn't say a word—they were obviously practised at this. Dave unchained Aziza from the bed, and together the two of them strapped her to the frame. It was made of thin wood, and formed two upturned V shapes connected by another small plank, like the base of a small trestle table. Steve strapped Aziza's arms to the front legs and Dave did the same with her knees at the back, all the while both of them slapping her, pulling her hair, and calling her names. Aziza ended up on all fours, secured and unable to move. The thin wood of the frame looked to be painfully cutting into her body. Tears were threatening to tumble down my cheeks and I blinked them away, determined not to show Aidan any signs of weakness. Aziza's distress was almost unbearable to witness, her anguished whimpers causing me more pain than the restraints cutting into my wrists.

Steve went around to her head and fumbled with the fastening on the back of the gag. Before he had even had the chance to fully remove the gag from her mouth, Aziza cried out, "Stop, please! No more, I can't take any more, please."

But everyone ignored her.

I couldn't watch. I could hardly bear to listen, but I had no choice in that. I screwed up my eyes and tried with everything I had to pretend that I was somewhere else, somewhere nice. But I couldn't even bring an image to mind. My senses were being assaulted by the high-pitched screams of Aziza, the pleading, the begging, interjected with the sounds of slapping and the grunts of the two men. And then I wasn't just revulsed, I was filled with an all-consuming guilt. What kind of a coward was I, closing my eyes and trying to pretend I wasn't there whilst Aziza was suffering horrific abuse at the hands of these men. But I didn't open my eyes. I clung to the restraints, my fingernails cutting into my flesh and I willed it all to be over. The shame was overwhelming, pulsing though me and mingling with the terror. Who knew how long it lasted, but it seemed to be a lifetime. When the noises abated, and all I could hear was the soft whimpering of Aziza, I willed myself to return to the room.

Aziza had been chained on her back onto the bed, this time with both her arms and legs spread out. Steve was trying to put the gag back in Aziza's mouth but she shook her head frantically from side to side. Steve slapped her hard across the cheek and forced her mouth open with his hands, thrusting the red ball into her mouth and strapping the fastener tight around her head. He then left her, weeping, spread-eagled on the bed. She turned to me, her eyes pleading for me to do something. I had never felt so utterly helpless in my life.

I looked over at Aidan. There were no signs that he was getting excited at what he had seen. In fact, he seemed completely devoid of any emotion at all, just standing there, with an air of detachment. He was putting on a performance. He was providing entertainment for men who were prepared to pay to watch it. This wasn't for him, it was for the punters who had found this site on the dark web and enjoyed what it was offering. Perhaps he was motivated purely by the money. He uncrossed his arms and stepped forward once more. "Enjoy that?" he asked the screens.

Nods and appreciative murmurs oozed down into the room from the televisions. "Great, well, let's make another bid then shall we?"

And the men nodded once more.

For the duration of the countdown, Aziza sobbed quietly into the mattress. The cuts on her body were still bleeding and dripping onto the sheet, and I was reminded of the picture I had seen of Gloria. As the countdown timed out, and I reviewed the words appearing on the screens at the end of the bidding, I knew with a sinking certainty what had happened to Gloria. I blinked heavily to push back tears that were fighting to form in my eyes. I would not let Aidan see me crying.

'Death', *'death'*, *'death'* said the screens. One after another, they were clearly ready for this. *'Whip'*, *'shag'*—a few of the men clearly wanted more before the inevitable, and I began to hope that the highest bidder had bid for something less final. But, as the *'HIGHEST BIDDER!'* sign revealed what was behind it I cried out, the sound muffled by the gag, and shook my head. I looked over at Aidan, imploring, begging for any ounce of humanity that he had. But as he returned my gaze this time, he remained expressionless. He turned to the screens and clapped his hands together.

"Well now, after three days, our fun is almost reaching its climax." He looked at all the eager faces, tongues hanging out, panting, leering into the room, excited for what was about to happen.

He scanned all the televisions, then declared, "I can see that there are some of you who haven't been here at this point before. So, just for your benefit, a quick recap"—and he leaned back against the wall and folded his arms—"to get you all up to speed on what happens next."

It felt as if he was about to explain the rules of Ludo.

"Now," he carried on, "I think you know that you're all allowed to put in a bid for a method and, don't forget to think about it. Some methods are messier than others and, well"—he drew a circle in the air with his finger—"some take longer. But, anyway, it's up to you, whatever floats your boat." He glanced down at the laptop. "But just to let you know there are five people waiting in the hallway, and—" He paused to look back up at the men on the screens. "Only the twelve highest bidders will be able to join us for the actual event. That includes those waiting"—he indicated the laptop—"everyone gets to bid on method, so make sure you bid high enough to be here. Yes, Peter?" He raised his eyebrows as one of the men clearly had a question.

"I was highest bidder. Do I still need to be in the top twelve to get in the room to watch?"

"I'm afraid so," Aidan said, turning up both palms. "Those are the rules that we all signed up to. But don't be too upset if you miss out, we have another willing participant over there, waiting to entertain us." And he gestured over towards me.

Peter licked his lips and unzipped his trousers.

"Anyway," Aidan carried on, "bidding will start in a few seconds." He paused, then held up the index finger on his right hand. "And, you'll have three minutes this time. Your screen will show up green if you are bidding high enough to be in the room, but it'll turn red if you're replaced by someone who's bid higher, pushing you out of the top twelve. You can bid again. You can keep on bidding until the three minutes are up, but if you're showing red when the timer finishes, you'll be locked out in the hallway."

Jesus, no wonder these people make money.

"And make sure you enter your chosen method. Remember, we go with the highest bidder on that one." He made it sound like they were bidding for a packet of dog chews on eBay.

I wasn't sure if the violent shaking in my arms and body was a result of hanging against the wall for so long, or whether it was the horror and disbelief at what I was witnessing.

Aidan went and stood next to the laptop; he looked up at the bank of screens and held up a hand. "Okay," he said, "bidding starts…now!"

And with that the clock faces returned to replace the twelve faces of the men bidding heaven knew how much to watch a young woman die.

Aziza had stopped sobbing, her limp body lying on the bed, her eyes closed against the awfulness of what was going on around her. She could see the screens from her position, but undoubtedly was trying to distance herself from what was happening. I tugged at my restraints, but all I succeeded in doing was to dig them further into my wrists. I was helpless, struggling uselessly and, if Aidan was to be believed, next up for this horrific form of entertainment.

Time seemed to switch into a different mode. With the inevitability of Aziza's fate, the hands on the clocks moved quickly, seemingly denying her of any extra seconds. I wanted things to slow down, they were moving too fast. Aziza needed more time. I needed more time. I slumped in despair from the shackles holding me against the wall. Desperation gave way to panic. There was nothing I could do but hang there and watch Aziza be killed whilst twelve men wanked as she died.

A fluttering in the corner of my eye caught my attention, and I turned my head towards it. Surely there wasn't another person about to enter the fray. I looked through the small window in the door. Something had moved in the room beyond, but nothing was there now. It was dark, still and quiet. The walls keeping secret the evil that was taking place within their confines. My heart plummeted. I couldn't stand any more of this. Perhaps it had just been the perspiration pouring past my eyes. But then another flutter, almost too quick to see, cast a brief shadow across the glass as something ran past the door. For a split second I was convinced that I had seen the face of Sam Charlton. Relief flooded through me, but then the face was gone. As quickly as it had arrived, my relief went too. Maybe I was hallucinating. Maybe the fear and terror, and the last vestiges of hope had combined to make me conjure up a vision. I looked back around the room, the clocks still counting down, Aziza silent on the bed. Aidan, Steve and Dave in a huddle over by the laptop, maybe counting the money they were raking in. I glanced over to my side again but there was no sign of anything, no movement, no face. I had to have been imagining it; dreaming up a rescuer. Even my hallucinations were disappointing me.

My attention was drawn back to the room by the clocks finishing their countdown. Once again the *'HIGHEST BIDDER!'* sign was displayed, this time on the middle row. And the grim reveal began, slowly, like the announcer on the X Factor, building up the tension. Every fibre in my body wanted to cry out. Twelve screens; twelve different men, twelve different ways to die, some gruesome and bloody. Finally we were left only with the highest bidder. I was struggling to breath around my gag and my lungs were straining. My head was light with the fear pulsating round my brain. I didn't want to look, but I couldn't tear my eyes away, and then it appeared— *'hanging'*.

And I whimpered with Aziza.

47

The men in the room began their preparations, and I knew that there wasn't much time left. Steve and Dave grabbed the meat hook from above the bed, which was attached to a thick rope that ran over a pulley. The rope was secured to a hanger with a clasp on the wall near the bed. Steve undid the clasp, unwound the rope and lowered the hook until it was hovering a few feet above the bed, and then resecured the rope against the wall. I couldn't believe what I was about to witness.

Then once again, and only very briefly, the face appeared. This time, even though I only saw him for a second, I was in no doubt that it was Charlton, shushing me with his finger against his lips and indicating that I shouldn't look. Keen not to alert anyone else to his presence, I averted my gaze, looking back around the room.

Before my eyes, the awful scene was unfolding. Dave took a step ladder from the far side of the room and climbed up to fetch a heavy noose down from the wall. He lugged it over to the bed before securing it to the meat hook. I wanted to scream at my inability to do anything to stop it. I wanted to scream at Charlton to get himself in here, right now. What was he doing? And I wanted to scream at Aidan for fooling me, and sweet talking and acting like a decent human being when all the time he'd known that Aziza was here, tied to a stinking bed and being tortured for other people's pleasure.

The men on the television screens were slavering, rubbing their hands together, openly excited at the prospect of what they were about to see. I took a chance and glanced over to my right, peering through the door with my eyes but trying not to move my head. I couldn't see anything. No sign of any movement, no faces. Nothing but darkness. I kicked back against the wall in desperation and frustration.

Steve and Dave started to unfasten Aziza from the bed. She struggled frenetically, lashing and kicking out and shaking her head. Steve removed the gag from her mouth and instantly Aziza began to beg.

"No, no no, please no," she pleaded as they dragged her towards the noose. Aziza's knees collapsed. Perhaps she was just exhausted. Or maybe she'd done it deliberately to make herself a dead weight, making it harder for the men to lift her into the noose. As the rope approached her face, she tussled and twisted her head, fighting to keep it away from her neck. This time, neither Steve nor Dave hit out at her; it seemed they were relishing the struggle. Maybe it made it more exciting for the people watching. Once they had her head in the noose, they tightened the knot until it was snug against the back of her neck.

They stood back to admire their work. Aziza was standing naked on the bed, the noose around her neck with the knot behind over her hair. She clawed at the rope, trying to loosen it, fumbling with the knot. Dave walked round to the wall, and took the rope out of its clasp. Slowly, slowly he started to drag it through the pulley, heaving the big hook upwards. Aziza rose onto her toes. Her screams were becoming more frantic as her feet scrambled to find the bed. Gradually, deliberately, Dave pulled her up. He was straining with the rope, even though Aziza was tiny, leaning back to take the tension of her weight. Aziza stopped screaming, her legs flailing in the air, her hands tearing at the rope, her mouth open as she gasped in what air she could take.

I screamed around the gag in my mouth, the sound muffled by the sopping rag. Steadily, Aziza rose into the air until she was about two feet above the bed. She was pulling herself up with her hands on the rope, desperately trying to keep the pressure off her neck, and her airways open. The muscles in her arms were clenching with the force of holding her throat clear of the noose, her fingers searching to get purchase on the inside of the rope. Dave leaned backwards, holding the writhing Aziza up, and then, without warning, he let go, and Aziza dropped onto the bed in a heap. She gasped for breath, huge gulps of air, her chest heaving in and out as her lungs finally filled with oxygen. And then, just as suddenly, Dave took up the strain again and lifted her up once more.

For the next few minutes, Dave repeated this process; dropping Aziza onto the bed until she had recovered her breathing, and then hoisting her into the air again. After a couple of times, Aziza was preparing herself for being pulled into the air by wedging her hands around the rope before it became too tight. All the time Aidan stood leaning against the wall, his arms folded, occasionally sweeping his hair back off his face. And then, almost imperceptibly he nodded and Dave took the rope, wound it several times around the hook on the wall and attached the end into the clasp. Aziza dangled in the air, her body twisting, her legs thrashing and her arms shaking with the strain of keeping her head up above the rope.

Tears poured down my face, I stopped struggling and rested the toes of one foot against the floor. It was useless. And it was me next.

48

At that moment, the door flung open. Aidan, Steve and Dave all shot round open-mouthed to see what was happening, as Sam Charlton and Mike Nash burst through the door.

"Police!" Nash shouted into the room, and a few of the televisions went blank.

Nash leapt onto the bed and knelt underneath Aziza so that he could hold her up against his shoulder. Once again she gulped at the air. Steve lunged onto the bed, knocking Nash to one side. Aziza had relaxed her grip on the rope and didn't have time to get her hands in position. She swung wildly from the hook like a pendulum whilst trying to grapple for some purchase on the rope. Charlton made his way over to me, but before he could get there, Dave had run around the bed and kicked out at him, landing a blow on the side of Charlton's thigh. Charlton was a tall guy, over six foot, much taller than Dave and he lunged back at him with his fists, landing a blow on Dave's cheek. Dave reeled back, and Charlton made another move towards me. He almost had his hands on my waist to lift me off the hook when Dave tried again, grabbing Charlton round the hips and dragging him backwards onto the floor.

Nash was, once again trying to lift Aziza up, so that the noose would come free of the hook. It wasn't going to work; the hook was too curved. The only way to free her was to unhook the rope and lower it down. But to do that, he would have to leave her hanging whilst he was working by the wall. He barged Steve out of the way with his shoulder so that he could jump off the bed and untie the rope, but he couldn't work the clasp. Aziza twirled and danced on the hook, desperately trying to keep her airways clear long enough for somebody to free her.

"If that bitch doesn't die, I want my money back!" one of the men shouted down from the wall. Most of the screens had gone blank now, although a couple of the men had remained, no doubt keen to still get their sport.

Charlton had landed on top of Dave and he hauled himself back to a standing position, pulling himself up to his full height. He drew back his fist and, as Dave leapt to his feet, Charlton punched him square on the jaw. Dave fell to the ground out cold, at least for now, and Charlton took the opportunity to hoist me up and lift me down from the wall. He pulled the gag from my mouth and I struggled to work my jaw.

"What the fuck took you so long!" was what I was trying to say, but I couldn't form the words. My mouth had forgotten how to function, my tongue swollen and rough as it rubbed against the roof of my mouth. I licked my cracked and dried lips and tried to swallow down saliva to loosen the skin at the back of my throat but both sides of my throat had welded themselves together. My wrists were still shackled together, but at least I was free. Charlton set me down on the floor, but my feet wouldn't hold me and I collapsed in a heap on the floor. Pain shot through my ankles as the muscles returned to a more normal position. I couldn't feel my arms at all and then, gradually, sensation returned in the form of an excruciating style of pins and needles spreading its way through my limbs like shards of glass cursing through my veins.

Aidan charged across the room and shoulder barged Charlton, knocking him to the floor like a rugby player, and the two of them rolled on the floor, fighting for supremacy, whilst I tried my best to stand up on feet that were reluctant to hold me.

Nash was still fumbling with the rope on the wall, but Steve was pulling him away. Aziza was losing strength; her body was just dangling and she had stopped clawing so desperately at the rope. Nash was struggling to work out how the clasp worked with Steve clinging to his back, trying to drag him away from it. I stumbled across the room, on feet that would barely function, before falling onto my hands and knees and then climbing onto the bed. I couldn't stand up but I crawled under Aziza and arched my back so that she could rest her toes on me. I prayed I wasn't too late, but then I felt her feet moving on my back, pushing herself up. Having me there gave her just enough help to release the pressure on her neck a little. The relief that I had got to her in time was immense, but she kept losing her grip with her feet. Nash needed to hurry up.

Dave had regained his composure and pounced onto the bed, knocking me out of the way and leaving Aziza dangling once more. I kicked up at him with my bare feet, and just managed to catch him on the side of his face. It didn't make much impact, and he grabbed at my ankles, tearing at the raw skin as he pulled me towards him. I swung my feet up again, this time hitting him with my heel on his jaw, which gave me long enough to reach up to the wall and grab the nearest implement, which happened to be a sturdy paddle. As Dave launched himself at me again I pulled the paddle behind me. My wrists were still bound, so I had to use both hands, like some tennis players did, and I swung with as much energy as I could muster at the side of Dave's head. He anticipated the movement and lifted up his arm, the paddle glancing off his forearm, leaving a scratch as it did so. I pulled my arms back to the other side of my body and swung again with a double-handed back hand. This time I was quicker and he didn't get his arm as high up. I caught him squarely on the side of the head and he flopped forwards, face down onto the bed.

Steve and Nash were grappling for ownership of the rope's clasp, and with renewed energy I threw my bound arms around Aziza's thighs as best I could and lifted her as high as possible. It wasn't much, but gasps and coughs indicated that she was at least able to breath. I wouldn't be able to hold her like this for very long. My arms were weak and, although she was only slight, it was a struggle to keep her aloft.

Nash was gaining control of Steve, and shoved him to the ground. Steve danced through the air as he fell onto his back, but as he flew backwards he grabbed hold of Nash's arm and used his feet to haul Nash into the air and lift him over his head. Nash fell with a tumble and rolled away before springing to his feet and this time lunging at Steve with force. Steve hadn't quite made it to standing and he was unsteady. He tumbled back, his head crashing into the wall, and he slumped, dazed, to the floor. Nash took the opportunity to grab the rope. I didn't think I could hold Aziza any longer, but then the weight of Aziza's body dropped onto me as Nash lowered her to the bed. I drew the sheet around her and lifted the noose over her head. She lay down, sobbing into the mattress.

"Thank you," she whispered. "Thank you."

I looked over at Charlton, but he was preoccupied. Aidan had managed to get the better of him. They were both on the ground, Aidan with his hands around Charlton's neck and Charlton trying to push him away by his shoulders. I turned to the wall behind me and grabbed the nearest cane. It was long, thin and flexible. I jumped off the bed, lifting the cane high above my head with both hands and I brought it down with as much power as I could marshal onto Aidan's back. His body recoiled and he shouted out with pain. He let go of Charlton's neck, clutching at his back with his hands, but I wasn't done. Again and again I brought the cane down, ripping through his shirt and tearing the flesh on his back. Charlton rolled out of the way, the cane glancing his arm as he did so. I gritted my teeth, my jaw set hard and I screeched with every hit.

"Verity, stop!" Charlton shouted as he clambered to his feet, but I was raining blow after blow on Aidan, his back wet with blood.

Steve ran round the bed and grabbed my arms, just as I was about to land another double-handed strike. Aidan staggered to his feet. Charlton curled over, his fist drawn back ready to land a punch the minute Aidan stood up. Nash was just about to run around the bed to help.

And then everything changed.

There was a deafening crack. It was so loud that it thumped a hole through the air as it travelled, punching my ears as it hit them like a physical blow. Everybody stopped. Nash and Charlton had crouched down, Aidan fell to his knees, blood still pouring down his back. Steve dropped my arms as I turned my head around, my ears ringing so loudly I couldn't tell if anyone was speaking or not.

Dave must have come to and climbed off the bed, because he was standing on the far side of the room, near the laptop, holding a handgun. He was holding it up high above his head. A cloud of dust and plaster was falling on his head. He signalled with the gun that Charlton and Nash should back off. Both of them held their hands up.

Dave was talking, but the words were quiet beneath the incessant ringing. "Over there." He gesticulated with the gun, pointing towards the wall just below the television screens.

A couple of the men on the screens were still watching what was going on in the room, eyes wide, mouths open. An added bonus; buy one death get a few extras free. Charlton and Nash took their time as they moved carefully across the room and stood by the wall, hands aloft, their eyes not leaving the gun for a second.

"Turn around, hands on your heads."

The two men did as they'd been told.

"On your knees," Dave ordered.

Charlton and Nash sank down, kneeling on the floor, their faces to the wall and their hands on the backs of their heads. Dave pointed the gun first at Charlton's head and then at Nash's.

Aidan got to his feet and walked around the room to stand behind them. He looked at Dave, and then over at me. He looked at me directly in the eyes and began to shake his head. "Big mistake—" Aidan started to say but he was interrupted by footsteps clattering through the warehouse beyond.

"Armed police!" came the call, as the footsteps stampeded towards the door. Several police officers wearing bullet-proof vests and carrying weapons ran past the open door, calling out their presence once again. I wasn't sure how many of them there were but they seemed to be assembling, ready for action. The policeman who had shouted was just beyond the doorway but his voice sounded small and distant, overwhelmed by the noise still swelling in my ears.

"Drop the weapon!" ordered a second officer. He stood in the doorway and leaned against the doorframe, his weapon pointed at Dave. Two other police officers crouched down in the doorway, sweeping the room with their weapons. The sound of further footsteps crashing towards the small room told me that more officers were arriving, rushing across the floor beyond. The welcome sounds of cocking weapons managed to drive themselves through the ringing still piercing through my brain.

"Drop the weapon!" the policeman demanded again.

But Dave stood firm. He was pointing the gun directly at the back of Nash's head. "Back off!" Dave shouted, and he moved the gun closer, so that it was almost touching the skin at the base of Nash's neck. "I'll shoot him," Dave screamed back at the policeman, his mouth wide, his cheeks red, the purple veins in his neck visible under his skin.

"One more time, drop the weapon." The policeman sounded calm, measured, but Dave took no notice.

And then, without warning, the policeman fired. In slow motion, Dave fell backwards, an arc of blood spurting out of his back and showering the wall behind. As he fell, the gun went off and Nash screamed out, falling forwards against the wall. Steve pushed me to one side as he ran past me to attend to his partner in crime. It was too late, Dave was dead before he hit the floor.

Aidan ran over and swept up the gun, before turning and charging towards the police officers, his arm outstretched, firing as he went. The policeman who had been shouting out the orders suddenly stopped, his mouth open as if he were about to say something, but he didn't get to say it. A hole appeared in the front of his forehead and almost instantaneously the back of his head exploded in a volley of blood and bone. Aidan only made a couple of paces before he fell to the floor, mid-stride. The policeman crumpled against the doorway, slowly sinking to the floor.

Steve threw his hands high above his head as half a dozen armed police officers entered the room, their weapons poised for action. Charlton followed suit. I looked at him across the room. He seemed to be miles away, at the end of a tunnel. I could see his mouth moving but I couldn't make out any words.

"Hands above your heads!" The words came piercing through the air like sharp arrows hitting my ears.

My perception was all over the place. People were moving, but staying still all at the same time; talking without sound. I was riveted to the spot and one the police officers pointed his weapon at me and shouted, "Hands above your head."

As my brain unscrambled what he'd said I raised my hands up, glancing down at the blood forming around Nash and wishing someone would do something.

49

Perhaps it was the shock of the gunfire, or the relief that it was all over, but I was really struggling to take in what was going on around me. It was as if I was watching everything from somewhere else, detached, not part of the scene. People were moving around me, but I was in a vacuum and their words were meaningless. There were police officers prowling around with their guns pointing ahead. Aziza was lying on the bed, crying softly, and I wanted to go and comfort her, but I didn't move. Charlton was huddling over Nash and calling to police officers, who in turn were shouting into their walkie talkies, their voices urgent and strained. I was vaguely aware of Steve being taken away with his hands handcuffed behind his back, cursing and swearing as he went.

In the doorway, a policeman leaned over the body of his colleague. He raised his head up high and shouted out in grief; a long, aching wail that drew me back to my surroundings. A combination of smells hit my nose in a rush, mixing together to paint some kind of horrific olfactory picture of events. The shackles had gone from my wrists, although I had no recollection of anyone removing them. I gulped in water from one bottle, then another. Someone took my pulse at some point, or maybe they didn't, my memories were becoming confused with the mixture of hormones mingling in my blood like a potent late-night cocktail.

Blood was everywhere.

There was a man prowling around taking photos of everything. Paramedics came running in pushing gurneys, rolling out Aidan and Dave in zipped up body bags. A helicopter arrived at some point, and Aziza and Nash were taken off to hospital. They ordered me to follow in an ambulance. I was told it was on its way. The police were combing through the building and men in forensic suits had arrived. Laptops, cameras, sheets, all the equipment that was hanging on the walls— everything was being put into bags and taken away. Charlton and I were alone in the room with half a dozen investigators. He came over and took me in his arms, stroking the back of my head and pulling me tight into him. I was too numb to cry. My mind was struggling to grab hold of coherent thoughts and it seemed as if I hadn't spoken for weeks.

I leaned back. "What the fuck took you so long?" I said, when I eventually managed to remember how my mouth worked.

We were asked to leave the room and let the forensic team do what they needed to do. They said we would need to provide fingerprints and DNA to help as the team tried to sort out which bodily fluids belonged to who. The vast emptiness of the warehouse took me by surprise; the upturned chair still laying on the ground at the far end. It was cold and dark and I shivered as Charlton steered me out into the night. The sun had set a while ago but there was still warmth in the earth and it wasn't unpleasant standing out there in the moonlight.

"We had to be sure we had the right place," Charlton explained when we found a spot to stand and wait, away from the swarms of police.

Blue lights lit up the sky with an eerie rhythm from a dozen police cars parked outside the building. I had no idea where we were.

"You saw me and then you disappeared. Aziza could have died." I wasn't sure whether to be cross that he'd taken so long, or relieved that he had turned up at all. We had saved Aziza and I supposed that was the thing that really counted.

"There was no point coming in until we knew that backup was on its way. Nash had to call in, and we needed to know they were coming. You saw what happened, we could all have been dead. They instructed us to leave it till they arrived, but…" He pulled me to him and held me tight.

"Yeah," I said, resting my head against his chest.

He held me there and we stood in silence for a while, watching people scuttling in and out in the pulsating blue lights.

"People are evil," I said, after some time.

"They always have been," he replied.

"Like this?"

"The gallows used to draw a crowd. Watching other people suffering, well, there'll always be people who enjoy that. It's just a more technological way of doing it."

"People waiting in the hallway to watch other people die…"

"And a line of people out there being drawn in to die for them…"

Friday

50

I sat on a bed in A&E. My loss of memory between arriving at the Five Two Two and waking up at the warehouse, my confusion about the sequence of events, and the significant blow I had received to my head, all combined to cause the doctors concern that I was suffering from concussion. They wanted me to stay there for a while. I'd had a thorough checking over. My foot had been bandaged to protect the deep cuts where it had rubbed against the rough warehouse floor, and my wrists had needed cleaning up where the shackles had worn the skin away. But there was nothing that wouldn't heal.

Nash was in another part of the hospital undergoing surgery to remove a bullet from his thigh. Despite the copious amounts of blood he'd left on the floor of the warehouse, the bullet had missed the main artery in his leg and things were looking promising for him.

I was bored in the hospital. I lay down on the uncomfortable bed, but I couldn't sleep. There was nothing to do but wait. Charlton came and went, taking phone calls, and bringing bottles of water.

"Don't you need to go home?" I asked him, not for the first time.

"You're not running away again," he said.

"I don't think I'm capable of running," I said, pointing to my bandaged feet.

"I'm not taking any chances."

"I'm not talking to you, not yet," I said, lying in the bed on my side and looking him in the eye. "Not here anyway."

And he picked up his phone and walked off down the corridor.

I couldn't shake thoughts of Gloria from my head, and the people who had played their part in her demise. I doubted Jack Clayton and Noah had had any idea what would happen to her in her ultimate chapter, but that didn't make them any less culpable; they had dragged her into that world to start with. I wanted to run through the hospital and rouse Nash from his anaesthetic so we could stitch it all together. Charlton had assured me that there were other police personnel in Lincoln who he was sure would be taking care of things in Nash's absence, and it wasn't too long before the news came through that the pair of them had been arrested. Mark Henry remained at large, though.

It was the early hours of the morning when a police detective arrived at my bedside. Charlton had returned. He was there, sitting next to the bed.

The detective introduced himself as Inspector Trevor Pierce. He looked like a relic from a seventies police series. He was wearing a tweed jacket and slacks and had a moustache that Groucho Marx would have been proud of.

"The signal was still being broadcast when the armed response unit arrived," he explained. "So we may well be able to get some good intelligence about what was going on, how they were getting subscribers and so on. Some of the subscribers weren't actually watching the action at the time, they were in some kind of virtual waiting room, and hadn't realised there'd been a raid so they were still connected. We think there might be enough information, well I say we, I mean the specialists think there might be enough information to set up a dummy event. Hopefully we'll catch some of the subscribers that way."

"They were signing in from all over the world," I said.

"I think there's good cooperation on these sorts of things across the different countries," DI Pierce stated, putting his hands in his pockets.

"Let's hope," I said. "It would be nice to see some of those bastards put away for a long time."

"The main reason I'm here, though..." He shifted his gaze.

"Yes?"

"Well, some of the stuff they had there aroused suspicions. You know, shovels and heavy-duty digging machines, and the like. We got some equipment sent over, a ground penetrating radar among other things, and located an area just outside the warehouse where the ground had been disturbed." He looked down. "We found a grave," he said. "A shallow grave in the grounds, just behind the warehouse."

"Gloria?" I asked.

He nodded. Charlton reached over and squeezed my hand.

"We think so, yes. We need to get an official ID, but there were identifying items found. And three other young people. Two females and a male."

"The man from CEOP said there'd been five different people in the pictures."

"Yes," he said. "So we were told. But they've searched and only found four so far. If there is another body, it's nowhere near the others."

"Do you know who they are?" I asked. "There was the young girl from Derby?"

"It's possible," he said. "Some of them were fairly well decomposed, and we're trying to match up personal items with missing person reports."

I sighed and leaned back against the bed, thinking of Linda and Sarah, and how they'd react when someone broke the news to them.

I fought with the sheet, not knowing where I was, an unknown terror lurking in the distance. I snapped open my eyes and took in my surroundings, relief flooding through me as I took in the hospital bed and the drawn curtain. Charlton had disappeared, but his jacket was still slung over the back of the chair. As I reached over for a drink of water, the curtains separated and a young doctor appeared. I hadn't seen her before and assumed there must have been a shift change.

"Morning," she said brightly.

The doctor perused my notes, pulling her mouth this way and that as she did so. "We have been in the wars, haven't we?" she said to herself, and put the notes down at the bottom of the bed.

Charlton appeared, two takeaway cups of coffee in his hands, and he lay them down on the little table.

"Ooh thank you," I said, reaching over and taking a sip. My jaw was stiffening up, and I was still struggling to produce saliva in the right amounts, so the coffee provided some welcome relief.

The doctor felt my head, shone a light in my eyes, and asked me if I had regained any memory loss.

"I think the reason I can't remember getting to the warehouse is because I was out cold," I said.

"It's very likely that you won't ever remember that, then." She looked up. "Any nausea?"

I shook my head.

"Headache?"

I shook my head again.

"Confusion?"

I looked at Charlton but said nothing.

"Is there someone at home to stay with you for a while?" she asked.

"Yes," said Charlton and I at the same time.

"I can ask my friends Robert and Keith to come over for a bit. I'm sure one of them will be able to, or I can go to them," I continued, looking at Charlton.

He glanced over the doctor's shoulder, his hands in his pockets, and clenched his jaw.

"Then I think you're okay to go home," she declared. She gave me a leaflet of signs to look out for. It was the same leaflet they'd given to Liam a few days' ago. "If you notice any of these, come straight back," she said, before turning around and leaving.

51

Before I left the hospital, I went to track down Aziza. She was in a ward with a couple of other people. Old ladies, lying silently in their beds, staring at the wall opposite. I'd asked Charlton to find out what ward she was on, and whilst I went to see her, he had gone down to the cafeteria to give me some space.

"Hey," I said to Aziza as I approached her bed.

"Hi." She gave a weak smile and pushed herself up a little so that she was half sitting, half leaning back against her pillows.

I pulled up a chair and sat down by the bed, resting my hand on top of hers. "Are you okay?" I asked.

She nodded. "Yeah," she said, "I'm okay."

"I'm so sorry…" I started.

"It's not…" she said. "Look, it's not your fault. You found me. You stopped it. You stopped that happening to anyone else." She studied my hand laying on top of hers, then looked up. "I don't think things ended that way for Gloria."

I shook my head. "They think they've found her body. Possibly others too." I didn't feel it was the right time to add that this was only at the warehouse. There were five people in the pictures the CEOP man told me about, and one of them wasn't there. DI Pierce had said that there may well be other young people in other locations. Aziza had been lucky, but I guessed that probably wasn't how she was feeling right now so I just patted her hand and stayed quiet.

She nodded. "They wanted to stop me from talking to you, didn't they?"

"I think so, yes. I think they thought once I'd started prying into what was going on, that I'd make the connections if you told me what had happened to you. As it goes, we made them anyway, but it just took us a little longer."

"You got there just in time." She wrinkled up the sheet beneath her hand.

"Who knew you were going to come and meet me?" I asked.

"Just Liam, and Amelia, that's all. I don't know how they found out."

I nodded. "Amelia," I said.

Aziza looked up, her brow furrowed in puzzlement.

"I don't know how much she knew about the people higher up the chain than Jack Clayton, but she may well have told him, and he could have passed it on. Or she may have got in touch with Mark Henry directly. I don't know."

"I think it was him who took me," she said.

"Mark Henry?"

"Yeah, Noah texted me. Out of the blue. He said he hadn't seen me for a while and missed going swimming. I stopped going swimming because Jack was there. I never told anyone about what he did, even at HSL. They helped me to see it was wrong but I was always too scared to tell them who had been involved."

"Did he threaten you?"

She nodded. "He said I'd done all sorts of illegal things and he could get me thrown out of Plumtree House, and probably the country. He said they'd send me back to Afghanistan with a criminal record." She looked up, her eyes wide. "I couldn't risk going back there." She paused for a while. "He said even if they found my family they'd never want anything to do with me after what I'd done." She hung her head. "He was probably right, my family would be ashamed."

"But he lost his hold over you?"

She nodded. "First it was Francisco. I don't know why but I trusted him, he was so nice. I didn't tell him exactly what I'd done, but I think he understood. He got someone from HSL to talk to me." She looked down, pulling her hands together, entwining the fingers. "I never dared tell them exactly what had happened, because I worried about what would happen. Jack had said anyone in authority would have to call the police to report me. But they helped me. I stopped seeing him, and after a while I threw away the phone he'd given me."

"How did he react to that?"

"To start with he kept texting. All the time. He'd say he loved me, he'd say he couldn't cope without me. Then he'd get angry and threaten me again. The thing is, by then, HSL had told me that that's exactly what he would do. That's when I got rid of the phone. And they helped me loads to stay strong."

"Where did he used to take you? When you were going out?""

Tears filled her eyes. "It just started as fun," she said. "He was charming and told me how gorgeous I was. He said he couldn't believe he'd met me and how happy he was that I had come into his life. He bought me presents and took me out."

"Did you know he was seeing Gloria?"

She shook her head. "He said he'd had a couple of casual girlfriends but that he had fallen head over heels when he met me. It was so nice. So nice to feel loved. To feel pretty and wanted. And sexy."

"And did you sleep with him?"

She nodded. "To start with I didn't want to. I'd just had my birthday and he said I should. That I was a proper woman now. He took me out for dinner and we had such a lovely evening and then he got really upset, said he'd spent all that money on me because he thought I loved him. He said he didn't want to see me anymore. He said I clearly didn't love him as much as he loved me. And it seemed like such a reasonable argument, so I agreed."

"How was it?"

"It was okay, it was nice. Then a few weeks' later we were drunk, at his place, and he said he owed his friend a favour, and his friend had told him he could pay him back by letting me sleep with him. I don't know if that was the truth, but he persuaded me. Then there were other friends, and there was always a reason, like the alcohol we'd had. He'd say a friend had paid for it and we needed to pay him back. He used to say, 'if you loved me, you would'. He'd look hurt, and I thought I'd lose him. Then after a while he stopped making excuses, and he stopped saying he loved me. He just told me I was a slut and to sleep with whoever he said."

"Did he ever hurt you?"

"A couple of times." She looked down and whispered into her chest. "A couple of times near the end, before I spoke to Francisco. I didn't want to do what he was saying, I'd plead with him not to make me, but then he hit me."

"Did he ever take photos or videos?"

"Only once," she said. "Well, not him. One time we were at someone else's house and I can't remember the reason now, but he had told me to have sex with a guy who came round and there was a camera in the corner of the room. Set up, on a tripod. The guy had started to take my clothes off, and we were on the bed and a man came in and started filming. I shouted out, telling him to stop, but I was held down. I think it was the same man that took me to the warehouse, but I can't be sure, it was a while ago."

"Mark Henry? What happened that night, when he took you? You said Noah had texted."

"Yeah he said we used to be friends, and he missed me and could we meet up. I said I was meeting someone in the afternoon and maybe I could see him after. So he said yes, but I think he was waiting for me to leave. I was on my way to meet you. Or maybe someone had told him I was leaving. Anyway, he caught up with me and took my hand. When I said I needed to be somewhere, he wouldn't let me go and the other guy was in a car across the road. He got out and between them they got me in the car. Noah took my handbag with my purse and phone in. I don't know where Noah went after that but I never got my bag back."

"I think he used your phone later to lure Liam out."

"Well, the guy, I think it was Mark Henry, took me to the warehouse." Tears were streaming down Aziza's face.

I stayed silent for a moment. There was no need to push her after what she'd been through, but she looked up and nodded. Maybe it was helping her, talking about it with someone who had been there. Someone who knew the horror of it.

"Who was there? Was Henry there at all? And Aidan?"

"I didn't see Mark Henry again."

"I think he was hiding at Noah's house. The police wanted to talk to him about attacking Liam so I think he was keeping a low profile."

"Aidan was always there when those screens came on." A shudder ran through her body.

I stroked her arm, goosebumps appearing up the length of it.

"But I don't know how often," she continued. "The room had no light and sometimes they left me in the dark. I don't know how long for, I lost track of the days."

I thought of Aidan entertaining me at the Five Two Two and Aziza lying there in the dark waiting for him to return and start things up again. I shook my head, but I didn't say anything to Aziza. I was struggling to comprehend the mental make-up of someone who could spend the evening chatting, apparently without too much to concern him, all the while knowing that he had Aziza there, strapped to that bed in that awful room. I could only assume it had amused him in some way, playing with my emotions. And presumably attempting to keep me off the trail long enough to carry out his task.

We sat in silence for a while. At length she said, "So was Amelia involved in this?"

"She certainly knew that Jack Clayton was picking on people. He was paying her to turn a blind eye. How much she knew of what was going on…" I shrugged. "I really don't know. More than she wanted me to believe I think. She was obviously peeved when Francisco put you in touch with HSL and you stopped seeing Jack. That thwarted their plan. Maybe Jack got cross with her. Jack would sweet talk people, play the boyfriend. Noah introduced people to him, both you and Gloria anyway. He was driving Gloria all over the country to be abused and filmed. I suspect Amelia was pointing the finger at who were the vulnerable young people. One way or another they knew who had no family, who had no one to chase up if they went missing. You thwarted their plans by going to HSL. If you hadn't, I think they'd have started taking you round to those kinds of places too. The thing is, if Gloria hadn't had Linda and Sarah to care about her, we might never have interrupted their activities."

I sat with Aziza a while longer. We didn't say very much. There weren't really words to cover what we'd been through, and sitting in silence was enough. We conveyed a mutual solidarity without

359

the need for words. After a while I decided it was time to talk to Sam and I gave Aziza a big hug, promised to check in on her in a couple of days and bid her a tearful farewell.

52

Charlton was happy to drive me home from the hospital, and we chatted as we drove.

"You figured out the venue," I said.

"It wasn't me," he admitted.

Apparently, the Lincolnshire police had been examining all the photos CEOP had sent over; there weren't many clues, but eventually they had matched up the distinctive zigzag pattern of the brickwork to a little row of abandoned warehouses just outside Sleaford.

"Nash rang me," he said, "and we agreed to go and check it out together. I tried to call you." He glanced over.

I hadn't picked up. I didn't need reminding. As far as I was aware, my phone was still lying on the ground outside the nightclub. It could stay there. I would cancel it and go and buy a new one. I certainly didn't want to see the front of that place for a long time.

I invited him in. I thought he might like to use the shower, as he was still wearing his clothes from yesterday. We both were, and they were spattered with blood; from Nash, from Dave, probably from Aidan as well.

Sam got his overnight bag from the car, and I led him into the house.

"I assumed you weren't picking up because you were still cross with me."

"I still am," I said.

He raised his eyebrows.

"Well, no I'm more cross with myself, really. Let's get showered and changed, Sam, and meet back down here."

Charlton was already in the kitchen when I went back downstairs, leaning against the counter. He'd put on some clean jeans and a ribbed top. He smelt of freshly washed skin.

"I didn't have you down as a whiskey drinker," he said, picking up the bottle of Redbreast 12.

"It was a gift," I said. "I never drink whiskey. I'll pass it on to someone else, or put it in a raffle or something." I took the bottle and put it out of sight at the back of a cupboard. I turned round to face him. "Do you think they'll find Mark Henry?" I asked him.

"'He's certainly going to be on their Most Wanted list," Charlton said, rubbing his jaw.

"I wonder if he and Aidan did fall out? I wonder if he had more of an active role with the other young people before Aziza."

"What makes you say that?"

"Well, he took Aziza to the warehouse, and then he never appeared again. It would have been a perfect place to hide. And to participate. I wonder if they were partners, more so than Aidan was letting on." I shrugged.

"I guess we'll never know exactly. His equipment has all been seized, there might be some clues on it."

"He'd taken a laptop with him, that probably had the most incriminating evidence."

"We'll just have to hope that he resurfaces before too long. He's lost a lucrative form of income, that's for sure."

"Now," I said, and I led him by the hand through to the sitting room. I took him over to the bookshelf and picked up the photo of John and I in Spain. "This is me and John in Spain, not that long before he died. It was a beautiful sunny day and we walked along the seafront to find this little bar."

I put it down and picked up another photo. "And this is us in Madeira. We'd just got off the cable car and took this selfie. Then we walked through some gardens and found the tallest vase in the world, and we laughed because it didn't actually seem that tall. We'd had a row before we got in the cable car, because he didn't like heights and wanted to get a taxi. I called him a wimp, in jest really, but it didn't come out as I'd intended. So we'd sat in silence halfway up, until I apologised. Or maybe he did, I can't remember that bit."

I picked up another picture, this one of our wedding. John was wearing a suit and me the long white dress that still hung in the wardrobe. In the picture, John was leaning me backwards, cradling my back with his arm, reaching down to kiss me, my dress flowing and billowing in the wind. I had felt like a movie star. "And this is the day we got married, the happiest day of my life." I put the photo down and dropped my head to my chest. I looked back up at him. "I have so many memories, Sam, it's not the time to let go of them yet."

Sam smoothed his thumb over my cheek and shook his head. He held both my hands with his. "I'm not asking you to let go of anything. You keep and treasure those memories." He picked up the photo of our wedding day and studied it for a moment. "He looks like a fine person," he said. He put the photo down and took my face in his hands. "Verity, you don't have to forget anything, or change anything, or leave anything behind. This is about making new memories, not replacing old ones." And he leaned in towards me.

I kissed him gently on the lips, and then pulled his hands away from my face.

"I'm just not ready to make new ones, yet."

-Epilogue-

I stood in the car park of the crematorium on what had turned out to be another glorious day. The sun glinted fiercely off the windows of the cars, sending dazzling beams of light across the car park. People were mingling, waiting for the service before Gloria's to finish. Nash was there, leaning heavily on a walking stick as he left his car and made his way to the waiting area outside the building. A gaggle of school girls gathered to one side, out of the way of everyone else. They had a teacher with them, but it wasn't Mr Moorehouse. Linda and Sarah stood chatting to a man who looked as if he might be the celebrant and I went over to say hello.

"How are you doing?" I asked Sarah, resting a hand on her elbow.

She nodded and swallowed. She opened her mouth, but closed it again before saying anything, and a tear ran down her cheek.

"We're okay," Linda said. "Grieving. It's just so hard to understand." She pulled out some tissues, passed one to Sarah, and then dabbed at her own eyes.

A few minutes later a car pulled up.

"Excuse me," I said to Linda and Sarah, and I went over to greet Liam and Aziza.

Aziza threw her arms around my neck and squeezed me tightly. "How are you?" I said, holding onto her shoulders and looking her in the eye.

"I'm okay," she said. "I have my moments, of course. I'm not sleeping well, but everyone's been so helpful. I've started volunteering for HSL and that's keeping me busy. I'm doing some training so that I can go into schools and tell people what to look out for. If I have anything to do with it, no one else, ever, will go through what I did."

I ran my hand down her arm. "That's amazing," I said. "To think some good might have come out of all this. You're amazing," I stressed, "you really are, Aziza." I was in awe of how she was coping.

She nodded and looked down.

I turned to Liam. "Liam," I said, "how's the nose?"

He laughed and touched it. "It's fine," he said.

The celebrant started leading people into the main room. Gloria's coffin stood at the front, a beautiful picture of her laughing placed on top. Each seat had an order of service, decorated with photos of Gloria. It was beautiful and I knew Sarah had spent some time designing it. I sat down near the back of the room. I had just finished reading through the order of service when Charlton came in, out of breath and sat down next to me. "Sorry," he whispered. "I got held up on the A46."

The celebrant read out a eulogy detailing Gloria's life, not going into any detail of what he referred to as her 'untimely death'. Linda read a poem and Sarah struggled to read a short speech she'd written without crying. The strains of Mozart's clarinet concerto started to drift around the room, and the celebrant invited us to each think, in our own way, and with our own memories, about Gloria and how she had touched our lives. I reached into my handbag and pulled out the plastic figurine of the Little Mermaid and walked to the front of the room.

"Keep watch over her," I whispered to the mermaid and placed her on top of Gloria's coffin.

From the author

Thank you so much for reading A Hallway of Gallows, I hope that you enjoyed it. As an independent author, without the marketing budget of a big publishing house, I rely heavily on reviews of my book and word of mouth to ensure that people hear about it. Reviews, especially good ones, help to push books higher up search results, so every comment helps.

If you liked the book, it would make me really happy if you could find the time to write a review, and tell all your friends about it. I do read all the reviews, and they help to make sure that future books are enjoyed by other readers.

Verity will be making another appearance soon in the next book, Unring the Bell, so if you are interested in finding out more about her next adventure you can follow me on Amazon. I am also active on Twitter and try to respond to all tweets and messages.

@ladyermintrude

Yours
Trudey

Acknowledgements

My heartfelt thanks once again to Sarah Smeaton for her editing, for her helpful suggestions and for assisting the story to flow. And to Margaret Swift for proofreading; your help was invaluable. Thanks also to all the friends and readers who read initial drafts and gave such constructive comments. I also need to thank the various professionals from the organisations referred to in the book, who happily took the time to talk to me, to read the manuscript, to show me round their departments and to give such helpful technical advice about the work that they do. These include Caroline Sanderson, Janice Spencer, John Horton, Deborah Crawford, Kate Richardson, and Steve and Sue Layton. Thanks to Marco Wilkinson for the map; and, lastly, to my longsuffering husband, who once again endured many hours of inattention as I prepared the book for publication.

Printed in Poland
by Amazon Fulfillment
Poland Sp. z o.o., Wrocław